CASTLES

CASTLES

Book 2 of
The Frencolian Chronicles

Carolyn Ann Aish

Horizon House Publishers
Camp Hill, Pennsylvania

Horizon House Publishers
3825 Hartzdale Drive
Camp Hill, PA 17011

ISBN: 0-88965-090-X
LOC Catalog Card Number: 90-86250
© 1991 by Horizon House Publishers
All Rights Reserved
Printed in the United States of America

91 92 93 94 95   5 4 3 2 1

Cover illustration © by Karl Foster

Scripture taken from
THE AUTHORIZED KING JAMES VERSION

Dedication:

In loving memory of my dad

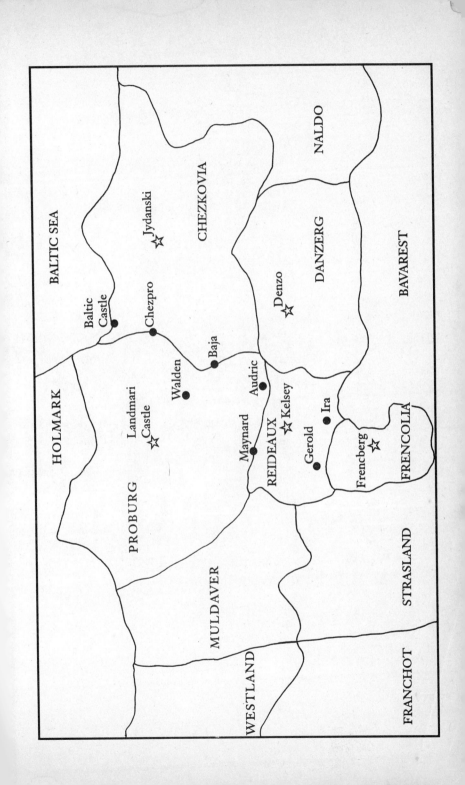

1

Jobyna Chanec felt the horse tremble as it climbed the steep, rocky incline. At the top of the ridge, the girl drew a sharp breath in exhilaration, dispelling her tiredness for a moment. Jobyna wished she could ride her own horse, Brownlea, but King Elliad made her ride with him on Speed. The mute slave girl, Ellice, rode Brownlea.

Exiled King Elliad, Jobyna's captor, urged the horse on down the rocky aisle of the glacier-carved, natural amphitheater. Stretched out before the girl's emerald eyes was a lush green valley nestled between embracing ranges. A thousand shades of green danced before her tired gaze, refreshing her turmoil-filled mind.

Far in the distance, along the edge of some woods, she could see the rest of their company setting up camp for the night. Smoke from newly lit fires rose lazily in the lengthening shadows.

Over three weeks of travel on horseback made the captive princess feel weary and sad. Every step Speed trod was one step further from her home country, Frencolia. Jobyna wondered where they were going? How much further would it be? She knew Elliad must have a destination in mind, but he did not talk to her except to issue commands.

"Eat, Sparrow!" or "Sleep!" or "Wake up!" he would bark at her.

At various stages on the journey, Elliad left the women, children, servants and slaves with several hundred soldiers and went off with the rest of his great horde of troops. He always returned triumphant, and it was some time before Jobyna learned the purpose and method of these excursions. Extra horses, carts and provisions were added to the assembly from this plundering and destruction. Scouting parties were sent ahead, constantly reporting back to Elliad, who, armed with maps, decided the routes they would take.

The awful truth was revealed to the tender-hearted girl one night when they had set up camp in a deserted manor house stronghold. Jobyna was sure the damp splatters in the main hall were blood. She noticed some of Elliad's soldiers were wounded. She had heard Elliad tell his knights to "terminate those unfit to travel."

Elliad motioned for her to be seated in the dining hall for a "celebration" dinner. A shrill scream disturbed the meal. It came from somewhere upstairs in the manor house and was silenced by a brief choking noise. Jobyna instinctively jumped to her feet with her hand over her mouth. A knight hastened to the open door, carrying the limp blood-stained body of a child under one arm like one would carry a sack of potatoes.

"Sorry, Sire, we found him hiding in a closet upstairs."

The sight of the mutilated child and the thought of what had so obviously taken place were too much for Jobyna. Fainting, she fell to the cold stone floor.

Jobyna awoke in a darkened room. The shutters had been boarded up and she supposed this was to prevent any chance of her escaping. Ellice brought food and juice, but the girl was too upset to eat anything. Jobyna's hatred for Elliad grew stronger. He was a monster, void of any human feelings, lacking in moral fiber. He was the most evil man she had ever known. A worm upon the dust of the earth was worth more in Jobyna's estimation.

Speed galloped the length of the valley floor. New strength filled his veins, and eagerness spurred him on. Brownlea lagged behind momentarily then gained a new surge of power. By now the horses knew the tents ahead meant rest, fodder and fresh water. The sooner they arrived, the quicker the ordeal of the day would be over. Elliad drove the beasts hard. At the end of a day, the horses' coats would be lathered in sweat. Failing horses were butchered to help feed the hungry multitude.

Jobyna sat beside the stream, soaking her tired feet and basking in the warmth of the sinking sun. Ellice combed the girl's long copper-brown hair, weaving it into one long braid. Jobyna flexed her left hand, exercising the weak fingers in the cool water. The memory of the torture she had suffered was indelibly stamped in her mind. Berg, King Elliad's closest bodyguard, had broken her forefinger because she would not sign a "confession" concocted by Elliad. This document stated that she and her brother Luke were traitors against the throne of Frencolia and were responsible for the death of the previous king, Leopold. Due to an interruption the torture was abandoned, but Jobyna knew he would have broken all her fingers had the distraction not occurred.

A week after leaving Frencolia, the exiled

4

King Elliad had announced to his captive that he was turning himself back into "Doctor John." The three stitches in her hand needed to be removed. Thick string-like thread had been knotted to stitch the incision made by Doctor Gilbert. Not only did the knots have to be cut but the thread twisted and pulled from the now healed wound. "Doctor John" had become angry and impatient with her during this operation. Due to the pain, Jobyna found it hard to hold still, and she had squirmed in discomfort as each stitch was removed.

Ellice dried her charge's feet, then replaced the woolen stockings and boots. Jobyna's green eyes met Elliad's cool blue ones as she rose from the rock. He was drinking from a goblet but his eyes followed her movements over the gold rim. Unnerved and annoyed, she threw him "the daggers," a newly invented look she reserved for him alone. If this beast prohibited her from speaking, she would show him her disapproval in another way. She could sense he was uncomfortable by the disdainful attitude she radiated, and this pleased her. She would never forget the dead child and how heartless Elliad really was.

The sun turned the clouds a milky orange as the company finished the evening meal. The silence in the gully was broken by soldiers rounding up the newly acquired horses to be branded with Elliad's mark. Jobyna decided she would retire to her tent. The thought of her father's horses—being branded by Elliad's men—her beloved Brownlea and Luke's horse Speed—filled her mind with renewed spurts of hate. The soldiers had branded the "E" over the Chanec "C" and branded another "E" on Brownlea's and Speed's foreflanks.

Jobyna's eyes met Elliad's as she stood. She stared at him with cold, icy hatred! Such a decadent and depraved person would never change! He just enjoyed causing misery, suffering and death to all in his way. Jobyna wondered how God could let such a person live and get away with the murder of innocent people.

"Sit down, Sparrow!" Elliad said gruffly, his heavy voice breaking into her thoughts.

Jobyna knew enough about his commands to obey. Ellice washed the utensils in the creek. Jobyna watched Elliad swill down the rest of his wine. He rose and walked to Berg, talking to him in undertones, turning her way now and then. She knew they were discussing her.

Elliad beckoned, "Come here, Sparrow."

Feelings of dread filled her mind. She hesitated, and a chilled sensation made her tremble. Jobyna knew she must obey; if she did not, Elliad's anger would be kindled against her. Each step in their direction filled her with

6

apprehension. Her eyes met Elliad's. His eyes had a look in them she recognized. He looked right through her as though she was nothing, nobody. Berg grasped her left arm, Elliad her right. They half led, half dragged her to the fires where the horses had been branded.

"I'm tired of the way you look at me, Sparrow!" Elliad's voice pounded in her head. "I want this to serve as a warning! You do not need to tell me how much you hate me when you look at me with enmity. I'm sick of it!" He spat on the ground. Berg twisted both her arms behind her back.

The exile-king took a brand from the fire. It was white hot. Elliad held it momentarily close to her. The heat touched her face and she felt her skin shrink back. She turned her head to the side and closed her eyes, trying hard not to scream out.

"Do you know what would happen if I held this close to your eyes for a few minutes?"

Shaking all over, Jobyna did not answer for a moment. Then, realizing he expected her to, she cried, "No!"

"You would never open them again, Sparrow."

Jobyna's legs crumpled under her, but Berg supported her and his grip tightened.

"Look at me!" Elliad shouted. His saliva splattered her face. Jobyna opened her eyes as her captor waved the branding iron in the air. She could feel his breath on her forehead.

"You do not treat your king with animosity, Jobyna! Do you understand?"

She could not answer. Her tongue was stuck to the roof of her mouth. Elliad screamed at her, "Do you understand, girl?"

"Yes, I understand," Jobyna answered feebly. An overwhelming desolation swept over her as she realized he enjoyed humiliating, victimizing and taunting her.

"How will you look at me, then?"

She searched her mind for an answer. Thoughts of his madness and his obsession with himself filled her with terror.

"Friendly, . . . with friendliness," she whimpered. Jobyna realized how much hate she had conveyed with her looks of malice. She had never imagined he would notice or care, but he was furious, wanting to destroy her pride. Sensitive to human reactions and cunning beyond description, he had interpreted her attitude as total insubordination.

A cynical grin pervaded Elliad's face as he pressed the brand into his captive's arm, just below her left shoulder. It burned through her dress sleeve, singeing the wool, burning through the skin into her flesh.

She screamed in terror and pain.

The moment he held it against her arm seemed an eternity. The searing pain made her nauseous. Berg held her against him, one arm around her body, his great hand clenching the branded arm at her elbow, holding it still, the other around her neck, holding her so tight, she could scarcely breathe.

The "E" brand permanently impressed, Berg suddenly released her. She fell to the sandy soil. Crying with weakness and pain, she vomited and gagged, losing her meal.

Afraid to be angry, feeling humiliated and wretched, Jobyna refused to allow Ellice to comfort her. All night she lay tossing and turning in her tent. Sleep was impossible with the searing pain in her arm. Never before had Jobyna been so homesick! Thoughts of her mother's reassuring arms made her sob. Arms no longer able to hold or comfort because Elliad, the monster, had taken away her mother's life.

In the past two months, Jobyna had lost her parents and her home. As self-appointed king of Frencolia, Elliad had sent out a decree stating all Gospel Books must be surrendered to him, or those protecting them would be executed. Jobyna's father did not believe Elliad would actually carry out the punishment. Louis Chanec had hoped to reason with him, but nevertheless had sent his children away to safety with a trusted servant, Sabin.

It was reported to Luke and Jobyna that Elliad had watched while their parents were executed. Jobyna now knew for sure her mad captor would enjoy watching such barbarity. Believing the message of love and peace in the Gospel Book had shut her mind from realizing the cruelty and depravity existing in the hearts of some people.

Her sheltered life was over. The brother-protector she once knew had a different role now. Luke Chanec was the new king of Frencolia. She was the captive princess, bearing the brand-mark of the arrogant demagogue, Elliad. Any kindness Elliad had shown her in the past was overshadowed with the unhappy knowledge that she could not even look at him but he knew her thoughts. Jobyna's parents had taught her to obey authority, and he was an authority over her. As long as his authority did not ask her to do anything against God, then she must try to obey. To speak or not to speak, to sit, to stand, to be pleasant and even friendly in his presence.

Jobyna fell into a fitful sleep, thankful she still had two eyes to see with and that he had not carried out his threat to remove her tongue.

"One day," she said to herself, "I will escape from him! God, please give me patience until then!"

2

Long live King Luke Chanec!"
"Peace to Frencolia!"
"God bless King Luke! God bless Frencolia"
Newly crowned King Luke Chanec visited
every town, village and castle in the kingdom
of Frencolia. His uncle, Sir Dorai, suggested he
pay these visits as the people of the country
were in dire need of a united display of leadership. The five lords of Frencolia and 14 senior
knights accompanied Luke whenever they
were able. Lord Farey, the oldest, did not journey to the towns near the farthest borders.

They traveled every day, changing horses at
midday, moving on to visit another town in the
afternoon, and if possible, a manor house in the

11

evening. Brief though the visits were, Luke obtained a clearer picture of the people and needs in Frencolia. Jubilant to recognize him, the people were eager to show their acceptance of the new reign of justice. Luke perceived the past oppression and hurt buried beneath the celebrations each village held for his reception. Elliad, as self-proclaimed king of Frencolia, had left a two-year trail of injustice and murder.

A few weeks ago, Sir Dorai had commissioned knights and soldiers to gather documented evidence against Elliad. Hourly, the gruesome list grew. Added to the murder of Luke's parents, Elliad was responsible for poisoning King Leopold Friedrich, first cousin to Luke's father, and Sir Samuel, the heir to the throne and the king's close friend. Voluntarily, knights and soldiers enlisted everywhere. They joined with those who would one day go out to bring Elliad back to Frencolia for the judgment he deserved.

Chanoine, Luke's home village, was decked out with elaborate floral decorations for the arrival of the boy king. People who had turned against the Chanecs were now acclaiming and cheering him. Luke remembered the plunder and burning of his home. The three Gospel Books his parents died to protect would have been burned to ashes, as they had been hidden in the wood-paneled walls of the manor house. Months of work copying the Scriptures for others to share were wasted as his home was razed. Standing on the rubble and broken soil that once supported his home, King Luke asked for monuments to be raised in memory of his parents. He commissioned the rebuilding of the manor house.

"Never again, in this country, will anyone die for believing in the message of the Gospel Book," the king declared. "Louis Chanec, my father, was a good man, kind and just to all. He wanted God's message to be here for my children, for your children, and their children. For this 'crime' he was murdered.

"In memory of my parents, I declare that everyone in Frencolia, servant or soldier, young and old, shall learn to read so they may understand God's Word for themselves. Those able, will make accurate copies of the Gospel Book for every family to have one. The Scriptures shall be read daily in every town and village square. God's Word will make us united and strong."

Luke realized the tremendous work ahead. A king's life was not easy. Everywhere he turned, there were decisions to be made. People needed encouragement. Documents required his signature. Sir Dorai supported Luke's decisions, advising and informing him when he felt it necessary. Luke thanked his uncle, reinforcing his own need for mature help and guidance. Lord Farey was a great source of counsel, and Luke was thrilled with the wisdom and understanding this man displayed.

The white-haired old man suggested that in each village and town a council be set up, consisting of those who believed or were sympathetic to the Gospel Book. Knights in charge of these councils were to be called "Chanec knights" and would report directly to King Luke. The days were filled with interviewing, appointing and commissioning the new Chanec knights to take with gravity the oath to install justice, righteousness and peace in Frencolia.

Upon departure from Chanoine, the royal procession was hailed by messengers with news from afar. Ruskin, a Frencolian knight, had returned from his mission. He and a group of soldiers and knights had located Elliad's trail and finally his camp which was on the move every day. Ruskin explained how they kept at an unobtrusive distance, following a path of massacre, plunder and destruction through three countries, Bavarest, Danzerg and Reideaux. Bavarest bordered Frencolia's eastern side, Reideaux, the north. Danzerg bordered the east of Reideaux and the north of Bavarest. Elliad was careful to leave no survivors; no witnesses. Sometimes the homes were burned to the ground, incinerating the bodies within. Ruskin suggested they meet urgently to decide a course of action. The knight felt messages must be sent to all countries in Elliad's line of travel, disclaiming responsibility for his insane actions.

"Maybe the other countries will join us in bringing this maniac to justice. They now have claims to his life. He needs to be confronted soon!" Ruskin announced.

"Ruskin," Luke asked, "What about Jobyna? Have you news?" Luke's thoughts were often with his sister and he was anxious for news of her.

"Yes, Your Majesty, we have. We managed to steal close to Elliad's camp one night, and in the morning, I saw her with my own eyes. A servant woman sleeps in her tent and three soldiers stand guard close by. We counted over a hundred torches burning in the night with twice as many soldiers standing alert on guard around the camp. Your sister rides each day with Elliad, on your horse, Sire. She seems strong and well." Ruskin reiterated the disadvantage of having to keep out of sight. "She is well guarded. Even when Elliad and the troops went off on their plundering, we were tremendously outnumbered by those left."

"It is just as well you did not show yourselves; they may have harmed her if they knew they were followed," Luke agreed. "We must pray the beast leaves her alone!"

Luke and the lords compiled messages, which were dispatched by Chanec knights. These knights were ambassadors for King Luke Chanec of Frencolia, and they carried tidings of peace with offers of condolence and help. The countries lying in Elliad's path, Proburg and

15

Chezkovia, were to be warned. Sir Dorai told Luke that Proburg was closely allied to Chezkovia, and both countries were hostile to Frencolia. One of these kingdoms, most likely, would be where Elliad was heading. This knowledge regarding the kingdoms was new to Luke, whose mind had never before gone beyond his realm. To think his country could be blamed for Elliad's butchery made Luke realize the implications and complications surrounding the madman's flight. It was imperative that word be sent immediately and help offered to restore wherever possible. This would all take time, precious time, and man power that could have been used to capture Elliad and rescue Jobyna. Luke was saddened. One could rebuild a house, but one could not bring back human lives. Elliad had done so much more to condemn himself since leaving Frencolia!

Luke completed his tour, returning to Frencberg as soon as he could. Meetings, convened with the lords and knights, continued on late into the night. Border castles to the north and east were stocked with food and reinforced with extra soldiers. New strongholds on the eastern border were commissioned to be built. Reports were to be compiled daily and instant messages sent if there were any signs of trouble. All communications received from outside Frencolia were to be treated with highest urgency.

Sir Dorai descended the steps to the back courtyard with the sound of clashing swords ringing in his ears. It was dawn. Ruskin was giving Luke lessons in sword fighting. Sir Dorai asked why his nephew was attempting to learn such a skill.

"I cannot defend myself, let alone my sister!"

"Your father would not approve," Sir Dorai said curtly.

Luke's father, Baron Chanec, had laid down his sword when he became a believer in the Gospel Book. He would not allow Luke's older brothers, let alone Luke, to train as knights. Therefore, Luke had no idea how to use a sword. The maneuvers and stance were foreign to the boy. Sir Dorai, the brother of Luke's mother, Elissa, had disagreed with Chanec's Christian philosophies, and the family was eventually estranged. Now, Luke and Jobyna, the only surviving Chanecs, were the responsibility of their uncle, Sir Dorai. Some weeks ago, when Luke was crowned king, Dorai had decided he would allow his nephew to develop the skills he wished. If Luke wanted to study books, then he may. If he wanted to go to war, so be it; but Luke would remain in the background with personal bodyguards at his side. *I want to honor my brother's convictions, but these are dangerous times*, Dorai thought, *and a king who could not defend himself? Well . . .*

Secretly pleased with Luke's initiative, he asked, "Why the change, Son?"

This familiar term secretly thrilled Luke. Smiling, he answered, "I have been reading in the Gospel Book. King David of Israel began his life as a shepherd boy. I was similar. Father often sent me to watch the sheep. I never killed a bear or a lion like David, but I remember chasing away wolves when I was just nine years old. David did not have early training in warfare, yet later on we read of him conquering many enemies. I most likely will not be the one to kill Elliad, but I want to show support for the men who are prepared to risk their lives for the sake of our country and my sister."

"Well said, boy!" Sir Dorai was impressed.

"Will you teach me, Uncle?" Luke asked. When Sir Dorai did not answer instantly, he continued. "We must each do all we can! With God's help, we will defend Frencolia and bring Jobyna back where she belongs. The knights tell me there is no one in Frencolia who can handle a sword like you, Uncle. Please, will you teach me?"

"I will." Sir Dorai put his hand on Luke's shoulder. "I want you to know, Luke, if I have any say, you will not be anywhere near the front lines. And if God were to hear my prayers, they are that you never face Elliad with a sword in his hand. The first skill you must learn is to defend yourself. That I can teach you."

Luke began his lessons with Dorai that very morning. They used the blunt practice swords and Luke realized the time and effort it would take to become proficient. But time was fast running out.

3

Jobyna woke late. The heavily clouded atmosphere made the day dark, and it seemed earlier than it actually was. Guilty at having overslept, she dressed quickly. Elliad's voice had not resounded, "Get up, Sparrow!" the usual morning command over the last three weeks.

Ellice poked the struggling fire beneath a small pot of broth which steamed invitingly. The slave glanced at the weary girl emerging from the tent. The burnt sleeve of Jobyna's dress was ripped off so it would not irritate the unsightly wound. Ellice fussed about, rummaging through a trunk beside the tent. She found what she was searching for, a jar of salve and a bandage. Jobyna was not in the mood to protest and while Ellice tended to her arm, the princess surveyed the camp.

All the tents were still standing and soldiers posted all around were on perpetual guard. Elliad was nowhere to be seen, and she noted that Speed was also gone. Knowing the other women in the camp had strict instructions not to talk with her, she said to Ellice, "Where has Elliad gone?"

Ellice pointed to the north, between the hills of the valley. "Do you know now long they will be?" Jobyna asked.

Ellice shrugged her shoulders. Scooping some broth into a bowl, the slave handed Jobyna a bread roll. The princess loathed to eat the bread, knowing it was stolen from the manor houses plundered the previous day. When Elliad's band had departed, the houses were left to burn. Cupping the bowl in her hands, Jobyna blew on the broth and sipped cautiously.

Ellice rolled up her own dress sleeve, pointing to an "E" brand on her arm. The purple scar was raised and ugly but long healed. Jobyna felt the suffering Ellice must have gone through.

"How long ago did he do that to you?" Jobyna asked.

Ellice held up four fingers.

"Four? Not four months?"

Ellice shook her head.

21

"Four years?" Jobyna exclaimed, not believing her. The slave girl nodded. "Four years! That's two years before he was king!" Jobyna struggled to work it out. If only Ellice could talk. She looked around. The soldiers watching them were out of earshot. This was the first time since leaving Frencolia they had been able to communicate for any length of time.

"Did you live in Frencolia?"

Ellice shook her head.

"Where then?"

Ellice glanced furtively at the closest soldier who was slumped against a tree; his eyes seemed to be half closed. Ellice smoothed the pine needles away from the earth. With her forefinger, she drew an "S" in the soil. Jobyna frowned. The slave completed the word Strasland, which was a country to the west of Frencolia.

"Did Elliad kidnap you?" asked Jobyna sounding shocked. Strasland was considered a friendly country.

They looked around again as a soldier strode their way. Jobyna finished drinking the broth. Kicking and scuffling with her feet, she smoothed the pine needles.

When he had passed, and his back was to them, Jobyna whispered, "What is your real name, then?" Ellice gesticulated with her hands and shook her head. "All right. I'll call you Ellice. You are worried Elliad would know we communicated if I slipped up and called you by your real name." This satisfied the slave girl. She shook her head to Jobyna's next queries: "Why doesn't he want anyone to talk to me? Is he afraid I'll organize an escape or something? If I didn't believe in God, I'd go insane!"

Much to the slave girl's concern, Jobyna helped collect wood for the fire. "I have to do something!" she declared. Jobyna stoked the fire, encouraging it to burn brightly. Thoughts of Elliad's treatment of Ellice made her feel angry!

Mist hung thickly in the valley, blocking out the sun. Long lone fingers of firelight kissed the treetops through the vapor. The mornings and nights were becoming cooler the further north they traveled.

Dispelling the haze, the sun shone brightly. The day had come out scorching hot. Fanning herself with a small branch covered in green leaves, Jobyna bathed her feet in the stream. Voices from somewhere behind her seemed to be growing louder. Several women were coming to cool off in the water. Ten or 12 small children accompanied the ladies. Jobyna noticed a boy and two very little girls, all with bright orange hair. Having not seen any of the children before, the captive girl guessed they traveled in the carts near the front of the cavalcade.

Recognizing two of the women, Jobyna spoke, "Ada." The woman looked at her cautiously, and Jobyna decided there was no point in showing animosity. The women probably had as much choice as she had to be there. "Are you traveling well?" Jobyna asked.

A woman Jobyna knew privately as "the sullen one" said, "Don't speak with her, Ada. I said we shouldn't have come over here." A false ring surrounded these words. The children were already splashing gleefully in the stream. One little girl fell right in, screaming and spluttering amidst loud laughter. The sullen woman hurried to pull the child out, scolding, then giving in and allowing her to sit, fully clothed in the stream, throwing handfuls of sand here and there.

The women moved just out of earshot. A feeling of suspicion came over Jobyna and she wondered why they had not stayed at the water's edge where they had previously been. A sudden dart entered her mind. *This is planned!* Her thoughts went back to a night in Frencolia, at the King's Castle, when these two women had betrayed her into leading Elliad to the secret passage to the treasure chamber.

Ada ventured to Jobyna, "I am sorry for you, Princess. I am sorry I had to betray you back in Frencolia. I know you understand." Her searching eyes met Jobyna's. The girl remembered the way Ada had cared for her when she was sick, and she recalled her nursing skills.

Jobyna looked across at the sullen woman. "I

do understand," Jobyna responded tenderly. "At least I think I do."

She remembered the way Elliad blackmailed even those closest to him, terrorizing them with death threats. "Tell me, Ada, what is that woman's name? Who is she?" she asked nodding toward the woman by the two little girls. As in the past, Jobyna had unintentionally brought up the very subject that this woman wanted to discuss!

"She is named 'Ranee.' You must be careful of her!" Ada whispered harshly. "She is very jealous of you!"

"Jealous . . . of me? Who is she?" Jobyna was intrigued.

"You must not tell anyone I tell you, no?" Ada waited for Jobyna to indicate. At her "victim's" shaken head, Ada spoke in soft undertones. Amused by Jobyna's naivete, she whispered, "She is Elliad's woman. Those two are his daughters. He will marry her when she gives him a son."

This shocked Jobyna. She wished she had not heard. It would be better for her not to know such things.

"Ada, you can tell Ranee that I am not the slightest bit interested in Elliad. I hate what he does, how he lives and his murderous ways!" she responded with a touch of anger in her voice. "I would rather be dead than have to ride with him!"

She looked cautiously across at Ranee who

turned her head their way and called loudly, "Ada, you come away at once, or I'll tell the king!"

Jobyna knew this was just a front. The information, the warning, had been passed on as intended. Ada moved away. The two little girls had Elliad's dark hair and blue eyes. Ranee's hair was fair. But for her sour look, Jobyna thought her attractive. They moved off further down stream. Jobyna sat watching them, wondering if her knowing about Ranee would show on her face to Elliad. She was not a good actress.

"I am too transparent," Jobyna told herself. "I must learn to hide my feelings." Ranee was not able to hide her inner feelings. No wonder the woman looked at her with unconcealed hatred. Ranee must wish she could ride on Speed with Elliad. Jobyna would gladly allow her. The puzzle of Ranee fit together now. Elliad trusted her, that was why she had been chosen to tend to Jobyna while she was sick. Why he didn't marry her was a mystery to the captive princess; but then, Elliad's character was beyond the scope of her imagination. She found it hard to pray for him, apart from imploring God to deal with him and bring him to a painful end. Guiltily she remembered the verses learned at home, words from the Gospel Book:

Love your enemies, bless them that curse you, do good to them that hate you, and

26

pray for them which despitefully use you,
and persecute you. (Matthew 5:43)

*To get even with Elliad, I need to do good! Impos-
sible!* she thought. Jobyna realized many of the
verses she had learned she just "parroted."
Maybe they were supposed to be more real,
more practical, than just words to be quoted.
She resolved to try and put the verses into
practice. The verses she memorized over the
years were useless to her unless she lived them.
In a loving family situation it had been easy to
show love and kindness. But now? She was just
like a hypocrite, showing a hateful attitude. She
must pray for Elliad. She must pray for an end
to the murderous crimes he was committing
daily. Could she do good, to him? No. She
hated him! What about Berg, the torturer? How
she hated him!

Leaning back on the rug that Ellice had
placed under the tree for her charge, Jobyna
tried to decide which one she hated the most.
Her mind raced as she lay in the afternoon
shade of the great pine tree by the tent, looking
up through the branches at the sky. The
tremendous tree traversed the bright blue sky
as the whispering wind blew expanding white
cotton clouds softly past. She asked God to
give her understanding. Did God love Elliad?
The answer must be "yes" for the Gospel Book
said "God so loved the whole world. . . . " The

rest of this verse, from the Gospel of John, ran through her mind.

"That's it!" Ellice looked up as Jobyna sat up suddenly and cried out, "I can ask God to bless Elliad, for with God's blessing, he may come to know God." She looked around at the soldier, thinking, *I must pray for these men, too.* Jobyna, communicating out loud, prayed a prayer she had never dreamed of before this moment:

"Thank you Lord for this persecution. It has shown me the truth about real love. To love only those who give love in return is human, but to love those who show hate is divine. That is what you did, Lord Jesus, when you forgave those who crucified you! Please forgive me for hating and for showing this hate on my face." *I am no better than Ranee,* she thought. "Help me to keep hating the injustice but not the souls of these people whom you love. Lord God, bless Elliad and Berg, Ranee and Ada. Bless all these people. Give me the chance to do them good even though they hate me. you love these people and you want them to believe in you! Teach me to pray for them every day and to show them your love. Bless them Lord, especially the children. Amen." As Jobyna lifted her eyes to meet Ellice's stare, she added, "Thank you, God, for my friend, Ellice."

4

Icy rain pelted down with gusting fury. The previous day's hail had chilled the air with freezing breath. Jobyna and Ellice huddled in the flapping tent. A knapsack of dried meat and fruit brought by a soldier was tossed in the tent opening. Bored beyond description, Jobyna wondered how Brownlea and the other horses were managing in the storm. She hoped they had found shelter.

Lightning lit up the charcoal sky and thunder crashed violently causing the horses to neigh with fright. They were terror stricken. It was nigh impossible to hear her own voice above the storm so Jobyna gave up trying to talk to Ellice. There was nothing to do but rest and wait. Elliad had not returned from his latest exploits.

Four days painfully passed. The laughing stream was now a raging torrent. Morning brought a strong southeast wind that blew the storm away. By midmorning the storm was retreating and Jobyna told Ellice she was going to check on Brownlea. Venturing out, Jobyna felt the wind grasp her hair and clothes, twisting and turning, tugging at the hem of her skirt. She drew her cloak around her.

Carrying dried apples and dates, Jobyna whistled and called for Brownlea. A soldier approached, blocking her way. The girl smiled at him saying, "I'm just seeing how my horse is. See, I have some fruit for him." Brownlea was no longer her horse, but Elliad's. *He will always be mine, in my heart,* she thought, comforting herself.

The horses were corralled by a number of men-servants and soldiers carrying whips. Jobyna wondered how they had all managed during the storm over the past few days. The men stood to their feet as she approached. With a gentle whinny, Brownlea lifted his head and began walking towards her. As she laid her head against his, her tears ran on to his rain-drenched nose. Brownlea licked her hands affectionately as he finished the fruit, nuzzling into her neck.

Raising his head suddenly, Brownlea pulled away from Jobyna. The girl looked around. In the distance, she could see horses approaching. *Elliad, it must be Elliad!* she thought and hurried back to the tent, breathless and concerned.

The arrivals, knights and soldiers on horseback, ordered camp to be broken and commanded they move off north as soon as possible. Jobyna found herself swept up by Berg, riding Speed. With a terrified backward glance at Ellice, they were gone, racing along the soggy valley floor. Berg urged the horse on at a startling pace. Jobyna almost cried out when he drove Speed straight into the turbulent waters, sending showering spray splashing upwards. She had worried about the way Elliad pushed the horse, but Berg was far more reckless. Using a short-cropped whip, he drove the horse to its limit.

After an hour or so, Jobyna could see the path they followed was growing wider, and they came to several crosspaths, turning north or east each time. Berg relaxed his tension and Speed traveled at a more comfortable pace.

Midafternoon, Jobyna's eyes focused on a large walled castle ahead. It was like nothing she had seen before. Compared to the Frencberg King's Castle, it was small, the construction and layout quite different. It had no

31

moat around it but was completely walled, enclosing towers that rose at each corner of the high walls. A conglomeration of buildings could be seen. They did not appear to be in any particular order; some were three stories high with thatched roofs. To the back was a huge arched building, reminding Jobyna of the stables back home. Large domed entrances graced the center. A paved road led through the narrow gate in the wall.

Pulling the horse up abruptly, Berg was met by soldiers leading another horse. Swinging Jobyna down off Speed, he lifted her on to the back of the other horse and then mounted behind her. Briefly, Jobyna cast her eyes around the courtyard. The sight made her feel sick. Dead bodies which had obviously been there some days were strewn here and there. Mutilated remains were bloated and purpling, soaked with the rains. Instinctively, she recognized Elliad's trademark of death. As the newly mounted horse galloped out the way they came, Jobyna wondered, *why the immense haste, and where am I being taken?*

The retreating sun radiated orange hues, which were slowly turning a deep red. Jobyna roused as the horse's hooves clattered on pavement. Her head was nestled against Berg's huge chest. Embarrassed, she pushed herself forward. Remembering her resolve, she looked up at the great hulk of a man. His graying beard and heavily lined face broadcast his brutal lifestyle. Even his name described him well: "Berg—a mountain!" Jobyna wondered if anything good could ever come from such a being. She prayed for him. Almost in the same thought, she heard her mind say, *We'll see what will become of that prayer!*

Outlined against the blood-red sky, great square towers with large battlements filled Jobyna's vision. The horse passed through various gates, and the similarities reminded Jobyna of the King's Castle in Frencolia. Many of the towers rose into pointed spires. Hundreds of small windows made an impressive picture. While the horse was led away to the stables, Berg walked with the captive girl to a small entrance. Inside, one of Elliad's knights beckoned Jobyna.

"Come this way." He indicated a spiral stairway. Miles, it seemed, of corridors were traversed, and Jobyna remembered the last time she walked in such a place. This time, she realized, she was in a different country, far away from home. Trepidation filled her as she wondered what lay ahead. Elliad was full of horrible surprises.

The soldier leading the way stood by a large arched door. He knocked loudly. The door was opened by a woman attired in a strange costume. Assuming the tone of a commentator, the knight announced, "The Princess Jobyna, Sister of King Luke Chanec of Frencolia, captive of King Elliad." Sweeping his hand in an extravagant way, he bowed, indicating her entry.

The room was filled with curtsying women. Jobyna jumped nervously as the door closed soundly. Motioning her through the foyer, the women took Jobyna's soiled cloak, clicking their tongues at her torn off sleeve and bandaged arm. They were chattering away in a language the travel-weary girl did not understand.

She was drawn through lavishly furnished rooms and into a sunken marble bathroom. Bathed, massaged with perfumed oils, powdered and pampered, her body had never known such luxury. None of their chatter made any sense to her. Consternation was shown when the clothes set out were all too wide. Jobyna was tall and very thin.

After comings and goings, she was dressed in a purple gown of more appropriate size. A sash tied around her waist took up the extra material. Her hair, still damp from being washed and towel-dried, hung loose down her back. Two of the women argued in a friendly way, obviously disagreeing as to how it should be done. Jobyna felt like a doll, not supposed to have a mind to think for herself. Her hair was braided and wound around her head; a strange

34

gold and silver domed jeweled apparition was brought and placed on the copper plaits. The braids were carefully arranged under the headdress so the fit was secure. Dangling gold and silver mesh-like nets of jewelry hung at each side, falling from her ears almost to her shoulders. Slippers of varying sizes were tried on until a small enough pair finally fit; they were encrusted with jewels, with a single diamond for each heel.

The women did not seem altogether pleased with the finished article. One of them rubbed rouge into Jobyna's gaunt, sunken cheeks while the others voiced and nodded approval. A looking glass was brought, and Jobyna took some powder, pressing it on her unnaturally bright cheekbones, trying to rub some of the rouge off. The girl worked on her face, blending and powdering until a more natural look was achieved.

A loud knock at the door indicated to the women their time was up. Dressed in a fresh, crisp knight's uniform, emerald green with gold embroidery, Berg held the door ajar, announcing, "King Elliad, exile-king from Frencolia, has come for the Princess Jobyna."

Jobyna drew in a deep breath. Elliad was there waiting for her, his arm extended to her. Dressed in a jewel-studded outfit, a simple gold crown sat on his head. Her heart told her to turn and run, but she remembered her resolution. To Elliad's surprise, she curtsied, saying, "Good evening, Elliad John." To her own surprise, she smiled as she placed her hand on his arm in the customary manner. On the arm of her captor, with Berg the bodyguard shadowing them, the long walk was not the ordeal Jobyna anticipated.

"It pleases me to see a change in your attitude!" Elliad declared.

She dared to speak, "I was wrong to act the way I did, Your Majesty. I apologize for my behavior."

"So, what brings this change, Sparrow?" he questioned, "the brand?"

"Not entirely," she said, catching her breath as they descended a wide central stairway. "I think, . . . it would be better for me not to say."

"Let me be the judge of that." He looked at her as they drew near to a landing. "This way." They turned down another long corridor, walking at a more leisurely pace. "Tell me!" he commanded.

"I remembered words from the Gospel Book." She paused, not sure if he would want her to continue.

"Yes, go on," he ordered, his eyes full of mockery.

"Jesus said, 'Love your enemies, bless them that curse you, do good to them that hate you, pray for them . . . ' "

Elliad was silent so Jobyna continued, knowing she was treading on dangerous ground. "I have been praying for you, Elliad John, and for

Berg. I was wrong to hate you when God loves you."

Elliad could contain himself no longer. His laughter echoing loudly, he stopped. Almost doubling up in the effort to control his mirth, he leaned on the wall for support and his whole frame shook at the hilarity he saw in her words. Jobyna looked at Berg. The towering man was not laughing but was staring at her in an inquiring, uncomprehending way. The great cavern of his mouth hung open and a deep frown distorted his forehead.

Elliad turned to Berg, still laughing. "Have you ever heard such rubbish? It is enough to be hated and despised, now we are pitied." He pulled himself together. His voice became sinister and menacing. "Have you been praying that God will strike me dead?"

"Oh no," she cried, "I pray God will bless you, both of you. I do!" Her green eyes were wide with truthfulness. She kept them on his for a moment then lowered her head in submission.

He tucked her hand through his arm and they continued in silence. The corridor widened. Attendants lined one side, bowing and curtsying. Elliad hesitated, turning to his captive. "Tonight we will dine with Prince Gustovas, the monarch of the kingdom of Proburg. He is giving me this castle, Jobyna. In return, I am giving him some of the treasures you helped me acquire in Frencolia. In a way, this castle belongs to you, too." The sarcasm reverberating in his voice was unbearable. His tone slid to a warning whisper and he moved his lips closer to her ear. "Just remember to act like the princess I have said you are! Speak only to answer questions!"

An announcement was made on their entrance to the massive dining hall. "King El-liad, exile from Frencolia. Princess Jobyna, Sister of King Luke Chanec of Frencolia."

The reception was different from any Jobyna had experienced before. People stood in one long line, waiting for the two guests to pass by. Elliad drew her along and they were intro-duced as they moved. She was not sure whether she should curtsy. *What protocol is demanded in this strange land,* she wondered. The men bowed, the ladies curtsied. Jobyna smiled at each one, trying to look them in the eye.

Elliad whispered, "When you are introduced to Prince Gustovas, curtsy." She was thankful for this instruction. She was captive, a hostage, but she reminded herself that Luke was her brother. He had been crowned king of Fren-colia; even Elliad conceded this. She must be brave and strong for Luke's sake, for Frencolia.

The prince grasped her gloved hand, pressing his lips to it. She curtsied, long and low, bowing her head. With his pressure lifting her hand, she rose, and met his inquiring eyes. He stepped back, slowly looking her up and down, from head to toe. Jewels gleamed from the prince's head and garments, dazzling Jobyna. But she would have liked to think she saw kindness on his fatherly face.

"And what message does the captive Princess Jobyna bring from Frencolia to the old Prince Gustovas of Proburg?" he asked. His kind, accented voice was deep and mellow. The room was heavily laced with breathless silence.

Jobyna kept her serious eyes on his. "I give a message of blessings for you to have long life and a happy reign."

This answer pleased the prince. Still holding her hand, he introduced her to his wife. "Her Supreme Highness, the First Princess Rhaselle." The lady was delicate looking, like a china doll. Her golden-brown hair hung in tight curls beneath a jeweled crown. Again, Jobyna's eyes were filled with sparkling jewels as she smiled into the pale brown eyes.

Prince Gustovas, full of a charm Jobyna had never been subject to, led her to the head of a long table where two thronelike chairs stood. With his arm around her narrow waist, he drew her to sit in the chair beside his. Jobyna caught the displeasure in Elliad's eyes, but she knew she had no choice. On the other side of the table, opposite the prince's wife, Elliad sat, after waiting for the prince to be seated first. Jobyna guessed Elliad had expected to sit by the prince.

The celebration dinner began. Course after

course was served and Jobyna was sure she could eat no more.

The goblets were filled and Prince Gustovas raised his, "To the success of King Elliad! May he throw off the shackles of Frencolia and enjoy a long, free life."

Jobyna wondered what story Elliad had told the prince. Whatever he had said, she knew would be filled with lies. She sipped from the goblet. Aromatic and sickly, the liquid made her choke. Drawing out her kerchief, she tried unsuccessfully to stifle her coughing.

The prince laughed loudly. "Tut, tut, Elliad. You haven't taught the maid to drink yet." He added words in German, clicking his fingers and a servant brought some fruit juice. Jobyna swallowed this thankfully, hoping her coughing would not make her sick. She had eaten too much after the meager rations she had grown accustomed to.

Raising his goblet, Elliad stood to his feet. "To Prince Gustovas and his beautiful wife, the First Princess Rhaselle. May they have a long and happy life."

Goblets were refilled. Prince Gustovas raised his once more and turned to Jobyna. "To Princess Jobyna. May she grow from an enchanting girl into a beautiful woman." Jobyna's eyes met Elliad's. He was looking at her in a different way, not through her, but at her.

The toasting complete, Prince Gustovas clapped his hands. Tables were removed and the seating rearranged. Entertainment was to begin. Such music was never featured in Frencolian life and Jobyna enjoyed the new sounds she heard from instruments she never knew existed. Jesters and jugglers performed. Their acts were met by much laughter and applause. Men in national costume did some energetic dancing to strange rhythmic music.

To Elliad's displeasure, Prince Gustovas sat close to Jobyna with his lips close to her ear. After a lively commentary of each act, he asked how she was enjoying the entertainment. She expressed her pleasure, commenting on his descriptions about each performance.

Prince Gustovas had a kindly face with a pleasant rounded nose and a gently furrowed brow. To Jobyna, he was the perfect fatherly image. His smooth chin made him appear younger than he was; his trim moustache was dark brown as were his eyes. Dark curls on his brow were speckled lightly with silver. He was an awesome, handsome man whose scented breath was remaining too close for Jobyna's comfort.

"How old are you, Princess?" Prince Gustovas asked. His eyes upon hers seemed black, like midnight.

"I turned 14 on our travels, five days ago." Her eyes traveled to the prince's left and she met the stare in Elliad's burning blue gaze. She knew this would be news to him. By her calculations, her birthday would have been the day he branded her.

Singers entered, first singing happy songs, then long, morbid ones. Their words Jobyna could not understand. Unaware of the late hour, and due to the ample meal consumed, the warmth of the room overcame her. Jobyna's head slumped back and she fell sound asleep. Elliad, perturbed, leaned over towards her. He hoped to rouse the girl who dared to break royal protocol.

Prince Gustovas grasped his arm and said to him, "Don't wake her. Has she not traveled far today? Only a true princess would dare fall asleep in the company of kings and princes!" He chuckled. Leaning sideways, his lips lightly brushed her forehead. "Keep your treasures, Elliad. I have enough. For the sake of your Princess Jobyna, I will give you this castle. Just you look after her, Elliad, exile king from Frencolia, and if you tire of her, send her to me. I will give you another castle for such a prize."

Jobyna woke suddenly as Berg collected her up in his massive arms. Everyone was standing, bowing or curtsying. Prince Gustovas kissed her hand once more.

"I'm sorry," she said sheepishly to the prince, her eyes including Elliad.

Berg carried her all the way back to the chamber she would occupy. Wide awake, Jobyna wished she could walk. Embarrassment swept her and she hoped Elliad would not be angry

42

with her for falling asleep. Not having heard the prince's last announcement, she imagined Elliad to be humiliated and furious.

Knocking loudly, Berg stood her by the door. The women Jobyna had previously met opened the door, curtsying as before.

Jobyna turned to Berg. Smiling, she said softly, "Thank you, Berg. God bless you."

The door closed behind her, but the great man stood for some seconds. Berg shook his head at the foreign kindness she radiated then moved slowly off down the corridor.

5

Messages Luke received from Proburg and Chezkovia were in favor of Elliad. This distressed the Frencolian King greatly. He could not understand the mentality of such kings and princes. The latest message from Proburg infuriated Luke.

Sir Dorai reminded him, "Elliad has great treasures. He can buy his way in or out of almost any situation. The treasures he possesses speak all languages."

"But he is using my sister as well. You said this Prince Gustovas in Proburg has four sons. How old is he?" Sir Dorai told him he was about 39 or 40.

"Thirty-nine!" Luke's voice grew louder, his

tone raspy and high, "and he writes such rubbish! If it wasn't for his law against polygamy, he would have her hand in marriage. This prince wants to know if we would agree to his purchasing Jobyna as a wife for his youngest son! What does he think she is? Some piece of jewelry to be bought or sold? He has the audacity to compliment me in such terms about my sister! He writes of the castle he has given Elliad, to 'keep the Princess Jobyna safe.' How dare he do this, when she belongs here in Frencolia! He is an accessory to Elliad's crime. We must write and tell him I want her returned here to Frencolia!"

Sir Dorai raised his hands, "Calm down, Luke, my son." Using the endearing term, he went on, "There are ways and means to work this out. Also, ways to make matters worse. Elliad would have filled the prince's head with lies, you can be sure of this. He will be in great glory, painting a wonderful picture of himself. Elliad may have told the prince that Jobyna is there willingly with him. How do we know what stories he concocts? We will wait until Elliad finally settles, then we will decide what actions to take. Prince Gustovas, I know, will be more sympathetic when he hears the truth! We must not spoil the future with rash statements and hasty decisions. It is good to know Jobyna is well. She must be holding up under great strain. Remember, too, Prince Gustovas is no fool. He writes such words from a safe distance. It may be a different matter were we face to face!"

A message arrived from the kingdom of Bavarest. They had suffered the most from Elliad's rampages. Their king was willing to join Frencolia in making him pay for his crimes. Bavarest was presently sending troops out to retrieve stolen goods, seeking revenge on murders committed in their country. King Jarvis pledged to keep frequent communication with Frencolia and would inform them how their counterattack went. Luke was more heartened by this response.

Days were filled with duties at court, decisions needing to be made, compiling of messages and the receiving and dispatching of information. The circle of communication gradually widened. Strasland, the neighboring country on the west, wrote of various raids Elliad had made over the past six years, always pillaging and murdering. The king of Strasland likened Elliad to a Viking raider, merciless and blood-thirsty. He offered allegiance, troops and help to capture Elliad, remarking, however, if the man had gone north, then good riddance. They hoped he would stay there and King Luke's sister would be safely returned.

Luke did not doubt Elliad would want to stay away from Frencolia. Thoughts of Jobyna's captivity troubled him. He felt helpless and impatient, bound by interkingdom intrigue, unable to rescue her.

"One day, Elliad, one day," he said to himself.

Sir Dorai addressed Luke later that day. "I have a request, Son." Luke waited for his uncle to explain. "My wife and children are at Leroy, and I have not seen them, but briefly, for months. I would like to bring them here to live. We could take up residence in the castle or occupy a place of our own in the city."

"Why, Uncle! You didn't tell me. I should have assumed you were married. I had no idea. But of course!" Luke was bursting with the excitement of the news. "They must live here in the castle. I will hear of nothing else." He paused to consider this new development. "How many cousins do I have?"

Sir Dorai told him with pleasure there were four cousins, three girls and a boy.

"And what is my aunt's name?"

"She is named Minette. I call her Mindy." Sir Dorai was pleased with his nephew's reaction.

"Uncle Dor, cousins are just like brothers and sisters! You have no idea how happy this makes me!"

The knowledge of his uncle's children made Luke feel as though a new dimension had been added to his life. He looked forward to their arrival and planned a great celebration to welcome them. Senior knights and lords were invited, and the diversion helped take Luke's mind off the troubles of the country. Lord Farey arrived the night before, and Luke spoke to him first and then to the other lords about a promotion for Sir Dorai.

"Lord Farey, if something happened to me, I have no heirs. Who then would be king in Frencolia?" Luke asked him.

Lord Farey stroked his long white beard. "That is something we have toiled long over, Luke." He smiled at the boy king. "The answer is for you to marry and have a son."

"I have no thoughts of marriage while my sister is a captive of the mad Elliad! Marriage will have to wait." He looked into Lord Farey's eyes, wanting to see his reaction. "I would like to nominate my uncle, Sir Dorai, as my successor. There is no one who has Frencolia's good in his heart so deeply as he. If something did happen to me, then the country would be in the best hands. For the sake of Frencolia, he saved my life and stood back, allowing me to be king!"

People lined the streets of Frencberg to welcome Minette and the children to the city. Sir

Dorai rode out to meet them, leaving Luke waiting in the castle courtyard.

The meeting of new relations was joyful, even tearful. Minette hugged Luke closely, whispering in his ear that she had prayed for this day. She looked younger than he had imagined as did her children. Uncle Dor had married a young wife. Luke was introduced to the children. He met his uncle's eyes as 10-year-old Maia curtsied for him.

"Yes, she is like your mother, my sister." He swung a boy from the cushioned cart. "This is Charles. He is eight tomorrow." With a serious bow, Charles raised his eyes to look at his cousin king. Sir Dorai collected the two little girls, one in each arm. "Doralin is six, and this is Elissa, named after your mother; she is four."

Luke seriously took each little girl's hand and kissed it. He turned to Sir Dorai, "You have not met Jobyna, Uncle. Were they the same age, your Maia and Jobyna would look like twins!"

The celebration dinner was convened early in the evening for the sake of the young ones. The festivity eased the ache in Luke's heart for Jobyna and the hurt he felt over the death of his parents. He beamed at his cousins, enjoying the younger ones' natural affection for him. After the meal, the king announced they were to move to the throne room. The lords, senior knights, officials and their wives stood for Luke to lead the way. Luke held his arm for

Minette to take, beckoning Sir Dorai and the children to follow.

Guests lined the walls of the throne room. Sir Dorai, with Elissa in his arms, stood with the senior knights. He was at a loss to know what was happening and chastised himself for not reading the program properly.

Five lords stood on the dais beside the throne. Lord Farey placed the Frencolian crown on Luke's head and handed him the scepter. The king rose and walked down the marble steps.

"By the power invested in me by the lords of Frencolia, I call Sir Dorai and his wife Minette to come forward." There was a shuffle as Sir Dorai placed Elissa down for Maia to take care of her. Minette took his arm and they made their way toward Luke. Two pages bearing cushions carrying crowns came forward. Luke commanded the couple to kneel. Gently, he brought the scepter to rest momentarily on each of their shoulders, one after the other, then passed the scepter to Lord Farey. Turning to Sir Dorai, Luke took one of the crowns and placed it on his uncle's head.

"You have been faithful and loyal to Frencolia. You shall be known as Prince Dorai, first in line to the Throne of Frencolia." He placed the smaller crown on Minette's fair curls. "You shall be known as Princess Minette, wife of the Crown Prince." Luke turned to the children, "Your children shall be Prince Charles, second in line to the Throne of Frencolia, and Princess Maia, Princess Doralin and Princess Elissa. May God bless you, each one. It is by Him kings reign and princes rule. Rise, Prince Dorai. Rise, Princess Minette." Luke embraced them one at a time, beckoning the children to stand by their parents.

A senior knight called out, "God bless King Luke Chanec." This cry was echoed by all present. Another called out, "God bless Prince Dorai and Princess Minette." They went through the names of all the children. When the cheers died down, Luke called out, "God bless Frencolia," bringing cheers and hearty affirmations.

Prince Dorai, Princess Minette and their children stood with Luke by the huge doors of the throne room as people left. When the last guest had departed, Luke said he would accompany his family to their quarters. The children, full of energy, played as they traversed the long corridors.

Luke's uncle turned to him as they strolled along. "You took me completely by surprise, Son. No doubt this was your idea?"

"Yes, you are correct. You saved my life, Uncle. There was nothing to stop you from chopping my head off back in the jail at Westbrook and claiming the Throne of Frencolia for yourself. You have the good of this country in your heart. Frencolia needs you in a place of leadership even after I turn 16."

Charles ran to Luke and touched his palm on his cousin's back, and said, "You're it," as he dove off ahead up the stairway. Luke ran after him with the girls squealing behind.

When they arrived at their suite, Luke said an affectionate "good night" to each, marveling again at how much Maia looked like Jobyna. It was hard for him not to believe it was her, they were so similar. Prince Dorai walked to Luke's apartment with him.

"I cannot express what you mean to me, Son. It is not just what you have done for us tonight; it is far more than that." He could find no other words to express his emotions. Luke drew him into his quarters and they talked into the night about the future.

"When I marry, and I do not plan to do so for some time, God may give me a son, and he will be heir. Until then, Uncle, if anything happens to me, you shall be king in Frencolia." The uncle shook his head. The thought was beyond his wildest imagination. Dorai had always intended to protect the throne for the one who had claim to it, never dreaming how close he would be to it himself this day.

"I am looking forward to seeing you marry and produce an heir. I am happy to support you, my king . . . my nephew. Frencolia needs you and your ideas for peace and unity. The people respond to your message, and you are much loved and respected already."

Their conversation soon included Jobyna, and

both reaffirmed their commitment to see her rescued.

"Tomorrow," said Dorai, "before the lords and senior knights leave, we are meeting to discuss the dispatch of a rescue party. Even if the group is only able to bring back more information, we need to be keeping a pulse on Elliad's movements. The party should go incognito. We will have to work out a strategy, a plan." With these thoughts whirling in his mind, Prince Dorai left Luke.

The monarch longed for his sister's return but was cheered by the thought of his cousins. *Cousins are like brothers and sisters*, he assured himself as he settled for the night. The castle was sure to be a happier, livelier place with his cousins here!

6

The next morning, Elliad woke with a pounding headache. He had stayed up too late the previous night drinking too much of the Proburg brew, kvass. It was difficult to steady himself enough to dress. He lay down, moaning.

Jobyna awoke early, still suffering embarrassment from her actions the night before. A pink satin and lace gown was laid out and the women helped her dress. Her hair crinkled attractively as they brushed the long braids out. She had scarcely completed dressing when there was a knock at the door. One of the women opened it. A knave spoke in German so Jobyna did not understand him.

"Prince Gustovas requests the presence of Princess Jobyna at breakfast." He handed the woman a red rose. She replied to him, telling him to wait a few minutes. The woman passed the rose to Jobyna. The name Gustovas was now familiar to Jobyna and she guessed the monarch wanted to see her. Shaking her head when someone gave her the pot of rouge, Jobyna pushed it away. If she couldn't go the way she was, maybe she shouldn't go at all! Holding the rose in her left hand, she placed her right hand on the knave's and allowed him to escort her where he would.

An exquisitely carved balcony with arched openings met Jobyna's delighted gaze. Displayed before her green eyes were the beautiful castle gardens filled with flowering rose bushes, trim hedges and cobbled paths winding their way among the foliage. Out beyond was the rolling countryside. Jobyna's vision was overcome with a hunger to keep feasting her eyes on the beautiful view.

Prince Gustovas rose to meet her. "This view pleases you?" he asked, kissing her hand too passionately. She curtsied, stating the affirmative. He held her hand tightly, looking at her face, hair and neck. "It pleases me, too, very much!" He gazed at her, watching a rosy hue creep into her cheeks at his obvious positive appraisal. Princess Rhaselle rose and Jobyna drew away from the prince, curtsying to his wife.

"My wife does not speak Frenc and you do not speak German. It makes for difficulty. I shall interpret." He motioned her to sit. "I have sent for your King Elliad, but he is, how do you say, 'under the weather.' Too much kvass, I think. So we have you with us for breakfast, which is good." He clicked his fingers in his characteristic way. Servants entered, bringing hot bread rolls and all manner of dishes Jobyna had never laid eyes on before. Prince Gustovas chatted while they ate, explaining the various ingredients and chuckling when Jobyna tried to show politeness at the strange flavors her taste buds were subjected to. Never before had she seen such food for breakfast! When the prince was sure Jobyna could eat no more, he stated they would go for a leisurely stroll in the garden.

Princess Rhaselle chatted away to her husband and he relayed the questions to Jobyna, passing the conversation back and forth. Jobyna enjoyed the discourse, the first sensible verbal exchange she had been involved in for over two months. A carved stone seat in the castle garden provided the perfect place to continue chatting.

"Rhaselle asks if you have ever seen the sea," Prince Gustovas inquired.

"I'd never left the borders of Frencolia before coming here," she replied. "What is the sea like?"

"It is something you have to experience yourself," Rhaselle replied through their interpreter. "One third of Proburg's northern-most border is the North Sea, and the most beautiful scenery in the world is along our coast. You must view the Baltic Sea from Proburg one day, Jobyna. It is like all the rivers and lakes of the earth rolling together to kiss the sky at the edge of the world."

Jobyna described the geography of her own country, the mountains, valleys and large luscious meadows. Rhaselle told her that Proburg was low-lying land with vast plains and rolling hills.

It was almost noon when Elliad appeared. He was perturbed to see Jobyna so involved in discussion, bright and full of good humor. His guilty conscience caused him to worry that she may have told some truths about him he wouldn't want them to know.

"Elliad, my friend. I was hoping to see you before we leave. We have a three-hour journey. You must come and visit my Proburg Capital sometime again and bring Jobyna to see a real castle, my castle at Landmari!" He took Jobyna's hand. "You must never think of coming without bringing Jobyna. Come and see us off, my dear." He swept the girl away with him, followed by his wife, who walked with Elliad.

How Jobyna wished she could leave with them. They seemed respectable, civil people who treated her like a human. The contrast was startling! The captive realized she had become accustomed to the cold, silent and indifferent treatment she received from day to day. She was scarcely more than baggage. The farewell was sad for her. Prince Gustovas' soldiers and servants made an impressive cavalcade. Princess Rhaselle kissed her on both cheeks, and the prince kissed her hands before gently kissing her forehead.

Prince Gustovas saluted Elliad, saying in German, "Do not forget my offer. I would increase it, if you so wish."

Jobyna did not remember the way back to her quarters. She was not sure where to go or what she was to do next. It was obvious that preparations were being made for arrivals, and she hoped Ellice would arrive soon.

"Sit there!" Elliad pointed to some steps at the side of the stables. His commands had returned! Jobyna hummed a pleasant tune from the night before, noticing Berg staring at her as he stood behind Elliad. She smiled at him, looking him in the eye for the first time. Several knights crouched with Elliad, poring over maps spread on the cobblestones. She would not allow her mind to imagine what horrible plans he was making. One of the knights looked over at her and she ceased humming. It would not be good for Elliad's anger to be kindled against her. Jobyna hoped they were not discussing her.

The next days were boring and uneventful. Jobyna was thankful about the lack of events, for Elliad's style of events did not thrill her in the least. The night before Ellice and the rest of the company arrived at the castle, Jobyna tossed and turned. She was alone in the large apartment and the air was hot and close.

Summer is here, she thought sleepily. Falling into a deep slumber, Jobyna thought she heard a click of the door. Her eyes failed to open and she sank deeper into sleep. Some time later she was disturbed and she was sure she could hear someone breathing heavily. Her eyes popped opened as a chill ran down her spine. She sat up, ready to scream out, wondering if anyone would hear her. A large hand wrapped quickly around her mouth, and her eyes widened in terror. It was too dark to see anything but she knew instinctively it was Berg. What was he doing in her room, in the middle of the night?

"I'm not going to hurt you, Jobyna," he whispered. "Just promise me you won't scream." He waited until she nodded, releasing her slowly, gently. Dragging herself up in the bed, she drew the blanket up, pulling her pillow in front of her as though a shield. Speechless, fear had frozen her tongue.

"Look, I'm not here to harm you." He put his face closer to hers. "Do you understand?" He glanced around at the closed door as he lowered himself to a sitting position on the bed. Holding his gigantic hands, palms up, in front of him, he continued. "I have not slept at all the past three nights. I have never lost a night's sleep in my life before. Every time I close my eyes, I see blood on my hands and it will not wash off." He looked at the cowering girl. "I'm not going to hurt you so please don't be afraid." Bringing the blanket down from her face, Jobyna tried to relax a little, yet she still felt like a trapped bird. "I am here because I want you to help me. You know what I am. Killing never worried me, until . . . " his deep voice, husky with emotion, broke off. There was a long silence. He hung his huge head, putting his hands to his temples.

Somewhat reassured he was not here on evil intent, Jobyna asked in a trembling voice, "Until what, Berg? Tell me, what?"

The huge frame did not move. He spoke into his hands, and his voice was muffled. "I killed your parents, and I cannot get them off my mind." He lifted his head to look at her. In the darkness, she could scarcely make out his face. "They were not afraid to die, Jobyna." Another long pause. "I am afraid!" His voice barely a whisper. "I am so afraid!"

Dumbfounded, the girl did not know what she could say or do! Berg flung his head back, his face turned to the ceiling. "I, the great Berg, am afraid!"

Tears rolled down Jobyna's cheeks. "You killed my mother and my father? They were so good and would never harm anyone. All they wanted to do was love people and help them." Sniffing, she wiped her tears on the satin pillow slip. "I miss them so much."

The bed shook as Berg slid off onto the floor. His head rested against the side of the bed. He did not speak. It dawned on Jobyna that Berg was suffering from the effects of over-powering guilt. But guilt could do nothing to bring her parents back! For a brief instant the thought of how she could make Berg pay for what he did surged through her mind but was quickly chased away with the realization that revenge would not bring them back either! She sniffed again, rubbing the tears with the blanket. She wanted to ask, "Are you sorry now?" but rephrased the question into more of a statement.

"You are sorry now, aren't you, Berg?" Her voice was soft.

"What good would that do? To be sorry?" Berg said thickly.

"Did you ever hear the message from the Gospel Book?"

"Yes. Many years ago. King Elliad invited the evangelist to his castle at Valdemar and we all heard what he had to say. The king laughed him to scorn and sent him on his way. His hatred for the Gospel Book began then." He did not tell Jobyna that Elliad's laughter and

61

scoffing of her had graphically reminded him of the evangelist's visit.

Jobyna's voice was soft. "What did you think about the message, Berg?" A silence broken only by his thunderous breaths pervaded the dark room.

"I did not think about it. There was no point. Elliad would not have allowed it."

"Do you remember the message, Berg?"

"Yes." Silence again.

"The evangelist said God can forgive sin." Jobyna waited apprehensively. Hot and clammy, the tension was incredible to her. Palpitating, her heart flew in prayer for strength.

"Yes, I remember." Berg remained slumped, head down.

"God will forgive you all of your sin if you believe on His Son and ask Him to forgive you." Jobyna waited, her heart was in her mouth.

"Would you forgive me, Jobyna?" lifting his head slowly.

"Yes, Berg, I forgive you. How could I not, when God will?"

The man sighed a mammoth sigh that made Jobyna jump. Instinctively, she pulled her "shield" up under her chin again. Though she knew she was not being tricked, it was impossible to dispel the intimidation she felt.

Berg was stifling, swallowing and smothering sobs that shook the bed. "I'm sorry . . . I'm so sorry."

"I forgive you, Berg. You need to tell God you are sorry. He will forgive you." A death-like quietness prevailed. Jobyna waited, her knees drawn up under her chin. She was clutching the pillow, her muscles tense. The silence drew seconds out into infinite minutes. Sobs, barely audible, continued to shake the mountainous structure of the man huddled on the stone floor. Jobyna trembled uncontrollably, waiting . . . waiting . . . not sure what there was to wait for. It was a long time before Berg pulled himself somewhat together. He stood, unsteady on his feet, moving slowly towards the door.

"I'll pray for you, Berg," Jobyna whispered after him.

Closing the door quietly behind him, he stole down the corridor. Jobyna slid weakly down into the bed, exhausted by the tenseness of the situation. She burst into tears, not sure why she was crying. Tears for her parents, torn away without her being able to express unrestrained grief at their going, unable to attend any funeral to help deal with the reality of their passing. Tears of relief that Berg the torturer's stony heart could become human flesh after all. God had stricken him with guilt for his wrongdoing. What would happen if Elliad heard of this? She must pray for Berg. His confession was a great blow to the image Elliad had of him. Jobyna knew all the crimes Berg ever committed were under orders from Elliad. The confession was a costly one for Elliad's right-hand man. A change in Berg could only be made at great cost. With these thoughts she fell into a fitful sleep.

7

Jobyna's long dark eyelashes lifted to view a room beaming with bright shafts of sunlight. Brilliant yellow burst its way through chinks in the shutters. Ellice rushed in the door. Boey, bustling breathlessly, was not far behind.

"There you are!" The servant woman opened the shutters. "My, have we had a time finding you! No one knew where you were!" She turned to look at Jobyna. The bed covers were in a heap. Her charge's face was drawn and dark rings circled her eyes. "What have they been doing to you? You look dreadful!" She issued orders to Ellice who scurried to the bathroom for a cloth and water. Boey sat on the bed, placing her ample arms around the girl's bony shoulders. Jobyna burst into tears and sobbed into Boey's cushion-like breast.

"The morning's half over and you're still in bed? The slave'll look after you and I'll be getting your breakfast." Boey gruffly pushed Jobyna away. Ellice placed a bowl and towel on the table. As soon as Boey had gone, she drew a tiny note, sealed with wax, from the folds of her cloak. Passing it fearfully to Jobyna, Ellice moved away. Staring out the window, the slave girl pulled off her boots and cloak. Jobyna wriggled her way out of the muddle of the bed, her head spinning. A note! Her first thoughts were of Luke. The seal was "K.E."! Frowning, she broke the seal and unfolded the parchment. It read:

J. The least I can do now is to take you back to F., that is what I plan to do the first chance I have. Keep forgiving me.

There was no signature, not even initials. Jobyna read the message a second time.

"Did Berg give this to you for me?" She asked Ellice. The slave girl nodded. "Where did you see him?" Ellice pointed and made the motion of horse riding. "We must burn it." The slave helped the girl find and light a candle, and they placed the burning parchment in the fireplace, blowing the candle out. Dressing thoughtfully, Jobyna noticed Ellice staring into space with a blank expression.

"You're tired, aren't you? Why don't you lie down and have a sleep?" The slave girl shook her head with finality. A knock came at the door and Ellice rushed to open it. Servants entered the room lugging several trunks. Boey waddled in behind them, placing a tray of food and juice on the table.

"Share it with me," Jobyna requested as she sat before the welcome meal.

"We had something before we left Baja Castle," Boey informed her.

Jobyna was interested to learn the name of the castle. Boey was in a congenial mood toward her and willingly answered the girl's questions.

"Yes, Baja Castle is on the border of both Chezkovia and Proburg. This castle is called Chezpro and is also on the border. They say it belongs to King Elliad now."

"Where have Elliad and his men gone today?" Jobyna asked, thinking of Berg.

"They are bringing the rest of the carts over here. Some of the servants are staying at Baja. There is another castle the king has bought. It is on the northern coast of Chezkovia. We will be moving there before the winter."

It pleased Jobyna that Boey had laid aside the stiff servant/princess attitude and was now talking to her more as a peer. Jobyna supposed the new warmth was due to the feeling of security she felt now that they had arrived at the country of their destination.

67

Chezkovia. If only she had a map. She could not remember such a country, yet the name was vaguely familiar and Jobyna wondered where she had read of such a place.

"How does the king of Chezkovia feel about Elliad living in his country?"

Boey answered, "Oh, I hear he is very pleased. You see, King Elliad has a dual citizenship. His father was from Chezkovia. It's not the 'king' of Chezkovia, either, Princess; he's called 'czar.' His name is Czar Kievik. King Elliad was evidently presented to Czar Kievik by his father when he was alive, and he has visited him since. There have been messages and gifts sent by King Elliad, and the czar is pleased for us to be here in Chezkovia."

Boey chatted on as Ellice helped her unpack the trunks. Jobyna learned that Elliad was worried about troops attacking from the south. He had taken most of the soldiers with him to bring the rest of the carts from Baja Castle. All the treasures arrived safely at Chezpro Castle with the company Boey and Ellice traveled with. The remaining carts contained the furnishings and food-stocks collected along the way.

"Doesn't all the plundering bother you, Boey?" Jobyna dared to ask the servant.

"I never let such thoughts cross my mind. That's up to them men folks. If they wants to do it, then let them do it, I says."

"Are you married, Boey?" the captive asked, changing the subject.

"I was once, years ago. But he got killed in a raid; we didn't have no children. So I'se just happy to go where I go. They'se head servant said I was to be chamber maid to Princess Jobyna. King Elliad's orders he said. 'N I asked him if'n I could talk to you now we was out 'a Frencolia, 'n he said please meself, so here I are!" Jobyna noticed the change in Boey's speech. She was rattling on, using some of the slang familiar among the servants, running all her words together.

"Who is Ada, Boey? Is she a servant?" Jobyna asked casually.

"Not likely. She's married to that Sir Berg. She's a class above the servants. You mind her!"

"What about that other one . . . Ranee?"

"You keep out'a her way, too. She's Elliad's woman."

"So they're not married?" Jobyna was checking out what she had heard from Ada.

"No. It's no secret he wants a son to carry on his line. She has to bear him a son, he says, and then he will marry her. Just two girls so far."

"It sounds a bit back-to-front to me."

"You better mind your tongue, miss, an' keep that to y'self, or you'll be 'n more trouble! No one dares to say anything again' Miss Ranee and the king. You mind, now. She's got 'er mind made up to be his queen some day, son or no son."

Boey unpacked some of the trunks, organized other servants to clean the apartment and changed the bed linen. Eager to excel in her new duties, she bossed and ordered Ellice. The younger woman complied with her every word. Jobyna, knowing she was expected to keep out of the way, lounged on the couch, thinking secretly of Berg's note and of escaping back to Frencolia. How good it would to see Luke again, her brother, the king! She tried to imagine him sitting on the throne in the Frencolian throne room of the King's Castle at Frencberg. In her delicious day dream, Jobyna was there with him!

Midafternoon, the door flew open. A breathless young soldier blurted, "Bo, you others, come at once! You'll all be needed. The men met with an ambush coming back from Baja. Troops from Bavarest. We had to abandon the carts. That's what they was after." Boey dropped the cloth she held. "The king's wounded, pretty bad. Over a hundred dead. Heaps more injured. There's a Chezk doctor on the way from Jydanski."

Jobyna followed them to the door where the soldier barred her way.

"Not you, Princess. You stay here!"

Ellice left with them and Jobyna was alone in the apartment. Surely there must be something she could do, she thought. How dreadful it was for people to fight and cut each other to pieces with swords and daggers. So Elliad was wounded! She did not feel sorry for him, but somehow she could not feel glad. He did deserve it though, she conceded. He had asked for something like this to happen for a long time!

Realizing she had better stay put, she unpacked a chest of dresses brought from Frencolia for her, hanging them in the enormous closet. She pushed the over-sized clothes to the back. No one was around to reprove her for helping and she was glad for something to do. Discovering the tiara and ruby necklace Elliad had given her in Frencolia, she felt nothing but hatred for them. To be the daughter of her baron father, safe in the manor house, was all the girl longed for. Jobyna reminisced on the happy times of her childhood, happily sinking back into her day dreaming.

The apartment was growing dark when Jobyna lifted the cover on the tray from breakfast. Bread rolls and fruit remained. She ate thankfully. Curling up on the couch, she began wondering how long it would be before Ellice returned. She felt unsettled, but was soon fast asleep.

It was late evening when Jobyna awoke. She felt refreshed and longed to go for a walk. No soldiers stood guard outside the door, but this did not surprise her. They were sure to be helping with all the casualties. Undecided, the girl stood in the doorway. Footsteps echoing in the dark made her mind up and she retreated into the apartment, fumbling to light a lamp. A young soldier entered.

"Come with me!" he ordered, moving off, expecting her to follow instantly.

"This is the story of my life," Jobyna grumbled under her breath. "Do this, do that, stay here, go there!" Daring not to do anything but follow, and chastening herself on her attitude, she rushed after the lad. *At least something was happening! Maybe Elliad was dead!* Chilled by this sudden thought, she tried to imagine what would become of her if Elliad did die. *Berg will take me back to Frencolia!* The thought of Berg and his change of heart cheered her and the passages did not seem so unfriendly as she hurried to keep the young soldier in sight. She ran to catch his quick march.

"How is Elli . . . King Elliad?" she asked the soldier, still running to keep up with the pace he had set. He did not answer. Jobyna became breathless and lagged behind. Rounding a corner, she felt as though she had circled the whole castle. The soldier stood before an open door, waiting. As she drew closer, he announced her, speaking quietly.

"Princess Jobyna."

The room was well lit. Jobyna entered slowly, cautiously, not knowing what to expect. Ada stood, staring at her, waxen-faced. Two men with their backs to her, leaned over a long table-height bench. The room reminded Jobyna of the one she had lain in when she was sick in Frencolia. It was some sort of sick-room, a recovery annex for soldiers.

Ada stepped towards her, "He . . . my husband . . . kept asking for you, so I sent for you."

Jobyna walked to the foot of the bench. Berg lay there, still wearing his battle-armor.

"Jo . . . by . . . na." His voice was racked with pain, each breath rasping with the immense effort to draw another.

Placing her hand on his, Jobyna said, her voice less than a whisper, "I'm here, Berg."

An arrow protruded from his chest, just to the left of his heart. Blood had oozed prolifically from the wound and the broken armor mesh was red. Congealed blood clung to his beard. Ada, her face stony, took up a cloth and sponged his forehead.

73

Jobyna said to her, "I'm sorry. I'm truly sorry."

There was movement at the door. The servants bowed as Elliad entered stiffly. His neck and right shoulder were swathed in blood-stained bandages. An older man, also with blood-stained clothing, followed. He cast his attention to Berg. Elliad turned his whole body towards Ada who rushed to the king's side. Drooping his left arm over her shoulder, he kissed her listlessly on the forehead.

With an uncomprehending look at Jobyna, who still had her hand on Berg's, the wounded king frowned and growled, "What are you doing here?"

Ada took his left arm and drew him to a far corner of the room. "Berg kept asking for her. He pleaded . . . begged." Looking away, she whispered, "He cried. I sent for her. He's been saying over and over how sorry he is . . . " Pausing, she looked furtively at Jobyna who could hear the words clearly. The girl kept her eyes on Berg's pain-riven face.

"About what?" Elliad demanded.

"Killing her parents."

Elliad beckoned the doctors over to him. "What would happen, if you removed the arrow?"

"It would hasten his death, Sire." The older doctor's accented voice was a whisper, but in the confines of the small room it carried to Jobyna's ears, "He has lost too much blood.

Removal of the arrow would cause more hemorrhaging. I have done all I can for him. It is only a matter of time . . . not much longer. I can prepare a draft, it would be better . . . "

"No!" Ada cried out, throwing her head back. She would have shrieked louder if Elliad had not placed his free hand over her mouth.

"Take her out." Elliad urged. "Leave us, all of you! Don't disturb us until I say." It took the two doctors all their strength to remove Ada from the room. Hysterically, she was sobbing, crying and fighting them.

Berg opened his eyes at the commotion. He saw Jobyna standing beside him. Her green eyes were horror-stricken and she was riveted to the floor.

The wounded Elliad ventured to Berg's other side. Taking his large hand in his own, he spoke earnestly. "You saved my life, Berg. That arrow was meant for me."

"It's over . . . now . . . all finished." Berg's voice broke. Elliad was struggling to control his own emotions.

"You have served your king very well. I shall never forget you. I will make sure Ada and the children are taken care of. Do you want to see them again . . . before . . . "

"No . . . I . . . have . . . seen them. I want . . . " His voice broke again.

Elliad put his face closer to the mortally injured man's. "Yes, Berg. Tell me. Anything."

"To . . . talk to . . . " His voice faded.

75

Elliad looked unbelievingly at Jobyna.

"You want to talk to Jobyna?"

"Yes."

Elliad looked at his captive. "Talk to him," he commanded, gesticulating weakly with his uninjured arm. "He wants to talk to you, girl! Come nearer."

Jobyna stepped closer to Berg's head. Drawing the stool up, she sat, her head level with his. Terrified due to Elliad's presence, she felt awkward and out of place. Elliad's blue eyes pierced her face and she blushed uncontrollably. The exile king sank down on a bench. Jobyna could see he was suffering excruciating pain himself. Beads of perspiration crowded his pallid brow.

"Berg, I'm here. How can I help you?"

"I'm . . . going . . . to die, Jobyna . . . soon. How do I know . . . for sure . . . God . . . will forgive . . . me?" He seemed to have summoned the strength to verbalize what was so vital to him in this hour. Jobyna looked across at Elliad who was glaring at her, his face hardened with pain.

"Tell him what he wants to know!" he demanded. Jobyna knew Elliad was allowing this as a "death wish" for his closest friend, the protector, who had saved his life. His eyes conveyed, "anything, just get it over with." For the first time, Jobyna saw emotion and pain in the blue eyes.

Moistening her lips with her tongue, Jobyna

tried to calm her voice. "Berg, when Jesus died on the cross, He was crucified between two thieves. They had done cruel, bad things." Out of the corner of her eye she saw Elliad lean on the bench and slump down in his seat. He dropped his head to rest in his hand. "One of the thieves believed on Him, and Jesus promised he would be with Him, that day, in paradise. The Gospel Book," she continued, glancing across at Elliad, who did not move, "says Jesus is able to save all those who come to Him, all who believe on His Name."

Berg's great frame shook as he tried to sit up. Elliad rose. He grabbed his bodyguard awkwardly, struggling to maintain his own balance. Berg reached out, gripping Elliad.

"Promise me . . . Elliad . . . you'll treat her well." Berg's spurt of energy was spent as suddenly as it came. Falling back heavily on the blood-stained bench, he wrenched Elliad with him.

Elliad, his eyes turned on the dying man's face, gasped, "I'll treat her well, Berg. . . . I promise . . . " The sudden jerk brought unexpected agony to the injured king. His face turned white and his eyes rolled back. Sweat now drenched his forehead, running down his face.

Jobyna read another meaning into the way Elliad presented his words. She thought, *He's really saying, "anything, I'll tell you anything, so you can go in peace."*

Berg released his hold on Elliad. The rasping voice came to her ears once more and Berg's head had slumped toward her. "Tell me more . . . about the Book." Jobyna looked across at Elliad again, but he was motionless.

"Tell him." Elliad's command held impatient resignation.

Racking her tense brain, Jobyna recalled verses she had memorized. Speaking slowly, decisively, she tried to be accurate in quoting the Scriptures. "Jesus said, 'In My Father's house are many mansions. I go to prepare a place for you.' He said, 'I am the Way, the Truth and the Life.' Also, 'I am the Resurrection and the Life. He who believes in Me, though he were dead, yet shall he live.' " The dying man gave a long, satisfied sigh. Jobyna was silent.

Berg's breath came in long extended rasps, then subsided until Jobyna wondered if he was breathing at all. Elliad did not move. "More" Berg breathed into her ear, "Tell me . . . more."

Slowly, Jobyna quoted the 23rd Psalm, her lips close to his ear.

"The Lord is my shepherd; I shall not want. He maketh me to lie down in green pastures: he leadeth me beside the still waters. He restoreth my soul: he leadeth me in the paths of righteousness for his name's sake. Yea, though I walk through the valley of the shadow of death, I will fear no evil: for thou art with me; thy rod and thy staff they comfort me. Thou

78

preparest a table before me in the presence of mine enemies: thou anointest my head with oil; my cup runneth over. Surely goodness and mercy shall follow me all the days of my life: and I will dwell in the house of the Lord forever."

His voice husky, the fading man exclaimed thickly, "That's . . . wonderful." Jobyna glanced at Elliad. He was unmoving. Berg swung between consciousness and unconsciousness, asking Jobyna to talk to him, to tell him more of the Book. Each time she hesitated, Elliad said, "Tell him." So she went through all the Scriptures she had ever memorized, until finally, in the long pause when Berg peacefully ceased breathing, all was silent in the room. Elliad, his head on Berg's arm, slept on one side of the bench, Jobyna on the other with her head against Berg's lifeless shoulder.

Light slowly began to permeate the chamber of death. It was as though morning was reluctant to hasten the discovery, unwilling to disturb the sleeping pair, who, though different as day and night, were briefly brought together by Berg's bloodstained body.

The door was flung open, the dank air was filled with a heart-wrenching scream. "Ohhh!"

Ada, wailing and sobbing, threw herself across the lifeless frame of her husband. Jobyna and Elliad simultaneously rose, the latter groaning as he weakly tried to stand. Two knights rushed to help their king.

"Ada," Elliad said to the distraught woman. He was unable to turn his head to look at her face. Still sobbing, she drew closer as he spoke. "Never have I seen a man die so peacefully." He spoke truthfully. With a knight on either side of him, he was helped from the room.

Forgotten, Jobyna rose cautiously. She walked around the bench, out the door and along the corridor. She was not sure later how she came to find her quarters but found herself crawling onto the bed, alone, tired and un-nerved. Her great would-be rescuer had died. What would become of her now, she wondered?

8

The view from the vast balcony where Jobyna had eaten breakfast almost a week previous with Prince Gustovas and Princess Rhaselle brought a small measure of comfort to the lonely girl. Over the past few days she had spent a lot of time walking to this balcony, pacing back and forth, not sure what else she could do.

This wing of the castle was deserted. Boey and Ellice had not returned since being called away. Jobyna tried several of the doors along the many corridors, hoping to find a library, but most of the doors were locked. A man servant brought her food twice a day, not answering her questions or pausing to converse.

Disinterest in food caused her to pick. She drank the fruit juice, but ate very little. From the balcony she could see some of the happenings around the castle. It appeared Chezpro was in a state of siege. All battlements and gates were well manned, no one leaving or entering. Graves were being dug in a grassy area of the garden. Soldiers' bodies were laid within these shallow graves and the turf haphazardly replaced. Jobyna imagined Berg would be buried there, without a funeral service. No one would read verses of comfort to Ada and his children.

Elliad's injuries were so severe that Jobyna imagined he might die. The girl wished she could be helping to care for the injured. The idleness made her feel totally useless. The previous day she had dared to walk down the stairs towards the chamber Berg had been in, but as she neared the doorway, she was stopped by two soldiers who ordered her to return to her apartment, telling her in no uncertain terms "to stay there!"

Jobyna remembered the plague, how she had taken care of her dying brothers and sister. She had nursed the servants stricken with the sickness of death. There were also orphaned children to care for. Jobyna and her mother had helped care for the many bereaved families in the village of Chanoine.

Leaning on the balcony balustrade, the girl reminisced on the times spent working with her mother. Happy hours spent looking after the affairs of the great manor house, talking about home making, learning of women's matters. All that seemed so long ago and far away, part of another life.

The sound of horses' hooves cut into her thoughts. She could hear the grinding of the chains, raising the portcullis. Forty or 50 horses mounted by men wearing Elliad's knights' armor rode through from the barbican. The company clattered across the courtyard toward the stables. Jobyna walked the circuit back to her apartment, pausing periodically to peer out the windows on the way, but she was disappointed to view only sky.

Loneliness swamped her with depression. If only she had a book to read, some embroidery to do or a pen and ink to draw with. Every sound venturing to her sensitive ears was received with interest, every creak, every rustle. Footsteps sounded and Jobyna hastened to the door. Stealing a glance cautiously around the doorjamb, her eyes focussed down the corridor.

"Ellice! Boey!" Relief flooded her as she saw the familiar faces. The girl's relief turned to concern as they drew nearer, tired and drawn.

"We have to pack everything, Princess. We are leaving within the hour," Boey announced with a hasty curtsy.

The apartment immediately became a flurry of activity. Boey did not argue as Jobyna took clothes from the closet and helped pack the chest and trunks. The servant talked at high speed the whole time.

"King Elliad is improving. He will be traveling in a special cart they have prepared for him. As soon as we are ready, we will be leaving. There is news of troops coming from the south. The king wants to be at his coastal castle by sunset today. It is a more secure castle, and he hopes to recuperate in peace. He's furious about them newfangled cross-bows the soldiers from Bavarest used. 'All cowards,' he said. They ambushed them, shooting from a ways off, killing soldiers and horses before they's even got a chance to defend themselves. Jest as well they abandoned the carts or it'd be far worse. Some of them poor soldiers, mind, . . . " She clicked her tongue, shaking her head. "Knocked him bad, that Berg dying. Took his arrow, too, they say."

Jobyna kept silent. She thought it wise not to say anything about being with Berg when he died. That would just give the servants something more to gossip about.

Boey rattled on, "They's worried 'bout the enemy coming from Frencolia. I jest hope we get clear 'fore they do."

She means my fellow country men, my friends. They're the enemy to her! Jobyna thought.

Before they finished packing, soldiers arrived for the trunks. Ellice gave Jobyna her crimson cloak, riding boots and gloves to wear. They

84

hurried along the corridors, down the stairs and out into the courtyard. Mounted knights and soldiers were already moving off. Carts packed up with chests, trunks, bags and packs were being repacked to utilize every inch of space. Such a scene reminded Jobyna of the time they left Frencolia. Frencolia. It was another world, far removed from the lifestyle she was forced to live now. A knight riding Speed drew near. He dismounted, and Jobyna recognized his voice as he spoke.

"King Elliad says you are to ride with me."

"Julian!" Jobyna murmured as he lifted her on the horse. He had lost a great deal of weight, but she remembered his high-pitched, rasping voice. She would never forget him. Julian was the knight who had captured her and handed her over to Elliad back in Frencolia. Jobyna hoped he had not been chosen to take the place of Berg. If so, escape would be much harder, even impossible. Wondering once more why was she not allowed to ride Brownlea, she asked herself how they could imagine her being able to escape. It would be impossible to go very far without being caught! With heart-rending dread, Jobyna turned her mind to the journey ahead, loathing the fact that every mile north was one mile further from her beloved home.

The road they traversed was wide, straight and well kept, not at all like the paths traveled previously. Good time was made, and Julian drew the horse ahead of the carts, riding alongside the soldiers in front. Jobyna viewed the countryside before her with a critical air. Unlike the mountains and hills of days gone by, it was rolling to flat, luscious and green.

Shortly before sunset, as Speed flew along the crest of a low rise, Jobyna noticed the sandiness of the soil. The grass was becoming more tussocky, such as she had never seen before. Lifting her tired eyes, she drew a sharp breath, and her spirits sunk lower. Outlined against the dark sky, etched into an isthmus-like clifftop was a great mass of castle—a fortress.

Several tiers made a striking, ominous picture. Jobyna counted four stories of balconies and windows. The keep, itself, did not have battlements but was roofed with layers of sloped shingles. Steep roofs would repel the winter rain and snow. The huge edifice touched the stormy clouds and Jobyna shuddered. This place would become her prison! There was one road to the castle with five sets of tower gates to pass through. Each gate was crowned with battlements. Already, King Elliad's soldiers were there on guard, keeping watch. The first and fifth gate towers were taller than the middle three. Jobyna heard the sound of water flowing under one of the drawbridges.

The last gate behind them, the company dismounted wearily. Escorted by Julian and two other soldiers, Jobyna walked up hundreds of stone steps, along narrow walkways and paths, through beautiful rockeries and gardens, amid statues of stone and arbors of vines. The terraced stairway to the castle entrance was extremely wide. Stone lions stood proudly on each side of the entrance, like fearless guardians. Breathlessness and fatigue overwhelmed Jobyna as they neared steps leading to open doors. The arched opening looked unwelcome, even forbidding. She found herself being ushered to a reception room to the side of the gray marble foyer.

Her cloak and gloves cast off, she allowed her gaze to circle the room. Her heart jumped with pleasure at the sight she beheld. Books! Books were chained individually to the huge shelves that lined two walls. The lamp light was dim, but Jobyna pulled book after book off the shelves, holding each one open toward the light so she could read the title page. They were all the same! All in the language of Chezkovia. She could not read them. Disappointed, she flung herself down on the couch to wait for her next orders.

Boey's voice came to the captive's ears as she felt herself being gently shaken. "Wake up, Princess! We're to take you to your room." Ellice gathered up the cloak and gloves as they hurried after a soldier. Walking the staircase was a dizzying experience for the girl. It was a narrow spiral, pulling her round and round, up and up. Still only half awake, Jobyna's head ached by the time they reached the apartment. Not pausing to explore or to cast her eyes around, she stumbled through the sitting room, into the bedroom. She fell on the bed with a sigh as Ellice hastened to pull off her boots and cover her with a rug.

Succumbing to her melancholy, Jobyna's last thoughts as she fell asleep were, *Lord, this is the end of the earth! Please be with me here, or I'll surely die!*

9

Unpacking, rearranging and resting filled the next few days for Jobyna and her two servants. A small chamber furnished with two bench beds was attached to the main bedroom. Jobyna's four-poster bed was surrounded with heavy, red, triple-lined drapes. Dominating the large sitting room was a huge fireplace with an elaborate chimney. Jobyna realized the winter here would be colder than any she had experienced before. The loathing she felt in her heart towards this castle fortress made her listless and dejected. Boey tried in vain to get her to eat the food she fetched twice a day.

The morning of the fifth day at this coastal castle Jobyna was ordered to be present at the evening meal with King Elliad. Boey and Ellice helped her dress with care, trying to lift her depressed spirits. She knew they would not understand how she felt, at least not Boey. Jobyna felt that if their circumstances had been different, she could be close friends with Ellice, but the slave chose to remain aloof. The attractive Ellice had been grossly mistreated, and her total submission to her station was a sign of her broken heart and crushed spirit.

Jobyna pledged to herself she would never let that happen. *I must learn to be more self-controlled, but I pray I will not suffer a broken spirit.* The girl felt wonderfully revived after the luxurious soak in the bath and the massage Boey gave her back.

"You'll be needing some meat on these bones, my girl," Boey said reproachfully as her large soft hands rubbed oil into Jobyna's spine. "There's nothing of you!" By the time she was dressed, complete with diamond tiara and ruby necklace, Jobyna's attitude had lifted.

Accompanied by a knight and a soldier who did not give their names, Jobyna noted the journey to the castle's dining room was by a different route than the one that had been used to bring her to the apartment. A shock of red hair poked from beneath the accompanying knight's cap. He also sported a red moustache and matching beard. Jobyna wondered if the three children she had seen at the stream belonged to this man. How frustrating to be surrounded by people yet not allowed to be acquainted with them.

The staircase was wide and elaborate. Jobyna's thoughts moved from the knight to her surroundings, and she guessed the other spiral staircase was a back entrance to the apartments and this was the main ascent. The grey marble floor reflected the great lamps with brilliance as she walked along, her arm resting on the knight's. Masonries along the corridors, balustrades and banisters were beautifully wrought and intricate patterns and designs displayed themselves. Jobyna's eyes grew wide with each delightful discovery. The ceiling was fashioned up into a high arched transom above the dining room doors, a tangle of exposed beams.

"The Princess Jobyna." She drew a breath at the announcement, not daring to imagine in what mood she would find Elliad. Knights and their wives were standing, bowing and curtsying.

Jobyna was overcome with humor at the charade. The corners of her mouth twitched at the thought, *I'm no more a princess than Ellice. It just suits this tyrant to call me such!*

"Come!" His voice brought motion to her feet. The knight escorted her to the seat beside Elliad. Her captor stood, taking her hand and kissing it. She blushed to think of having to endure such mockery. Wondering what her portion of commands and orders would be this time, she sat, remembering other times when he invited her to dine just to shock her with information of his plans. She well remembered his announcement of the plan to leave Frencolia, taking her with him as hostage. Her mind recalled the tearful farewell she had whispered to her homeland as they traversed the border from her country into what she felt now was oblivion. Jobyna wondered how long she would remain "valuable" to Elliad; how long he would continue to allow her to be called "princess."

"Eat, Sparrow." The familiar command sprang from Elliad's lips. Jobyna directed the food automatically to her mouth, unseen, untasted. Determined to chew slowly or she would be sick, she looked cautiously around the room. Ranee's eyes met hers. Hatred and resentment seethed from the brown depths of the woman's stare. Jobyna swallowed then smiled at her, trying to convey a mutual feeling of the desire to exchange seats, hoping her smile would not be misconstrued as gloating. Ada was picking at her food, her face hollow and empty. Jobyna wondered what happened to the children on such occasions.

"So. What does Sparrow think of Chezkovia?" Elliad inquired.

"Is that the name of this castle, Chezkovia?" Jobyna asked innocently, "It's very . . . ominous."

"Chezkovia is the name of the country. This

is the most secure castle I know of. There is only one way in and one way out, unless you want to fall hundreds of feet into the Baltic!" He laughed, cutting the mirth off suddenly.

"How is . . . your injury?" Jobyna asked. He still wore his left arm in a sling, a smaller bandage across his neck and shoulder.

Ignoring the question, he turned to the red-haired knight sitting next to her and asked, "What is the name of this place, Brian?"

The knight struggled to swallow his huge mouthful, then answered. "There are several names, Sire. The most common is Baltic Castle."

"Then we shall rename it! Let's do it." He waved his left hand as he spoke. "Suggestions from the court . . . " The names came thick and fast, each knight trying to outdo the other to please Elliad. They voiced some ridiculous names, and others such as Victory Castle, The Lion's Palace, Treasure Chest Castle, Storm Castle. Elliad turned to Jobyna. "And what would Sparrow call this ominous place?"

All eyes turned to the girl. She was tempted to say, "The Chezkovia Prison!" Sudden memories of where she had seen the name Chezkovia flooded Jobyna's mind. It had been written in the back pages of King Leopold's Gospel Book and linked to the name of Elliad's father. Elliad's name had been recorded there with its meaning. She pulled her thoughts back to Elliad who was expecting a reply.

"I would name it Elliad." Her voice was decisive, triumphant and final. Her green eyes glowed as she thought of the meaning of the name. Elliad, in spite of enjoying the sound of his name, was rendered speechless. He caught the sparkles in her eyes, and he knew there was far more to her declaration.

"Why would you name it after me?" His violent tone shocked her. The exile king was demanding an answer! She suddenly went hot, feeling the intense stare of Elliad's court burning her face. Realizing the truth would make mockery of the God she believed in—it would shame Elliad in front of his despicable company; also it would invite his deepest anger upon herself—she dropped her head and wished she had not spoken. It was too late to backtrack now.

"Why, Sparrow? Tell me why?" He lifted her chin, his blue gaze piercing her watery green pools.

She shrugged childishly. "I like your name, Elliad John, I do." She smiled at him. The room broke with nervous laughter, then applause. His eyes locked hers in fierce combat. He knew she was concealing something, but it would keep.

Brian raised his goblet, calling, "To Elliad's Castle, and to King Elliad. May his strength return like that of a lion! Long may he reign!"

10

At the completion of the meal, the dining room was filled with buzzing conversation, wrapped with laughter here and there. Elliad rose from his place and moved around the long tables, pausing at intervals to talk to this one or that one, kissing the ladies and slapping the men on the back. It was obvious to see his strength was returning fast.

Jobyna was tired. She felt tense and thirsty. They had been so occupied with their food and drink that no one had noticed her abstinence. When Elliad's back was toward her, she caught the eye of a servant and discreetly beckoned him to her.

Requesting fruit juice or water, she found

herself promptly served with a clean goblet and jug of juice.

Ignored and satisfied to be so, she was able to study the people. People interested her. This bunch seemed empty, their faces void of real care and affection. Her father had called it "dog-eat-dog" when people climbed on each other to succeed.

Julian had drunk too much. His face shone red, his nose almost purple. He fell off his seat, and his laughter resounded like the bray of a donkey. Jobyna guessed his mirth would be at a bawdy joke. Ada was also drunk, her indulgence for other more obvious reasons. Ranee was sober. She sipped from her goblet, aware of Jobyna's gaze. Elliad walked to his mistress and whispered lingeringly in her ear. He sat, kissing her cheek, then her neck. Jobyna looked away, feeling disgusted. Having studied her company long enough, she poured more juice.

Elliad whispered in Ranee's ear, who in turn threw a sneering look at Jobyna and rose, leaving the room, followed closely by Ada. Silence slowly stole over the atmosphere as people noticed their departures. Elliad strolled leisurely around the main table to Jobyna and extended his arm. Everyone stood, bowing and curtsying as they made their exit.

"Chezkovia is over three times the size of Frencolia. It has five times the population," Elliad informed her as they walked. "The king in Chezkovia is called the czar, Czar Kievik. He has two sons. The eldest son of the czar, the heir to the throne of Chezkovia, is called the czarevitch. His name is Czarevitch Kenrik. I want you to remember that name, Jobyna. In a few day's time, Czarevitch Kenrik is coming with his entourage to visit me and discuss my future here. He is coming as his father's representative. I am preparing a welcoming banquet for him and I want you to be present. You know now what is expected?"

"To be seen and not heard," she said in a jovial manner, immediately biting her lip for being so outspoken. They approached the corridor leading to her apartment.

Elliad motioned behind for the knights, Julian and Brian, to wait. Turning to face her, he asked in threatening tones, "Why did you want to name this Castle after me, Jobyna? You did not fool me with such flattery! I detected unspoken meaning in your words."

"I honestly do like your name, Elliad John. But it's true. You would not approve of my reasons." She was blushing and could not meet his icy stare. His rough hands shook her violently, making her jump with fear. The pressure of his strong left hand gripping her shoulderblade made her gasp with pain. All the nightmares she had ever dreamed flashed across her terrified mind as Elliad pinned her against the door to her room. His right arm pushed up hard under her chin, and the girl felt sure she would be strangled. Ellice and

Boey stood back in fright as Elliad threw the door open and flung Jobyna violently backwards. The force of this motion caused her to sprawl sideways, falling helplessly to the floor. A strangled cry escaped the girl's lips as one leg twisted under her, receiving the full weight of her descending torso.

"You make fun of me, girl! How dare you mock me!" he yelled, ordering Ellice and Boey out of the chamber. Jobyna shuddered as the door slammed shut. They were alone.

"I do not mock you, Elliad. If you would just listen . . . " Gasping with the agony of her twisted leg, her voice broke. His blue eyes were blazing with fury. He waited, towering above her.

"Your name has a very special meaning. I did speak out of turn at dinner, but realized it too late. It would have been the wrong place to have explained . . . in front of your friends." She pushed her hands on the slippery marble floor, sliding backwards, away from him. At last she felt the tabletop against the back of her head and she halted the awkward process. "I read the meaning of your name in the Gospel Book belonging to King Leopold." Elliad put his hand to his forehead, his eyes rolling back in their sockets. *Would that book never cease bothering me?* he wondered.

"I . . . I realized, too late, you may not like . . . you would not like me to tell you the meaning the Gospel Book gave to your name. I . . . I call the slave girl you gave me Ellice, which is the feminine for Elliad." She struggled unsuccessfully to contain the torrent of tears threatening to break free. "I do not mock your name, Elliad John." She sobbed.

His voice was controlled as he asked, "What was the meaning of my name?"

Between the sobs, she continued to try and stall. "It was listed with the names Elijah, Elisha . . . and Elliot. My mother's name Elissa was there."

"What was the meaning of Elliad?" he demanded, growing impatient.

"Elijah, Elisha and Elliot mean 'Jehovah is my God'; Elliad means 'Jesus Christ is my God.' That is why I like your name." Jobyna hung her head and the tears ran unhindered down her cheeks. The truth was out. His expected mockery and anger, mingled with the pains shooting up her leg, were too much and she allowed the pent-up emotions free rein.

"You lie! You make it up!" he shouted as his countenance ruddied with rage. "My name cannot mean such rubbish!"

Like a cringing child, she shielded her head with her hands, closing her eyes. Her frail frame trembled uncontrollably as she expected him to strike her with his raised fist.

This was not the answer Elliad had expected. Like a caged lion, he paced back and forth. He hated her sincerity, and strangely enough, it dawned on him that she was telling the truth.

It was hard to believe, but she had protected his name from certain mockery in the dining room!

Elliad realized, for the second time of late, how wrong he had been about her. Aside from her religious stupidity, she was no threat to him. This was plainly obvious when he heard her comfort Berg, uttering words of kindness for her great enemy. Ranee's list of grievances sprang to his mind. He remembered the seeds of hate she had sown. He had been poisoned by Ranee's ridiculous jealousy. Ranee's lies, yes lies, he thought, had been listened to willingly. She began the trail back in Frencolia. Slight pangs of remorse came over him as he saw Jobyna huddled on the floor, her face white, pained and terrified.

In the ensuing silence, Jobyna cautiously uncovered her head. Licking tears from her lips, she whispered, "It was in King Leopold's own handwriting. He wrote beside your name how much he loved your mother and you. You were the only child of your mother who was the king's first cousin. Her name was Alice, meaning 'truthful one.' Your father was named Elliot, and he was born in Chezkovia."

Elliad stiffened, glaring at her once more.

"King Leopold wrote much more about your parents in the pages at the back. There was an account of a visit to your home in Valdemar when you were a boy. The king gave you your first horse. When you were eight years old, he

100

gave you a sword." Elliad was speechless, his thoughts became frozen in the past.

Jobyna verbalized the next thought as it entered her mind. "I could write to Luke and ask him to send the Gospel Book. Luke would send the Book to me; I know he would. You could read . . . what was written . . . for yourself. . . . " Her voice tapered off as her tormentor strode to the door. Throwing it open with a resounding crash, he stormed away.

"Leave me! Don't touch me! Go away!" Jobyna cried when Ellice and Boey tried to pull her to her feet. Sliding under the table, she pushed them away, sobbing. "Go away! Go away!" The girl screamed as Ellice tried to draw her from her retreat. Finally alone, Jobyna leaned on the cool, stone wall, crying softly. Mustering all the strength she could, the girl crawled to her bed, dragging her injured leg limply behind.

Jobyna's knee throbbed painfully all night. Finding it impossible to sleep, she relived the terror of the evening over and over. Boey was wakened by Jobyna's moans. Lighting a lamp, she fetched some liniment. Carefully, the servant tried to massage the sore leg and knee, but Jobyna pushed her away fiercely, crying with excruciating pain. Boey knew better than to persist or to ask questions, so she sat silently with the sleepless girl until dawn.

"You'd better rest today. You have a swelling the size of my cap coming up on your knee. It don't look right at all!" Boey declared. Jobyna did not argue but gladly let herself be tucked again into bed, seeking vainly for a comfortable position.

"I twisted my leg back as I fell." Elliad's treatment the night before still filled her mind. "He hates me," she murmured.

A loud knock resounded on the door. Brian spoke to Boey, ordering that Jobyna come with him. "The king commands her presence at his breakfast table." Boey dared not disobey this order. She roused Jobyna, helping the reluctant girl to the couch. With Ellice's assistance, they dressed her. Ellice combed her hair and sponged her pallid face. Both servants noticed the girl had become cold and shivery. Brian hammered impatiently at the door once more.

Boey moved into the corridor. "If you wants her to go to breakfast, then you'll have to carry her! She's hurt her leg real bad and can't even stand on it. She's not well at all."

Entering the sitting room, Brian collected Jobyna up in his strong arms. Her body went stiff as she gasped at the pains shooting through her leg. The cripple begged him to put her down. Ignoring her pleas, Brian carried her out.

11

The breakfast room of the royal suite was silenced by the announcement: "The Princess Jobyna."

Surprise shadowed Elliad's face when he saw Brian with Jobyna in his arms. It was obvious the girl was in great pain. Her face was gray, her eyes sunken and cheeks hollow. Beads of perspiration speckled her ashen brow. Elliad took her hand solemnly in his, kissing it. Jobyna's eyes met with Ranee's icy stare. The young girl was in too much pain to notice, but for the first time, Ranee's gaze held great fear.

"What happened?" Elliad queried.

"I fell and twisted my knee," she replied, her pained eyes saying, "as if you don't know."

Jobyna tried unsuccessfully to stifle a cry as Brian placed her by the chair she was to occupy. She swayed and would have fallen if Brian had not steadied and supported her.

Elliad ordered Brian to carry the girl to the couch. He wanted to know how much she was putting on, to see if she was pretending. "Let me look at it!" he commanded.

"No! Please don't!" she cried, trying to sit up. Elliad pushed her back, beckoning his mistress. Ranee sat beside the girl, firmly pinning her shoulders down. Jobyna felt too weak to struggle. She felt her skirt and petticoat slowly being raised.

"Get Sleven, Brian," Elliad commanded.

"Clear the room! You too!" he declared, giving Ranee a shove. He sat, waiting until the room was empty. Jobyna saw Ranee complying reluctantly. She was walking backwards, obviously upset at being dismissed so curtly.

"Did I do that?" Elliad asked.

"My leg twisted when you pushed me," Jobyna murmured.

Elliad walked to the door and peered out into the corridor. Closing the door softly, he crossed back to the couch. Taking his prisoner's limp hand in his own large one, he whispered, "You made me angry last night. I wanted to hurt you, but not like this."

Misinterpreting his words as an apology, Jobyna thought his illness must have changed his mind drastically.

"I was going to tell you, after breakfast, that you can write today to your brother and ask him to send you King Leopold's Gospel Book. I'll have some messengers take the letter to the nearest Frencolian knight they can find." He put his finger to her lips. "This is just between me and you." She nodded dumbly, believing she was dreaming and her ears were deceiving her. This was the first kindness he had shown her since his great pretence of playing "John the Doctor" back in Frencolia. The thought of being allowed to write to Luke made her able to smile through her tears.

"If Luke sends a letter, will you let me read it?" Jobyna questioned.

"But of course," he replied, frowning as he raised his finger to his lips. Footsteps resounded in the corridor. "Sleven is the best doctor I have ever known." Patting his shoulder, he continued, "He fixed this and says it will be good as new soon."

Brian entered the room with a doctor, who bowed to Elliad. Jobyna recognized Sleven as the man Elliad had spoken to about removing Berg's arrow, the one who uttered those fateful words, "I have done all I can."

"So, this is the little princess I have heard so much about." His accented voice was cheerful. He looked at the girl's face, then directly at Elliad. "Don't they feed you very well? Or don't you eat what they give you?" Not expecting an answer, he looked at her knee, pressing it firmly here and there, prodding it this way and that, making her writhe and moan.

"What happened?" his kind voice questioned.

"I fell backwards and it twisted," Jobyna answered, her voice void of emotion.

"Did you fall down the stairs?" When no answer was forthcoming, he turned to Elliad. "The kneecap is dislocated and will need some work done on it. A few days off her feet should see it on the mend." He stood up and drew Elliad into a side room. Jobyna's keen ears heard the doctor's muffled voice, then Elliad's, raised.

Her mind drifted to thoughts of Luke. She hoped Elliad would not change his mind about allowing her to write to her brother. She dared not imagine how good it would be to have the Gospel Book to read. Maybe Elliad was just taunting or humoring her. Maybe, when it arrived, he would burn it for some sadistic joke. The pain in her knee swamped her mind and tears ran down her cheeks.

What a crybaby I am, she thought. *I seem to be crying all the time lately. Now I've dislocated my knee. What next?*

Sleven and Elliad came back into the room, the latter calling Ranee and three servants who were hovering at the door, waiting to serve breakfast. Elliad ordered Ranee to fetch "the girl's servant." The doctor issued instructions in undertones to the servants, who nodded, moving quickly to fetch what he required.

Sleven sat by Jobyna once more with a friendly look in his eyes. He took her hand in his, but her feelings of trust were shattered as she remembered Gilbert, the doctor in Frencolia who, though kind, had betrayed her.

"Do you eat well, Princess?" Sleven asked. Giving the hint of a shrug, she shook her head. Eating was not really a concern any more, except when Elliad commanded her, like last night. "Do you sleep well?" he queried.

"Not very well," she said, thinking of the bad dreams which constantly disrupted her sleeping patterns. Although Jobyna could not see Elliad, she was aware of him, listening to her answers.

"What do you do most of the day?" Sleven continued.

"Nothing . . . I guess. . . . " She faltered, unsure as to why there were so many questions.

"Apart from going back to Frencolia, what would you like to do the most?" She was silent, so he carefully rephrased the question. "Let me ask you, Princess, apart from the people you left behind, what do you miss the most?"

Jobyna remembered her boredom and replied, "Oh, riding my horse, Brownlea. I used to go riding every day, . . . and reading." She would have added "from the Gospel Book," but swallowed these words, "and drawing pictures . . . embroidery . . . cooking with my mother. . . . We used to . . . " Her voice broke. Memories of her mother brought more tears to her already brimming eyes. Biting her bottom lip, she closed her eyes and turned her head away from Sleven. Boey bustled into the breakfast room, curtsying to Elliad.

"Sleven, this is the woman who minds the girl. Answer the doctor's questions, Borena," Elliad said.

Jobyna looked around at the sound of Boey's full name, Borena. She had never heard the name before.

Sleven's voice broke into her thoughts. "How well does the princess eat?"

"Oh, sir, I keep telling her she's fading away and needs more meat on her bones, but she just picks a little here and a little there, not enough for a fly. She fills up on that fruit juice. That won't keep her going forever. I tells her that," she said glaring at Jobyna, "don't I?"

"How well does she sleep?" the doctor asked.

Clicking her tongue, Boey closed her eyes and said, "Oh, well, that there's another story, that is!"

"Let's go in there." Sleven nodded towards a side room. Elliad and Boey retreated with him. Jobyna strained to hear them, but their voices were just a muffled hum. She hoped Boey wasn't telling them about the nightmares she suffered from. Jobyna wasn't too worried about her dreams because right in the worst part she would pray and reassure herself it was only a dream. She would wake to find Boey leaning over her anxiously. Jobyna always apologized to Boey for screaming out and waking her. That they were in the other room, discussing her, disconcerted Jobyna.

She let her mind wander and wondered, if she were badly hurt, whether Elliad would have her life ended as he did his soldiers. Maybe it would be better to end like that. It certainly would be good to get away from this dreadful place. Life in heaven must be far better than enduring the pains in her leg and her continued imprisonment.

Boey reentered the room. Squeezing Jobyna's shoulder softly, she whispered, "You'll be all right, luv. You're a survivor, you are. I'll see you later."

Boey had unintentionally left the door slightly ajar and Jobyna could hear Elliad and Sleven talking. She wondered which country Sleven was from. She was sure he was not Frencolian.

The doctor's voice grew louder. "It is up to you, Sire, whether you want the maid or not. I'm telling you the truth! It is plain to see she is pining away. She herself doesn't even know it is happening. If changes are not made quickly, then by the winter you will not have her. The signs of malnutrition are clear, and what's more, she has given up. She may even, subconsciously, hope to die, as some sort of happy release from the pain of living in captivity."

"No one wants to die, Sleven." Elliad shook his head, not believing what he was hearing. He followed the doctor back to Jobyna's side.

Quietly and with deliberation, Sleven asked, "Jobyna, are you afraid to die?"

"Oh, no," she said staring painfully at him, "I'd be much happier."

Sleven's reproachful eyes met Elliad's surprised stare. Several servants arrived with a crude pallet, a wooden platform with handles on each end, used for transporting wounded soldiers.

The physician took a tray from one of the men and mixed powder into a goblet. "This is just to help you relax, and it will take the pain away." Placing a cushion behind his patient's back, he helped her to a sitting position so she could drink. She complied, thinking, *there's nothing to lose, anyway*. The effects of the drug began instantly. Jobyna could feel her tense muscles relaxing. Sleven told a servant to hold her ankle and another to sit on the couch holding her shoulders. He put the stool close to the couch and began to work on her knee, ordering the servant to put more traction on her leg.

Rousing briefly with the excruciating pain, Jobyna screamed out in great torment, "No. You're hurting me. Please don't! . . . No . . . " The doctor's face blurred into the ceiling. Swirling in black holes around her, the room became part of a blackness, merging together until everything was overcome completely.

It was late in the afternoon before Jobyna became fully aware of the thick bandage on her knee. The doctor was concerned for his patient and made his fears well known to Elliad. Sleven was a doctor from Jydanski, the capital city of Chezkovia. The exiled king was his employer, and Sleven was paid handsomely to supervise Elliad's recovery and the recuperation of his injured men. The doctor's one stipulation upon his employment was that Elliad was not to meddle with his decisions as a physician. Therefore, Elliad showed respect to this man who helped to heal his injuries with expert ease.

Sleven's number one recommendation for the exiled king was to send Jobyna home to Frencolia. He advised his boss to be content with a ransom. Elliad said this was impossible. He told the doctor Jobyna belonged to him and he would be the one to decide what happened to her.

Sleven's second recommendation was for him to have her cared for properly; her physical health as well as her mental and emotional well-being must be tended to. Elliad was mortified to hear his "captive treasure" was fast fading and in a few weeks might no longer be his, or anyone else's.

"You will bury her in the garden with the soldiers you have lost if you do nothing! She needs tender love and care to blossom," Sleven told Elliad. The doctor discussed at length how Jobyna could be helped. The physician said that if Jobyna had three to six months with the right food and a stimulating environment, then he, King Elliad, would have a totally different princess. The doctor asked for extra payment and he would have his wife help supervise her care. Jobyna was growing from girlhood into womanhood and at her age, a woman's help and company were vitally important.

Sleven questioned Elliad about his captive's sickness in Frencolia and his treatment of her on the journey. Elliad reacted greatly to the questioning but calmed down somewhat when Sleven told him he had heard it all anyway from the soldiers and servants. It was no secret that the girl had been subject to torture and torment. The negative influences she had been under in the past weeks were staggering.

Demanding that Elliad give him a free hand, the doctor stated he would take total responsibility. The girl needed to be treated like a princess, if that was what he called her. She was not to be treated like a slave, a prisoner or a disposable piece of furniture. Elliad told Sleven about the pneumonia which almost took her life in Frencolia. The doctor, Gilbert, had not expected her to live and he had warned Elliad that she might never really be strong. Sleven reminded Elliad that human beings could only take so much.

Elliad conceded. His treatment of Jobyna had been particularly harsh. Impressions of her stubbornness and hate were formed incorrectly by Ranee's lies. He did wish to keep his treasure. She was, after all, the sister of the King of Frencolia, and was, therefore, valuable to him. As long as there were threats of troops from Frencolia, he needed her. Remembering Prince Gustovas' reaction to her also reinforced her worth.

Jobyna tried to focus her eyes on her surroundings. The room was small and emitted a comfortable feeling. Warm aromas together with the smell of newly baked bread permeated each corner. A woman she had never laid eyes on before sat in a rocking chair, knitting. The lady's face was lined and weatherworn, but she radiated a certain kindness and serenity. Her black hair was flecked with grey, like salt and pepper. Jobyna tried to sit up, the effort making her groan. Her leg felt like a lead weight.

The woman rose quickly at Jobyna's cries and came over to the bed. She patted her charge's hand. "Well, good afternoon, Princess Jobyna. I'm Brenna, the doctor's wife. How are you feeling now?"

"Much better, I think. Did . . . my knee . . . "

"My husband put your kneecap back in place and bandaged it. He said it will be as good as new in no time at all. You must be hungry."

Sniffing deeply, Jobyna inhaled a deep breath, giving a sigh of pleasure. *That's fresh bread!* She remembered the letter Elliad said she would be allowed to write to Luke. A long sigh escaped as her head hung down and sadness covered her face.

"What is it dear?" Jobyna was silent. Elliad had said it was to be "just between me and you." Before Jobyna could speak, Brenna said in her pleasant voice, "I think I know what you're wondering about. Well, King Elliad has told us that you are going to write a letter to your brother. He asked us to help you with it. As soon as you eat some food and feel stronger, I will help you write to him." The look of pleasure that raced to Jobyna's face confirmed that the older woman had guessed correctly.

Jobyna was ecstatic. She must pray the letter would not only be written but would go to Luke in haste, and she would be able to receive word from him. She scarcely dared to think that Elliad might let her hold and read the Gospel Book. These thoughts cheered her more than any that had crossed her mind since she had been happy at home with her parents and Luke.

12

The letter was more difficult to write than Jobyna had imagined. So much had happened, yet she could tell Luke so little. How could she tell him about the brand? About her dislocated kneecap? She longed to write of her dislike of the plundering, to complain about the tedious journeying. How she hated the miles separating her from Luke. She wanted to tell of Berg's death and Elliad's injury, but she knew the offender would censor her letter before it was sent.

Disappointment replaced the joy of writing to Luke. The knowledge that her words would not be just between the two made her feel like giving up. However, she persevered and was able to put her signature to a piece of work she regarded as satisfactory.

Jobyna held her breath when Elliad came to collect the small piece of parchment. She was sure he would want her to make changes. The girl had been with Sleven and Brenna for three days and accepted their bribe to eat satisfactorily before writing the letter. Sleven had replaced her fruit juice with milk and the improvement to her health was already showing in the rosy hue of her cheeks. "Eat little, and often," the doctor commanded and tempting morsels were served six times during the day. Brenna did not force Jobyna to eat or complain when she didn't, but she insisted the girl drink the milk. Brenna quickly learned the food Jobyna enjoyed most and increased the quantities of these dishes. Bread rolls and vegetable soup or stew were favorites, and Sleven saw with satisfaction that this part of his work would be the easiest.

Homey comfort and warmth surrounded her in the doctor's apartment. The rooms were far less elaborate than the ones she had occupied on the third floor. Situated on ground level between the kitchen and servants' quarters, mouth-watering aromas of baking pervaded the six rooms. Tantalizing odors wafted from the castle's great ovens. Sleven brought his patient a simple, crude pair of crutches, encouraging her to explore the rooms. There were three bedrooms, a sitting room, a dining annex and a small bathroom. Great arched windows with huge shutters looked out toward the vegetable gardens of the southeast. Savory smells of seaweed in the salty air blew softly into the windows and Jobyna wondered what the Baltic Sea looked like. So far her eyes had not seen past the stone statues and walls.

Elliad rolled the parchment up. His face was stony and unreadable to Jobyna who sat on the couch with her bandaged leg on a footstool. Her captor sat at the table. Brian stood outside the door. Sleven paced back and forth, his hand on his chin, waiting. He had rehearsed with Elliad the king's next words and watched while his employer pulled his chair nearer Jobyna.

"We will send the letter off today. It will take between one or two weeks to reach Frencberg, and about the same time for your brother's reply." He could see the light dancing in Jobyna's emerald eyes. Drawing a deep breath he was still unsure how to word his next statements. Sleven had told him the girl desperately needed to know she would never be deliberately harmed again.

"I have been wrong about you, Jobyna. I listened to lies from . . . the womenfolk. They told me you often said to them you wished you had a dagger so you could kill me." Her green pools widened at this disclosure. "I wanted to destroy your hate and insubordination." His hand clasped his injured shoulder. "This is the first injury I have ever had. The first time I

117

have known pain. Recuperation has been a time where I could think deeply, without distractions." He was silent for a moment. "I cannot change the past. I cannot bring your parents back to you." The deep hurt in her eyes was obvious as he spoke of her parents. Elliad continued, his eyes on hers. She could not meet his cobalt stare and looked away.

"I want you to know I have changed. I am in a new country with a new life and will be doing things differently." The statement Sleven was waiting for came next. "You must never fear being hurt again. I will never let anyone harm you, Jobyna." She refused to look at him. Elliad wanted to grab her head in his hands and force her to watch him, but he waited and then said, "No one is going to hurt you, Jobyna; I won't let anyone. Will you believe that?" He reached out cautiously and turned her head until their eyes met.

"I'll try to," she whispered submissively. Too much had happened, too much pain, for her to really believe him. If he truly meant what he was saying, why didn't he send her home? She reminded herself what her father had said, "Always give people the benefit of the doubt." Looking into his searching blue eyes, she added, "I do believe you, Elliad John, and I want you to believe me when I say I have never wanted to kill you." She wanted to cry out, "All I ever wanted to do was to go home," but she didn't dare. Instead, she said, "I am glad that you are feeling better." She wished she could add, "and I pray for you and ask God to bless you—not lately—but I will again." But she thought better of it and kept silent.

Sleven listened, watching with great interest. He was aware of great intrigue and sensitivity in the clash of Elliad's will against her submission. Jobyna wanted to please this monster, but he did not accept her attitude as that of subjection. Elliad believed she was mocking him when in fact she was showing a strange care and concern. The doctor decided to talk to Jobyna further and also to discuss her with Elliad. For Elliad to accept her, and for her to know he accepted her, even in the smallest way, would heal some of her emotional problems. Maybe he had taken on an impossible task.

Jobyna spoke again, "Thank you for sending the letter. Will . . . will you let me read the Gospel Book when it comes?"

"The Gospel Book shall belong to you, Jobyna. You can read it as much as you like."

Sleven was awestruck by the reaction these words brought. Jobyna's face broke into a great smile. Her emerald eyes sparkled and she looked delicately beautiful. Laying her small hand on Elliad's large one, she said, "Thank you, oh thank you!" The doctor had no knowledge of the decree Elliad had sent out against Gospel Books and those who possessed them. He had no idea how uncharacteristic it was for Elliad to allow Jobyna to have one in her possession, in his own castle.

Jobyna wondered curiously if Elliad really was changing. Maybe the words she had quoted to Berg had made him realize there was something worthwhile in the book after all.

Elliad himself was not entirely sure why he was allowing her to write to Luke and why he was letting her have the Gospel Book. No doubt his injury and Berg's death had stamped an indelible scar on his life. Maybe he was growing weaker as he grew older, he thought to himself. It would revive memories of his past family life to read what King Leopold had written about his father, Elliot. He pondered on what could have been if he had made different choices when he was younger. He stood to his feet, kissing the back of Jobyna's hand. His mind recalled the pain she had been through and he had the strangest sensation of wanting to please this maid, to see her beautified with happiness. Shaking the foreign thoughts from his head, he went to stare out the windows.

13

"Czarevitch Kenrik will be arriving tomorrow." Elliad turned from his repose by the windows. "Jobyna will come to dinner." This was not a question, but a statement.

Sleven counterstated, "Princess Jobyna will not be going to dinner! She will be resting and recuperating."

Jobyna saw Elliad's angry look return as the two men strode out into the hallway. Arguing and contentions filtered through the closed door to her ears. Hopping about, she picked up a crutch for support and crossed to the door, pushing it open. Staring at her in surprise, the men ceased their shouting.

"Excuse me, but I hate to hear you arguing,

especially about me. Do you want to know what I think?" Sleven laughed heartily. The girl had more spunk than he had first imagined.

"Why would we want to know what you think, Sparrow?" Elliad's tone was impatient and angry. His icy blue eyes chilled her to the bone. Jobyna immediately hung her head to escape his angry gaze.

"I'm sorry. I'm always talking out of turn," she murmured, thinking to herself, *of course they're not interested in what I think*. Turning with the aid of the crutch, she hopped back to the couch. Sleven obtained a glimpse of Elliad's impatience with the girl and of her giving up in submission. He watched Elliad, knowing the problem was with him, but then, so was the power. Elliad enjoyed displaying his unrivaled and unrestricted power and authority. He gleaned delight from lording it over those subordinate to him. The exile struggled to prevent himself from grabbing her viciously and forcing her to talk instead of moving away. Sleven stood in the doorway blocking his way.

"Sire, . . . King Elliad. Can't you see her submission to you?" The doctor's voice was quiet lest she hear. "She is no threat to you. She is trying to calm you, to smooth things over, and you react violently as though she is wanting to destroy you. Sit down." He indicated the bench in the hallway. "Go," Sleven ordered Brian.

Elliad calmed down as Sleven administered some psychology laced with home truths. He then said to his fuming employer, "Come with me, and keep quiet. You will see she wants to please you."

Jobyna sat on the window seat, staring out at the garden, watching gardeners pulling weeds and turning horse manure into the sandy soil. Turning at the sound of the men entering the room, she braced herself, and lifted her eyes to look at Elliad.

It was Sleven who spoke. "What would you like to do, Jobyna? Would you like to go to dinner and meet Czarevitch Kenrik?" As he expected, she remained silent. He rephrased the question, urging a reply. "King Elliad and I want to know exactly what you think about it. Tell us truthfully." His grey eyes encouraged her, giving her confidence to reply.

She bit her lip with uncertainty. Turning back to Elliad, she spoke. "I will do what you want, Elliad John." She hung her head. The king was ready to give a cutting remark, but was intercepted by Sleven.

"You're not telling us how you feel, Jobyna." The doctor spoke kindly. Jobyna looked at Sleven, then at Elliad, wondering if she dare voice her true feelings.

"Well, I must admit, I'm not excited about the dinner part, or about meeting the Czar's son, but if you want me there, Elliad John, then I'd rather be there." She looked away, not sure she was making sense.

Elliad sighed, turned, picked up the letter

from the table and stalked away. Jobyna was truthful, unpretending and guileless. She had always been honest. She wore her feelings on her face. Sleven's words were right. It was tremendously difficult for Elliad to comprehend someone who did not pretend, especially a female. It amazed him that she did not put on a false, hypocritical front. Sleven maintained that she was terrified of meeting with his disapproval and displeasure. He must try and remember she told the truth.

Elliad halted in his steps, standing stone still. Brian grabbed him in concern. Elliad pushed him away, staring at the view of the countryside from the royal suite. What did a sparrow matter to him? Who was she anyway? Would it really bother him if the waif withered away and died? He could not banish her earnest green eyes from his mind. As soon as he completely recovered, he must get out of this castle, he told himself. The emerald-eyed princess had disturbed his usual feeling of total mastery. She had disrupted his absolute power and domination.

The next afternoon, a round wooden bathtub was carried into the sitting room. The sight of it made Jobyna feel more at home. Ellice and Boey helped bring the hot water.

Jobyna said to Ellice, "I've missed you." A look of pleasure rushed to Ellice's eyes. Boey thought the words were wholly for her and beamed at Jobyna. Sleven was not happy about the extra activity. He wanted Jobyna to rest. Upon returning from his "sick rounds," he beheld Jobyna dressed in a loose blue and silver satin evening gown with a ruby necklace at her neck and glittering tiara on her cascading wavy hair. Sleven caught a vision of what the princess could be.

Brenna, helping the girl sit on the couch said, "Now, you do look more like a princess." (To her husband she later declared, "You can see why the king wants her there! Imagine what she'll look like in a few year's time, Sleven. It's not only her striking beauty, it's more her demeanor. She radiates something.")

A knock came to the door. Boey bustled off, mumbling, "If that's for her, then they's early, they are!" She was ready to give Brian a piece of her mind, but the bodyguard immediately announced Elliad's presence. Hurriedly gathering up the towels, the women were embarrassed that the bathtub was still in the center of the room.

Ignoring Elliad, Doctor Sleven bound a fresh bandage around Jobyna's knee. "We may have to do something about that swelling. There is too much fluid building up under the kneecap. I was hoping it would be going down by now."

"We have received a surprise today," Elliad

said, speaking to Jobyna. "The czar's daughter, Kenrik's sister, has come along with him. She is a little younger than you, Jobyna, and from the moment of arrival, she has been asking to see you. It seems your fame has traveled." He bowed, mockingly, then straightened suddenly. "I could not bring her . . . here . . . " he said indicating the humble rooms, "so you must go to meet her. She declares she cannot wait until dinner tonight." Sleven opened his mouth to speak, but Elliad quieted him with a fierce gesture. "Czarevna Cynara grows more impatient by the minute!" He pointed to Brian, waving his forefinger in Jobyna's direction. The knight collected her up carefully in his strong arms. Jobyna wondered what it was going to be like to meet a real princess.

The castle's reception lounge was buzzing with a variety of people dressed differently from anyone Jobyna had seen before. The men, standing in a long line at the door, wore red and white embroidered suits, with trousers under their buttoned tunics instead of the Frencolian-style tights. A cloak, falling in pleats from heavy shoulder pads to the hip, was worn over the tunic. The ladies wore colorfully embroidered dresses, low cut with huge puffed sleeves.

As Brian carried her through the foyer, the announcement was made:

"King Elliad. Princess Jobyna."

The ladies curtsied and the men bowed.

Jobyna looked for the princess. Elliad walked toward a couch where a young woman was reclining. Bowing low, he kissed the czarevna's hand. Brian placed Jobyna on another couch. Ranee arranged Jobyna's skirt and the cushions behind her shoulders. Jobyna winced once or twice, trying to get comfortable. The Czarevna Cynara rose and walked to her on Elliad's arm.

In his usual disparaging tone towards Jobyna, Elliad said, "Czarevna Cynara, this is my Princess Jobyna."

Cynara grasped both Jobyna's hands and she kissed each cheek, seriously. "I have heard much about you, Princess Jobyna. I am sorry you have not been well." Turning, she pointed to a footstool. One of the Chezkovian men carried it over and she sat close to Jobyna's couch. Elliad and Brian stood close behind the couch. People in the room began to help themselves from a table covered with small finger snacks. Wine was served. The ladies chatted discreetly, obviously summing up the princess from Frencolia.

Knowing it was her turn to say something, Jobyna wanted to be friendly and said warmly, "I'm very pleased to meet you Czarevna Cynara. You speak perfect Frenc. Did you have a pleasant journey today?"

The conversation moved back and forth. Jobyna was asked how old she was and her birth date. Jobyna learned, despite all of her outward maturity, Cynara was only 11. The czarevna was short, but grown up both in looks and manner. Her raven black hair was styled elaborately on top of her head. A sparkling gold crown sat like a halo among ebony curls. Cynara's face was a mask of heavy make-up. Jobyna's brown hair, shining with bright copper hues, hung naturally to her waist. Her cheeks and lips radiated a natural rose pink. Thus the two girls were a noticeable contrast between extravagant decoration and breath-taking simplicity.

"But you're so very thin, Jobyna. You have no shape at all!" Cynara's childish jealousy made her cruel. Her voice quieted. "I have heard," she said placing the back of her hand beside her lips, "that you have suffered . . . torture!" Jobyna became instantly aware of Elliad's listening presence.

"You don't believe everything you hear, do you?" Jobyna was quick to answer. This did not deter the czarevna, who persisted on the subject.

"I'm sure that what I heard has some truth."

"Tell me about Jydanski, your capital." Jobyna succeeded in an abrupt change of subject. They discussed Chezkovia and Frencolia, Cynara declaring her country more advanced and better in every way. The conversation was laced with tension. Every question Cynara asked implied her superiority. When a knave announced it was time to move to the dining room, Jobyna stifled a sigh of relief. Cynara rose suddenly, without a word to Jobyna, and left the room with her ladies-in-waiting, followed by a number of Chezkovian bodyguards.

14

Tiredness, verging on exhaustion, made Jobyna glad that Brian carried her to the dining hall. She would never have managed the distance on crutches. To Brian's massive frame she was just a featherweight. She stared up at his pinched countenance, his thin, sharp features and shock of orange hair. His long strides kept pace behind Elliad without effort.

After being announced to the people assembling in the dining hall, Jobyna was placed on a couch, near the tables. The knights and their ladies formed a reception line like the one at Chezpro Castle. Jobyna thought of Prince Gustovas and Princess Rhaselle, wishing she could be with them. Anywhere away from here! Most of the Chezkovians spoke in their native tongue. Jobyna felt sure she would never remember any of the names. Some of the ladies uttered short Frenc phrases, obviously well memorized. When the introductions were complete, all eyes turned to the entrance.

The moments of silence made Jobyna feel sad. *All these people, yet not one friend who cares for me more than they care for the couch I sit upon. We may as well be statues in the garden for all we mean to each other! What emptiness, how lonely it is! It is more lonely to be alone in this company than to be alone in the wilds. I'd rather be on my own in the valley, at least I would feel my own company and that of God's presence. Here, I feel like a caged bird on display!* She pondered, shaking her head, trying to pull her thoughts away from her surroundings.

The knave was making an announcement: "His Imperial Highness, Czarevitch Kenrik, Imperial Heir to the Czardom of Chezkovia. Her Imperial Highness, Czarevna Cynara, sister of Czarevitch Kenrik."

Jobyna watched as Elliad introduced his court to Czarevitch Kenrik and his sister. The captive knew she would not be able to curtsy to the Czarevitch, it would be foolish to try. *How unprepared I am for such an occasion. I have never had any training on how to act while in the company of royalty. I wish I were a sparrow and could fly back to Frencolia to hide in my nest,* she thought.

Her eyes studied Czarevitch Kenrik. She wondered how old he was. Eighteen or 19 was her guess, maybe even 20. He was broad-shouldered, very tall and as dark as his sister. His black beard was short and trim, and his curly hair was cut very short in a definite style, unlike Frencolian men. The crown he wore was the shape of a gold dome, covered with precious stones and edged with ermine. The Czarevitch's clothes were the same as the other men, red and white, but around his shoulders and neck hung rows of jeweled medallions, reminding Jobyna of the Seal to the Kingdom of Frencolia. Each of Kenrik's fingers, on both hands, bore at least one elaborately jeweled ring.

Thoughts of the sparrow filled Jobyna's mind and once more she wished she could fly away. The room felt hot and close and she was conscious of the blush creeping up her neck. Some of the ladies had fans and were using them discreetly. If only she could feel the coolness of moving air against her hot face. Elliad turned toward her couch for his final introduction.

"Princess Jobyna from Frencolia, now of Elliad's Castle, in Chezkovia."

Czarevitch Kenrik turned towards the girl. She bowed her head and when she raised her eyes, she saw his extended hand. On placing her hand on his, he leaned his face toward the back of it, barely allowing his moustache to brush it. Pungent smells of perfume emanated from his being, and for a brief moment, his black eyes met her green ones. Jobyna was sure his eyes were filled with amusement toward her. Elliad accompanied the royal pair to the guest positions at the table. Brian carried Jobyna to the chair beside Cynara. Elliad sat beside Kenrik. Jobyna felt immensely relieved that she was not sitting by Elliad.

Eating a little of this and a little of that, Jobyna noticed Cynara taking large helpings time after time. She also noticed the controlled silence under which the meal took place.

"No wonder you're so skinny, Jobyna. You eat like a mouse!" the czarevna chastened, her voice very quiet, almost a whisper. Jobyna was glad she had not said "like a sparrow." *And no wonder you're so well rounded, you eat like a horse,* she thought smiling back at Cynara. Jobyna looked around at the waiters, catching the eye of one she recognized. A few moments later he brought her some fruit juice. Cynara, whose goblet had been filled several times with the bubbling beverage, said with a giggle, "You don't drink kvass?" Jobyna did not answer, but poured the fruit juice and drank from the golden goblet.

Once the leftovers of the last course had been removed, Elliad and Kenrik became deeply involved in a discussion about new inventions in armor and weaponry. Elliad broke into German and Kenrik laughed loudly. Cynara joined in their conversation for a while and then was

133

quiet. She said something in a cutting tone, then turned away from them towards Jobyna. The men continued talking and laughing.

Cynara turned to Jobyna and rattled softly in her native tongue. Then, "Oh, I'm sorry, Jobyna. I forget, you cannot understand me. Just as well, I suppose." She held her goblet up and the waiter filled it. Sipping from it, she continued, "My brother and your Elliad are as bad as each other!"

"He's not my Elliad," Jobyna whispered.

"Oh." Cynara looked at her in surprise.

"What are they talking about?" Jobyna asked this behind the back of her hand, knowing it was not good manners to talk in undertones.

"Women! Of course!" Cynara retorted. Jobyna was embarrassed, for the Chezkovian men and women were listening to the men's conversation with great interest. Cynara whispered again, this time behind her hand, "I don't suppose you want to know what they said about you?"

"No!" Jobyna responded, too loudly. The men ceased their conversation, staring across at her. Cynara stood to her feet, followed rapidly by the Chezkovians and copied by many others, a chain reaction.

"I'm tired! I'm going to retire." She nodded to Elliad. "Good night, Elliad, king-in-exile." Cynara curtsied to her brother. "Good night, Brother." Turning to Jobyna she said, "I hope to spend some time with you tomorrow, Prin-

134

cess Jobyna." With her ladies-in-waiting following, Cynara swept from the dining hall. Jobyna drew a deep breath which was noticed by Elliad. Before she knew what was happening, Brian lifted her from the chair. She said a weak, "Good night," and was borne on her way back to Sleven's and Brenna's quarters. Jobyna realized she had dined with Czarevitch Kenrik and Czarevna Cynara, of the czardom of Chezkovia, and wished she could tell her brother all about the royal occasion.

15

Prince Dorai carried the tubular package into King Luke's office. Marked "confidential," the package was sealed with Elliad's K.E. seal. This was the first communication from the exiled king since he had left Frencolia. The uncle longed to break the seal and open the tube, but it was addressed to "Luke Chanec of Frencolia." Elliad did not address Luke as "king."

Luke strode breathlessly into his office. He stared at the tubular, leather-bound package. Breaking the seal, he untied the leather cord asking, "Who brought this?"

"Two of Elliad's knights. We are questioning them, but we have to be careful. They say your sister's safety is at stake for their being well treated and given a safe return," his uncle replied.

Luke unrolled the parchment. "It's Jobyna's handwriting!" he exclaimed. "Dear Brother Luke," he read to himself; then he read aloud, knowing his uncle was anxiously waiting,

Dear Brother Luke,

I am so excited to be writing to you that I hardly know where to begin. So much has happened since I left Frencolia that it would take much paper and ink to write about it all. The important thing is that I am able to "talk" to you in this way, and you can write back to me. Please write and tell me how you are.

I am glad to be at a settled destination. The journey was an ordeal I am glad is now over. I am being well cared for and trust you do not worry. King Elliad allowed me to write this letter to you. He said I may have the Gospel Book of King Leopold's which was in the treasure cave. I hope you found it. It was hidden in a cleft up on the same side of the valley as the cave. Please send the book to me with your letter so I may have the comfort of reading the greatest words my mind can ever take in.

Luke's voice broke here. Handing the letter to

his uncle, he sat down, his head in his hands. Prince Dorai took the parchment, his eyes searching to find the place where Luke had broken off.

> I pray for you every hour and for Frencolia. May God keep you in His care, not as I am, but free . . .

His voice trailed off. Then he resumed reading,

> We will see each other, Brother, if not here, then in heaven. Write soon. My deepest love and affections go with this letter.
> Signed,
> Jobyna Chanec.

Luke's mind was filled with the dominating thought that Jobyna was desperately ill, maybe even dying. Elliad, with some strange compassion, had allowed her to write such a letter. Even his uncle had to admit there seemed to be no real purpose for Elliad to have allowed her to write. No trickery was apparent. There seemed to be nothing he could gain from her requests. Luke asked for counselors to be brought to read the letter and give their opinions. While this was being arranged, he went with his uncle to talk to the two knights who had brought the letter. This proved rather fruitless. They had seen Jobyna, and apart from looking tired and thin, she was well, they said. The people spoke of her as "The Princess Jobyna from Frencolia." They told them she had been introduced to Prince Gustovas and Princess Rhaselle, and she was to meet the czar's son, Kenrik. Eventually she would go to Jydanski and be presented to the czar himself.

Luke commanded the two men to be escorted to the guest quarters. Although treated as guests, they were to be under strict guard and all communications with them were to be limited to essentials. No information about kingdom matters was to be passed.

The Gospel Book, which had been retrieved within two weeks of Jobyna leaving Frencolia, was brought. Counselors perused it thoughtfully. Notes at the back, written in King Leopold's handwriting, were of special interest, and scribes were ordered to make a copy of all Leopold's words, lest the late king's writings be lost forever. Otherwise, it was an ordinary Gospel Book, containing 23 books of the Bible. The scribes worked through the night, using bright lamps and changing writers every two hours. Luke read the references to Elliad's childhood, the birth of his father, Elliot, in Chezkovia. There were also notes made of the time King Leopold and Luke's father were close confidantes. The lists of names with their meanings were carefully copied, but nothing could be seen that seemed to be of particular benefit or value to Elliad.

Sorrow overwhelmed Luke as his counselors agreed with him that the book must, indeed, be for Jobyna. It was possible it was a death wish allowed by Elliad. Luke felt bereaved of his sister once more and was certain he would never see her again. He paced the floor all night long, trying to form words in his mind to put in his letter to her. He knew for certain that Elliad would read the communication.

Eight different letters came from his pen. He tore each one up as he read it. He revealed too much, writing as though they were his final words to her. Too much grief was conveyed, too much longing for his sister's presence with him at the King's Castle in Frencberg. Abandoning the letter writing, the frustrated king went to watch the scribes at work.

Prince Dorai found his nephew there in the morning. Luke told him, "I cannot write the letter. Adequate words evade the parchment. I wish I could take the book to her myself."

"Try again after breakfast, Son. Keep your mind on Jobyna's last few sentences and the hope she has to see you again. Write of your hope to see her. Let her know you have not lost faith. She needs that much. Tell her of the good things that are happening in Frencolia."

Luke took up fresh parchment after breakfast and wrote,

My very dear Sister, Jo,
If it was hard for you to write to me, it has been just as hard for me to reply. I would far rather be bringing this Gospel Book to you myself. May God's words give you strength, faith and hope every hour of the day.

How much love can one send in a letter? Then I wish to send more.

I am well and trust God for the future, for Frencolia, for myself and for you. Remember, dear one, there are no mistakes with God, only appointments He sets for us.

It would take weeks to write down all that has happened. I am looking forward to the time we can talk and be together once more. Apart from your absence from Frencolia, everything happening in the kingdom has been positive. The Gospel Book is read daily in each village, town and in the great square in Frencberg. Children are being taught to read. Can you believe, Sabin is learning to read and write and is making great progress? We have sent a message to the evangelist who is in Spenola, inviting him to come back to our country. There is a great thirst for teaching from the Gospel Book. I have

wished every day for your presence here
to enjoy the things God is working out.
All that Father wanted for our family is
being shared with everyone.

My love and prayers go out to you. We
will meet again. Remember, even in your
captivity, you are free in Christ. My
brother-love for you grows stronger every
day.
Signed,
Your affectionate brother,
King Luke Chanec, Frencolia.

Prince Dorai read Luke's letter several times.
"It will be a miracle if this gets past Elliad," he
murmured, his eyes upon Luke's claim as
"King Luke Chanec." This possession of title
pleased the uncle, but he knew it would in-
furiate the exile.

"I just wish we could do something to him.
Something very final," Luke said with the
sound of hopelessness in his voice. "He has got
away with everything, and our hands are tied
from making him pay for it!"

Knights had been sent out several times, and
the messages brought back were the same each
time. "Elliad was ahead of us all the way." "Elliad had too much strength and power." Now
the country he was in, Chezkovia, was suppor-
tive of him. They had even allowed him to live
in the stronghold of the Baltic Castle.

"We must have the support of other countries

if we wish to go to war against Chezkovia. Our army is less than one quarter the size of the Chezkovian forces. They have the latest armor, weapons and battle equipment. We must bide time, build up our own strength, and see what alliances we can form. It would be better to have Jobyna rescued without bloodshed," Prince Dorai told Luke and the counselors. "We must see what a smaller group can do traveling incognito. Maybe they will execute a successful rescue and Elliad can be assassinated secretly. Whatever we do must be well thought out and meticulously planned."

Luke added, "Yes, and we must pray. God can choose to use many or a few to do what He purposes. The way He works is His way, not the way of men."

The Gospel Book, with the letter tucked safely in the front cover, was carefully bound in a leather binding and addressed, "To Jobyna Chanec, care of Elliad John Pruwitt, exile king, The Baltic Castle, Chezkovia."

Escorted to the border with their important package, the two knights left that day with the careful conveyance.

16

The coffin was being slowly pried open! Jobyna could hear the reluctant nails screeching discordantly against the wood. She turned over in bed, struggling to pull herself from the strange dream and the fearsome pictures filling her mind. Awaking to the welcome sound of Sleven and Brenna conversing in their native tongue, Jobyna wished she could understand them, though she knew they used their language to speak privately together. An unfamiliar voice came to her ears and the girl decided to rise and discover what the conversation was about.

Sounds of nails being drawn from the imaginary coffin came once more to her surprised

144

ears. The noise was not from a dream! Taking a crutch, Jobyna entered the sitting room. Sleven was unpacking a large crate. The awesome looking contraption he was bolting together was for real. At first, she imagined it was some kind of instrument for torture! A servant was helping the doctor attach it to the wall. Several round lead weights lay on the floor. Jobyna's look of surprise pleased Sleven. He wanted her to be interested in all that happened.

"Do you know what it is, Jobyna?" Sleven asked.

Jobyna tried to think logically, to prevent her vivid imagination from seeing what was not there. "It looks something like the balance used to weigh bags of grain at a market place."

"You're right. It is a balance, but this one is not for bags of grain." Jobyna watched as Sleven fidgeted with the thing. Brenna brought breakfast to the table and they sat together to eat. After the meal, Sleven told Jobyna to stand on one side of the balance. He put three of the weights one upon the other. Checking the gauge, he added a smaller one.

"When I can put two more large weights and one small on this side, Jobyna, you shall be strong enough to go riding each day on your horse. . . . What was its name?"

Jobyna looked happy, but doubtful, "Brownlea? How long will it be?" she asked.

"Oh, I'd say maybe a month or six weeks. It could be more, or less. It depends on you."

145

"I don't know your seasons here. When does the winter come?" she asked, concerned lest the snows came before she could go riding.

Sleven continued tightening the screws and bolts on the balance. "In Chezkovia, we have six seasons. We are in the summer season now. Next will be the sunny, warm autumn and then a foggy, humid period which will signify the approach of winter. The heavy snows last one to three months, and as you have guessed, there will be no riding then. But the spring can have alternate days, cold and wintry, or warm and sunny. The snow melts fast. We are not as snowed in as Frencolia." He smiled at her, having finished with the balance. "There are at least four months yet before the snow will keep you indoors. Plenty of time for you to get completely well and ride your horse."

Jobyna was happy with the thoughts of riding Brownlea. Memories of horse riding on the manor farm were precious to her and she was impatient to begin. Brownlea was the second horse she had owned and he had been her most prized possession.

Sleven took the bandage off her knee. He was concerned. The swelling was not diminishing. "I think you should rest today, right off your feet, all day! The activity has been too much, too soon. I will inform King Elliad that you are not to be disturbed. I plan to take the stitches out of his shoulder this morning. He will want to rest. It will be quite an ordeal for the king."

The doctor almost added "and for me." King Elliad was not a good patient. Each pain, each twinge was like torture. His pain tolerance was very low. There were 39 stitches to deal with and it would take half the day!

"How many stitches did he have?" Jobyna remembered the stitches she had had in her hand.

"Thirty-nine," Sleven murmured, replacing the bandage on Jobyna's knee. He crossed the room to a smaller crate, the top boards having been pried open. "I have had some things sent from my home in Jydanski." He pulled out some books and brought them to her. "Brenna will show you what else I have brought. There are tapestry and embroidery threads, all sorts to keep you occupied. You must keep both feet up and try to rest." He took up a chest with a handle on the top and left the room.

Browsing through the books, Jobyna discovered much to interest her. There were maps of Chezkovia and the surrounding countries; names of kings, queens and their children were given. Jobyna decided she would find the books interesting, especially one that had an explanation of the German language with parallel Frenc and Latin words. She knew she could rely on Brenna to sound out any difficult pronunciations for her. The doctor's wife brought the girl milk and fruit, pleased to see her happily occupied and content to be resting.

Heavy knocking rapped on the door which was thrown open before Brenna could stand to her feet. Brian strode in. Without a word, and ignoring Brenna's protests, he carried Jobyna off. The girl found herself upstairs in Cynara's suite. The Czarevna was waiting impatiently for her arrival.

"Anyone would think you are some sort of prisoner or something!" Cynara was peeved. She expected her commands to be obeyed instantly.

Jobyna, pleased that Elliad was otherwise occupied, was also thankful the women in the room were paying no heed to them. She could talk openly with the Czar's daughter.

"Actually, Cynara, that is exactly what I am. I am Elliad's prisoner," Jobyna replied.

"Oh, I forgot. But then, in many ways aren't we all—prisoners I mean—to our parents or our country?" Cynara said, not wanting to be outdone. "Have you ever been betrothed?" Not waiting for an answer, she continued, "I have. Twice. And both times to the same person. The first time, Father tore up the contract because he was mad with Prince Gustovas, and . . . " She paused for a breath.

"You were betrothed to Prince Gustovas?" Jobyna was amazed.

148

"No, silly!" she said laughing, "To his son, Konrad. Anyway, the second time, Konrad tore up the contract and made his father furiously mad with him. Konrad disappeared into the Proburg mountains for weeks. Then, when they wanted us to be betrothed again, I talked Father out of it. I will never marry Konrad of Proburg! It is unforgivable to do what he did! Right now I'm quite free and enjoying it. Father is not too sure he wants his only daughter to live in Proburg anyway. Now, if Konrad would have been more agreeable and had come to live here in Chezkovia . . . "

"Is this Konrad, Crown Prince of Proburg?" Jobyna asked.

"No. You don't know anything, do you? Konrad is the youngest son. Prince Gustovas has four sons, and Konrad is the only one who is not married. He's really different. Not like a prince at all, quite strange, actually. He'd rather put his head into a book, or go climbing mountains than be in court. People in Proburg say he is mad. They call him 'The Crazy Prince.' But then, I've only met him a few times, and each time the whole of Father's court has been present. We have not even spoken to one another. Konrad ignored me as though I did not exist. I heard through my ladies-in-waiting that he does not wish to marry me, either." She gave a sigh, as though it were frustrating to think of him. "What is your brother, Luke Chanec, like, Jobyna?"

Jobyna talked about Luke and Frencolia. She told Cynara about the letter she had written and how much she missed her home country. When she spoke about Brownlea, Cynara interrupted her, a disgusted tone filling her voice.

"You have your own horse? You ride a horse?"

"Yes, I love to ride. Don't you have a horse, Cynara?"

"You mean . . . you sit up on top of it, right on its back, like the men do?" Cynara's thick black eyebrows were raised, her dark eyes wide with amazement and distaste. Jobyna, interested to know the customs of Cynara's home country, asked her how she traveled.

"I have my own carriage," she replied disdainfully. "Any lady of consequence in Chezkovia rides in a carriage! I don't think I've ever seen a woman on horseback!" She stared at Jobyna, trying to form a picture of a princess riding a horse. She shook her head and giggled.

"What is a . . . carriage . . . like?" Jobyna asked, revealing her ignorance. Cynara described the horse-drawn carriages, explaining the many different shapes and sizes, some half covered and some fully covered. She told Jobyna of fancy carriages that could even be slept in. Jobyna asked about the roads in Chezkovia and discovered the country was flatter with wider roads. In Frencolia, the roads were narrow, hilly and rocky. A carriage would be all right in the city or the towns, but not so practical out on the countryside. The carts used in Frencolia had to be very strong and well built. Ladies often traveled sitting on seats in a more elaborate type of cart. They called it a "birota," but there were no carriages as such. The nearest Jobyna had seen to such a vehicle was a covered gypsy wagon. Cynara wished she could take Jobyna on a tour in her carriage and introduce her to some of the cities in Chezkovia. The czarevna exclaimed she would take her to visit some of the sights of wonder along the Baltic Sea coast.

"You will simply have to come and stay with me in Jydanski!" Cynara was enthusiastic and determined. "You must try to eat more, Jobyna. Skinny women are so unfashionable. I declare I have never seen anyone as thin as you!"

They talked non-stop for over two hours, and their friendship grew as Cynara realized Jobyna had no desire to be competitive. The Czarevna was deeply impressed by Jobyna's caring disposition, her honesty and kind frankness. A sudden revelation flashed into Cynara's large brown eyes. "It has been said that you are religious, Jobyna. Are you?"

"It depends what you mean by 'religious,' Cynara."

"You know what I mean! Gods, and all that stuff," she voiced impatiently.

"Well, yes. I do believe in a God. Don't you?" Jobyna asked.

"Oh, I suppose so. Not that it would affect me

151

at all. God can't have much time for people, really. He's sure to have much more important things to take care of. In my life, I have plenty of people who look after my well-being. I wouldn't know what use I would find for God." She tittered as the words fell from her lips without her thinking. "He's God, and I'm Cynara! There's not much more to it than that! But then aren't there hundreds of gods? That's what people I know believe."

"No, I am sure there is just one God. One Creator of the world. Have you ever read the Gospel Book?" Jobyna asked.

"That's what I mean!" Cynara exclaimed triumphantly. "Religious people believe that book!" They both turned their heads as footsteps sounded at the door. Without knocking, Sleven and a servant entered.

"Excuse me, Your Imperial Highness," Sleven said, bowing to Cynara. He raised his head to look unapologetically into the Czarevna's eyes. "Princess Jobyna is ill and needs rest. I am her doctor and must do my job. She is recovering from an accident to her knee."

"You haven't changed, Sleven! You're always bossing your patients around! Talking is not exactly straining Jobyna's knee, is it?" Cynara questioned tartly. She pulled a face when the servant collected Jobyna carefully in his enveloping arms.

"I'm sorry, Cynara. I do hope I will see you again some time," Jobyna said before she was carried from the apartment back to Sleven's rooms.

There were no interruptions for the next two days. Off and on, between dozing, Jobyna enjoyed a hobby she had missed greatly, drawing. She drew an ink picture on heavy parchment, a waterfall cascading down the cliff entrance to the valley. She edged the mountains with misty clouds, carefully watering the ink down so it was gray, not black. Brenna asked her if it was a real place, and Jobyna described the valley to her. The next drawing was of a lone lily, reflected in a small pool of water. She drew the stream in the valley as a background. Describing the color of the lily to Brenna, Jobyna said it was between pink and blue, almost lilac. The memory of the beauty of the valley in Frencolia helped her rest peacefully.

Sleven was pensive when he looked at her knee the next morning. Jobyna told him it had throbbed unbearably in the night. Leaving it unwrapped, the doctor laid out a tray, taking instruments from a cupboard. He sent Brenna to the kitchen for a goblet of milk.

Stirring a small amount of powder into the milk, he told his patient, "I know you have been through this before, Princess. The scar on your hand has healed very well and so will this one. You have too much fluid on your knee and I must relieve it. Then the knee will be able to heal properly."

Late that afternoon, Elliad, recovered from the removal of his stitches, came to the apartment extremely angry with Sleven. "You have been rude to Czarevna Cynara! How dare you! She is furious with you. Each day she has requested Jobyna's company and you have refused. She has decided to return to Jydanski earlier than planned. The girl will come down for the farewell!" Elliad stormed across the room. "Where is she?"

"The princess is in her bedroom, resting. I made an incision in her knee about an hour ago. There is fluid that needs to drain off. Tomorrow, I hope to stitch it. Sire, you well know what a new wound is like. She must not be moved." Sleven's voice held an anxious warning. He followed Elliad and Brian as they strode into Jobyna's bedroom. However, at the sight of the open wound in Jobyna's knee, the thick wad of towels under her leg soaking up the oozing fluid and the clammy pallor of her face, Elliad backed away to the door. Wordlessly, he motioned Brian to leave with him.

17

The kingdom of Frencolia was in a frenzy preparing for the celebration of the century. King Luke Chanec was "coming-of-age" in a few days. On Luke's 16th birthday he became the legal, absolute monarch. His uncle, Prince Dorai, became increasingly pleased with his part in the decision which had proclaimed Luke as king. Never before had such peace and unity been experienced in Frencolia; though the kingdom was poor in tangible riches, it was rich with spiritual benefits.

The day of the birthday was a warm, early autumn day. Over five long months had passed since Elliad's abdication. Luke dressed in the robes laid out for him and Prince Dorai placed the Frencolian crown on his head. The king was to walk to the throne room where the lords and senior knights would individually proclaim their allegiance to him as king and to the kingdom.

Feasting would follow and food would be distributed to the poor. It was still harvest time and food was plentiful. Each town and village in the country would have celebrations on this, the king's birthday. Three days' rest from all work except the necessities had been declared. Luke decreed that all slaves were to be given their freedom on his birthday. If they chose to stay with their master and the master wanted them, they would be paid a fair day's pay for a fair day's work. The remuneration could be in the form of food, shelter and material benefits. Violations of this decree would be dealt with by a special council commissioned by Luke.

King Luke Chanec rode through the streets of Frencberg with Prince Dorai, Princess Minette and the children following. People cheered loudly as the royal procession passed by. Numerous children tried to keep up with the parade. They trailed garlands of flowers behind them, singing and skipping. It was a wonderful day of unprecedented celebration.

In the kingdoms away to the north, the air was becoming cooler. The message, "summer surrenders," softly scampered on the northern breeze.

Transfixed by the view of the beautiful Baltic Sea, Jobyna was aware that today was Luke's 16th birthday. Her heart prayed longingly for him to have a joyous time. Seated on Brownlea, she watched with wide eyes as the waves washed the sandy shore. This day was the happiest she could remember in a long time.

"How beautiful," she breathed, inhaling the spicy, salty air. Sleven and the soldiers who were with her looked on in silence. The princess made a beautiful portrait, enveloped in the rich, red crimson cloak. Her long hair played gently in the breeze, fanning her fresh young features. Sleven knew the battle was won. The change he had hoped for had taken place. The doctor thought back over the past few months. It had taken three months for Jobyna to gain the satisfactory weight. Her knee had healed and the horrific nightmares had ceased. Jobyna looked like a different person. Sleven was not sure if it was the Gospel Book, the letter from Luke or Elliad's departure to Jydanski. He realized it could well be a combination of all three. Elliad had gone to the capital with Czarevitch Kenrik, announcing his intent to stay for three or four weeks. He was yet to return.

Once on the firm sand, Jobyna patted Brownlea's neck, urging him into a gallop. The girl raced him the length of the sandy shore. At one place Brownlea sped through shallow waves, sending salty spray shooting in all directions. Jobyna wheeled the horse around as they came to a large cluster of jagged rocks. She could see Sleven and the soldiers coming, but they were still halfway down the beach.

"You're as good as ever, Brownlea," she said, patting the animal's sleek neck. He nodded his head up and down, and Jobyna knew he enjoyed having her on his back once more. He, like she, would never forget the feeling of an exhilarating ride. Jobyna cantered Brownlea back towards Sleven. With a shake of the reins, she galloped him to the far end of the long sandy seashore. Breathless, she drew her mount to a trot and returned to the company.

Her eyes beheld the cliffs towering high above them. The gray castle walls grew sheer above the cliffs at the end of the beach. It was an awesome sight. Apart from the many narrow, shuttered slits of windows, there were no exits, no stairways, no doors or balconies on the northern side of Elliad's Castle. Once one was inside the gates, there was no escape. Jobyna turned her eyes to look across the curling waves. The sun shimmered through them, turning the billows a delicate shade of aquamarine. Sparkling white foam played mischievously around Brownlea's hooves. Jobyna drew a shuddering breath at the sight of the sea swirling around the distant islands. The

Baltic was so big, and she felt so small and in-
significant in comparison.

"You must not overdo yourself, Princess,"
Sleven warned. He had never seen anyone ride
as Jobyna rode. She, a woman! To imagine
what would happen if she fell would be to
think of all his work being in vain. The more
time he spent with the girl, the greater his ad-
miration for her character and courage grew.
Sleven had previously made up his mind that
he must treat her as his patient. He would
make her well, but there was no way he would
help her escape from Elliad. The captivity was
not his business.

Sleven had asked her about the injury of her
hand, also about the brand, and Jobyna told
him what had happened. She knew there was
nothing to gain by hiding the facts. He asked
her about her parents and her home, and she
related to him the evangelist's visit and her
father's conversion to the beliefs in the Gospel
Book. Tears assembled spontaneously when
she recounted the facts of her parents' murders.
The doctor was silent when she told him how
Berg had requested her to quote the Gospel
Book, having previously invoked forgiveness,
from both Jobyna and God, for killing her
parents.

Sleven noticed the great happiness Jobyna
gained from reading the Gospel Book. When
she was asleep at night, he borrowed the book.
Holding it close to the lamp, he read, trying to

work out what strength there could be in such simple words. Brenna looked up at him from her rocking chair where she had been dozing. Her husband read a verse out loud, then said, "That's true, isn't it?" She agreed with his deductions. Sleven always remembered to return the book before morning.

Each day Jobyna rode Brownlea out under the five towers, through the many castle gates, along the road and down the beach access path to the shore. She enjoyed exercising and galloping the horse. The girl was fascinated by the many changes in the tide, the differing colors of the sea and the Baltic shore itself. Riding for a longer time each visit, she became faster and fitter. Sleven did not try to keep up with her. He sat on his horse with the mounted soldiers, enjoying the Baltic view, savoring the spicy air and beholding the beautiful princess who rode the gleaming brown horse.

The air continued to cool, and one day there was the tinge of an icy chill at dawn and dark clouds hung threateningly in the heavy air. Sleven announced at breakfast that if they were to go riding, it must be that morning before the storm came. Jobyna quickly fetched her cloak and riding-boots, struggling to fit the footwear on.

"I'm needing larger boots. These are too tight. And to think they were so big on me they would almost fall off!"

"We can send them to Jydanski when the winter comes, for a bigger size in exchange. You won't need them until the spring," Brenna told her.

That day, Jobyna made up her mind about the Baltic. She decided she did not really like it at all. When it was calm, it seemed wondrously soul-stirring. But now, with great waves crashing onto the beaten shore, the breakers coughing up monstrous shapes of driftwood, it was wild and angry.

Huge dark gray waves crashed upon the rocks as she turned Brownlea to canter back along the beach. Spray, dirty with silt and sand, shot out into the air. It stung her cheeks and she felt moisture all around. The wind tore at her hair, swirling it high in the air, across her eyes, blocking her vision. Wishing she had plaited it, she drew the great mass together and twisted it into a knot, tucking the lump inside the back of her cloak.

Brownlea needed no urging. He galloped at breath-taking speed along the shore, turning before reaching the rocks, spinning back the way he came. Jobyna sensed that the horse, too, realized this was to be their last ride along this beach.

Sleven, watching her, heard horses coming over the rise to the beach access. Elliad drew his horse near and sat speechlessly, watching Jobyna ride.

"How often does she ride like that?" the king asked, not taking his eyes off her.

"Every day, Sire. She has amazing strength now. You will notice changes in the princess."

From the other end of the beach, Jobyna could see a large company of knights, some in the green and gold uniforms of Frencolia, but most wearing the red and white of Chezkovia. Her heart raced suddenly. Even from this distance, she could tell by his purple cloak and the outline of his bearded face, it was Elliad. She changed her position on Brownlea from sitting astride to that of sideways, rearranging her heavy skirt over Brownlea's lambswool covering. Holding the disappointed Brownlea in check, she cantered him along the shoreline and up toward the company.

Before she arrived, Elliad, seeing her obedience in moving toward them, turned his horse, and with his men, rode off toward the castle ahead of her. Sleven started his horse back up the beach as Jobyna drew Brownlea alongside. They rode silently, Jobyna apprehensive, Sleven pensive.

Upon arrival at the stables, Jobyna saw signs of a move at hand. Horses were being prepared for riding, carts moved to harness the waiting animals. She knew these activities very well and wondered where they would be going this time.

"What is going on, Ben?" She asked the stable boy who took care of Brownlea.

"I'm not too sure, Princess, but I think the king is moving to the capital, Jy . . . Jy . . . the capital . . . Jy . . . "

"Jydanski." She completed the name for him and he nodded. "Yes," she added, "It is quite a tongue-twister."

Brenna helped Jobyna pull off her boots. The girl wondered whether Elliad would send for her or if he would come for her himself. Sleven was absent. Jobyna had seen him detained by two men at the stables. Boey bustled in with a food tray and Jobyna ate hungrily. Riding had increased her appetite and she ate everything on the tray, pouring a second drink of milk. When Sleven arrived, he was pleased to see the plates on the tray empty. It was some hours later that the expected knock sounded on the door. Julian stepped insolently inside.

"King Elliad requires your presence, Doctor Sleven," he announced. His ogling eyes stared passed the doctor, at Jobyna. His small mouth hung open, the fat of his triple chin drooped down to hide his short thick neck. Sleven left with Julian and Jobyna felt an overwhelming sense of relief. She wondered if she would have to go for the evening meal, but no such summons came and she continued working on a tapestry with Brenna.

Sleven returned later in the afternoon. He spoke to Brenna in his native tongue. Jobyna wondered if she should go to her room as she could now understand enough of their conversation to gather most of the meaning. Brenna had been giving her casual lessons in German and Jobyna found it easier to understand than to speak the language herself. The couple talked for a long while and Jobyna sensed the conversation was tense at times. They were speaking of unrest in Chezkovia, of dissension among leaders whom they named, calling them "emirs."

Dinner that night was served in the cozy cottage-apartment. Jobyna was sure food had never tasted so good and the crackling fire was comforting and homey, the perfect setting. Knowledge that Elliad was otherwise occupied brought radiant relief, making the meal more enjoyable. Sleven returned when they were half way through dinner. This time, in his dialogue with his wife, Brenna was more in agreement, but Jobyna noticed tension when the words "Jydanski," "Czar Kievik" and "Chezkovia" were mentioned. The name Elliad came up often in their conversation, but due to the speed of their speech, Jobyna missed too much to comprehend the meaning.

The girl was concerned. She knew Sleven and Brenna to be very patriotic. They shared a great passion for the affairs of Chezkovia. However, due to the double meaning Jobyna read into their discourse, the uneasy eavesdropper wondered how loyal they were to Czar Kievik.

When they had exhausted their desired communications, Sleven turned to Jobyna as Brenna cleared the table. He spoke in Frenc. "Princess, I am going back to Jydanski with King Elliad. I am not sure how long I will be away, maybe two or three weeks. Borena will move in next door while I am gone. Brenna and I have nine children and 24 grandchildren. I wish to visit some of them before the snows come. It would have been good if Brenna could have come, but I realize it is too far for such a short time."

Brenna had explained to Jobyna that all of their children did not live in the capital but that they were near by. Two married daughters lived in Proburg. Elliad had requested that Sleven return for the winter to the Baltic Castle after visiting Jydanski to care for the seven soldiers still recovering from the ambush. He said he wished Sleven to continue taking care of Jobyna. The doctor did not tell Jobyna of Elliad's compliments regarding her health. The king had been most pleased with the improvement, although his thoughts were principally occupied with affairs in Jydanski. Brenna assured Jobyna they were enjoying taking care of her. The more acquainted they became with her, the greater satisfaction they had in their princess patient's well-being and happiness.

The next morning, immediately after breakfast, Jobyna walked down to the stables with Brenna and Sleven. The air communicated decisively of the rapidly approaching winter. Sleven kissed Brenna, long and passionately. He turned to Jobyna, taking her small hands in his. "Remember, there is to be no more riding, and if the snows come early, you must cease walking in the gardens and stay indoors."

Elliad rode around from the precinct where his horses were housed. Cool blue eyes briefly connected with Jobyna's sensitive green ones as he critically looked her up and down. His lips curled with a smile which disturbed the girl, but he was obviously eager to depart, for which she was thankful. Signaling with his hand, he led the cavalcade, Julian and Brian following close behind him. Jobyna breathed a long, loud sigh of relief. Her eyes met with Brenna's and the girl read sympathy and understanding on the lady's kind face. Brenna blew a kiss as Sleven rode by. Turning, she put an arm around the captive's shoulders and they went back to Elliad's Castle, up the many steps, along the stone walkways and paths.

Every meal that week was a celebration to Jobyna. Her adversary had departed! She hoped Elliad would forget about her and would never want to see her again. Maybe he would send her back to Frencolia. This hope made her heart celebrate all the more.

18

Winter struck early, in full force. Blankets of dazzling snow lay thick in the castle grounds. Brenna told Jobyna this snow could melt away quickly, then there may not be any more for two or three weeks.

Hagen, the knight in charge of the castle, dictated to Jobyna that she was permitted to walk about the castle wherever she wished, with one or two conditions and exceptions: she was not to go near the servant's quarters or speak to the children; and he warned her not to send any messages to anyone, either written or verbal. Disobedience in any area, Hagen decreed, would mean loss of every privilege and he would have her confined elsewhere in the castle. The only other stipulation was that she must have Brenna or one other woman accompanying her. Jobyna was not authorized to wander about on her own.

Jobyna submissively complied to Hagen's demands and she enjoyed the liberty of the castle. Long walks were taken twice a day as she desired to keep up her feeling of fitness and energy. Brenna would stroll with her in the morning and Boey in the afternoon. Sometimes Ellice went with her and Jobyna was pleased to have her company. She learned from Boey that Ellice was working in the kitchens. Boey was the best source of news to Jobyna and the girl learned much from conversing with her. The servants shared every tidbit they could glean from their peers, harvested from messengers and soldiers venturing in and out of the castle.

Elliad had moved into the Czar's Palace in Jydanski. Jobyna found this information intriguing. Boey informed her that Ranee and Ada had moved to the capital as well, but their children had been left here. The czar had assigned a whole floor for Elliad and his court.

Elliad living in the Czar's Palace at Jydanski! Suspecting Elliad of ulterior motives, Jobyna wondered what dastardly scheme he was up to. *At least the czar was powerful with secure control over his czardom,* she thought.

Next the girl took herself to task for not giving Elliad the benefit of the doubt. She must hope he had changed. Questioning Boey as to how many people were left at the Baltic Castle, the servant woman told her Elliad's Castle was protected by only 30 or so soldiers, the rest having gone to be with the exiled king.

"Not that it needs many to look after this place. They tells me it can be secured with 10 soldiers, two at each gate, and no one can enter forcibly or otherwise!"

The Gospel Book continued to strengthen Jobyna's spirits and Brenna asked her to read aloud in the late afternoons before the light retreated, leaving evening darkness to rule. Jobyna often conjectured what Elliad thought about the words King Leopold wrote in the back of the book. The stitching binding that whole section had been cut and the king's writings removed. Brenna helped Jobyna secure the Gospel Book once more in the leather casing, sewing it with strong thread to keep the pages together.

It was six weeks before a message came from Jydanski for Brenna. The doctor's wife told Jobyna that Sleven had been detained and would come as soon as the snow eased off.

The new year began almost unnoticed. Jobyna thought wishfully of the joyful celebrations enjoyed in Frencolia to welcome the new beginning.

January passed. Many days were spent sitting by the fire, craft-making, embroidering, knitting, reading and chatting. The weeks merged into a long respite, and Jobyna was pleased to be occupied. She asked Hagen if she could spend some time in the kitchens to do some baking and he consented reluctantly, stating it was not the sort of occupation expected of a princess, but if she kept the rules and was happy, then he had fulfilled his job.

Ellice helped her mix up dough for bread and she racked her brain to remember the biscuit recipes her mother used. Tasty pastries and tempting cookies turned out from the oven by her hands were enjoyed by all who sampled them. On the pretence of checking up on his charge, Hagen came to watch. The knight was warmed by the kitchen ovens, tempted by the aromas, and he enjoyed watching the beautiful princess work. She became well liked among the servants and soldiers left behind at the castle. Unbeknown to Jobyna, they gambled over the scrumptious morsels she manufactured. The fact that the princess baked them made each one very valuable. It became the highlight of the day to gamble with high prices over a jam tart or a nutty cookie.

The children were kept in the servants' quarters. Jobyna gleaned this fact from Boey, but Hagen reinforced his command that she was not permitted to go there.

Wishing she could read them stories from the Gospel Book, Jobyna watched the children from the cottage-apartment window as they played in the snow. They waved to her, and she waved back, smiling. Jobyna asked Hagen if the children could come to the cottage sitting-room, even a few of the littlest ones, and she would read stories to them. Hagen emphatically gave her a negative every time, and she saw he was getting angry with her persistence. He called it "nagging." Timidly deciding on a last attempt, she requested he have some of her baking taken to them, and when he said this was acceptable she went to the kitchens every day to bake the sumptuous delights she used to like as a child. There were 27 children so she made 54 gingerbread bears, complete with eyes, ears, mouths and noses. It was such fun! The kitchen was a wonderful place to be and Jobyna sampled all she baked as she had watched her mother do. She grew bigger and taller.

February was almost over when Sleven returned. The hint of an early spring hung in the breeze. Snow lying on the castle grounds was sparse, more like heavy frost. Scooping Brenna into his arms, the doctor spoke in Frenc, telling her he never wished to be parted from her again. He kissed Jobyna's hand and cheeks, exclaiming how wonderful she looked. "You have turned into a woman, and very beautiful, too."

He did not voice his thoughts, but he was not sure he wanted Elliad to see her now. Gone was the thin, gaunt wisp of a girl, too tall for her weight, looking like she would blow away with a breath of wind. Here she was, taller than Brenna, rounded and womanly. Jobyna would soon be 15 and she had blossomed into the flower she should be, as a woman of child-bearing age.

Sleven was tired and easily agitated. The first day after he arrived, Jobyna went to the kitchens to keep out of his way. That night she heard him pacing the floor. Brenna and he had talked over dinner, speaking in German. Brenna became upset and exclaimed loudly several times. Elliad's name was slotted here and there in the foreign conversation and Jobyna wished she knew all they were saying, especially when Sleven also spoke her name, linking it with Frencolia. Gaining enough of the discussion to know they were fearful for two of their sons who were in the Chezkovian Cavalry, Jobyna was surprised to hear that there were serious divisions among the Chezk troops.

After baking the next morning, Jobyna decided to walk and she asked one of the woman servants who was free from duties to go with her. She continued this practice each day, trying to leave the apartment free so that Brenna and Sleven could have time alone.

Four days after Sleven's return, she was walking with a servant named Lora who said her husband had returned for a short visit with others from Jydanski including Sleven's company.

"King Elliad wants them to take a couple of carts of stuff back, in spite of all that slick icy snow around. They's gain t' go when the storm stops."

Jobyna was interested in this, for here was someone who would have firsthand information. She chose her words carefully, speaking casually, "What does your husband think of Jydanski?" she asked.

"Oh, 'e says its not like Frencberg. Too prim and proper them Chezks. Everything must be done just right."

"What does your husband do?" Jobyna asked Lora.

"He's jest a 'go-fir.' Y' know, go fir this, go fir that. He takes messages for the king. Kind of dangerous too, if I knows nothin'."

Without comprehending the seriousness of her disclosures, Lora began verbalizing matters not meant for Jobyna's ears. The servant's voice slid to a soft whisper as they sat on a bench in the clerestory. Jobyna shivered, crossing her arms to draw her cloak around her, holding it closed because it no longer overlapped.

"The king sends him on missions all over Chezkovia. My Frewin has met a lot of important people in this here country. We's had them knights and lords back in Frencolia, but they's nothin' compared to this lot. Them emirs, I mean. The king's got a lot o' friends here, if I knows nothin'. Why, my Frewin reckons 'e's got jest about as much support as that czar there." She drew a breath of satisfaction, enjoying being able to gossip to new ears, obviously proud of her husband's progress.

Drawing another deep breath, she rattled on, "Frewin's got a special mission that takes 'em to a castle in another kingdom. It's a such a secret, 'e didn't even tell me, 'e didn't 'xactly say what for eiver." She frowned, realizing he had outwitted her. "He's been there a'fore . . . mind there, y' mustn't talk to anyone 'bout all this. My hubby says it's all like, like, y' know, confidential like." She glanced at Jobyna's white face and giggled. "But then, yore not gain' nowhere to say nothin' are ya?"

"No, I'm very much part of the furniture here." Jobyna answered, her mind racing. "Tell me, Lora, why do you say King Elliad's got as much support as the czar?" Lora did not answer right away, so Jobyna added congenially, "He must be well liked and popular. Maybe he's being kind and good to people so the czar will like him and be happy with him."

Lora whispered once more, enjoying stating her opinion of what her husband had no doubt told her, not suspecting it would go any further. "Him? Kind 'n good? There's no place for that stuff. It just don't work! My hubby ses 'e rules with a rod of iron 'n I'se agrees it's necessary in days what we live in! No, don't you see? The king will be taking over Chezkovia, jest like 'e did in Frencberg, that's obvious, if I knows nothin'! My Frewin ses this time 'e's right in the palace itself and 'e'll work from the inside out! The hardest part, hubby ses, is to get rid of that there czar wivout no one s'pecting! I fink that's what hubby's next trip's about. 'Til have to be real soon too, the rate it's all gain' now."

Jobyna's mind flipped over as she tried to digest Lora's words. A chilling sensation gripped her. She froze as Lora continued, "An' my hubby's gain' t' get promoted, that's what 'e ses. Frewin's such a good go fir, he's valuable to our king, that 'e is." She laughed, "An' it won't be 'king' much longer, if I knows nothin! It'll be czar!"

Jobyna's thoughts raced to Frencolia and the way Elliad became king there. To express to Lora her hatred of Elliad's ways, to speak against these horrendous, dreadful plans, would surely bring verbal abuse and disapproval. Frewin would likely hear that his wife had spoken to her! She must hide her feelings and pray she could use this information to prevent another murder! But how?

Rising shakily to her feet Jobyna asked, "Will your husband take you back to Jydanski with him?"

"No, I don't fink so. I'se jest happy to stay here anyways. I don't travel too good y' know. Got a bit of that there 'rites in me legs, an' anyways, if I knows nothing, 'e's so busy 'e don't have much time for me, 'e's got 'pointments all over!"

"Did your husband do the same sort of work in Frencolia, like message taking?" Jobyna asked innocently, placing one hand on the wall as though for support. They moved slowly, descending the stairs. Jobyna struggled to keep her voice calm and controlled.

"Yes. That's when he was noticed by the king for 'is, 'ow you say, 'is 'bilities. . . . He . . . ah . . ." Lora's voice trailed off. Her simple mind discerned a little of Jobyna's position.

Jobyna's thoughts suddenly turned to bitterness, *I wonder who Frewin betrayed? Someone with a Gospel Book? Maybe Father?* Trying to prevent the sarcasm she felt rising, she surprised herself with the way she hid her internal turmoil. "Frewin's come up in the world, hasn't he, Lora? I guess you will move to the palace in Jydanski eventually."

Lora, an unsuspecting soul, did not read anything into Jobyna's well-guarded comment. Shrugging, she murmured, "Well, I s'poses if it all goes 'cording to plan, that I will. But I's don't think I'll like it much, if I knows nothin'. Too big if what hubby ses is true."

Jobyna thought it wise not to question the servant woman again. She did not think she could suffer any more revelations from Lora without exploding. It seemed Frewin's spouse had unloaded the relevant, up-to-date items and further discussion might only arouse suspicion. Jobyna chatted away about her baking recipes, asking Lora to share her favorite ones. She told the servant how she made her gingerbread bears. They disputed in a friendly manner as to mixing and kneading bread dough, the stoking of the ovens, the glow of the embers and how to rake them so the heat was even. Jobyna took the long way back to the kitchens, directing discussion completely away from their previous conversation.

Nearing the kitchens, Lora whispered, "Mind, Princess, what we's talked about was jest 'tween you an' me."

Jobyna replied coolly, "Oh, I never give away anyone else's secret recipes." They parted as Jobyna reached the doctor's door.

Jobyna shut the door behind her and leaned against it. She felt exhausted and ill, and put her head back, closing her eyes. Her thoughts were in Frencolia. She visualized the village of Chanoine where Frewin and Lora had come from, traitors to their country! *Maybe they had been in league with Todd against Mother and Father! The monster, Elliad, is at it again! He has changed, but for worse! Czar indeed! What will he call himself,* she wondered, *Czar Elliad?*

Believing all that Lora had so innocently spilled, Jobyna realized there was much more to it. The matter was far more complex than Lora's simple mind could fathom. In a foggy distance, the captive heard Brenna's concerned voice, but she sounded miles away. Thoughts crashed in her head as she had seen the waves crash on the rocks.

"Jobyna," Brenna came over to her and put her hands on her shoulders. "Jobyna! What is wrong? You look ill." Jobyna looked down at the woman with unseeing eyes.

"I feel ill. I really feel ill, Brenna." Jobyna walked around the doctor's wife and into her bedroom. Flinging her cloak on the chair, she threw herself on the bed. Great sobs shook her body as she remembered her parents, vibrant with love and life, brutally murdered. She thought of Cynara and Kenrik with a realization of how helpless she was. There was nothing she could do, a prisoner of Elliad's Castle. For all she knew, Sleven may even be a traitor, he was in Elliad's pay, and Brenna . . .

The doctor's wife stood in the doorway, listening to Jobyna cry. She moved the cloak and sat on the chair. "Jobyna, what happened? Did someone hurt you?"

"No." Jobyna sobbed into the pillow. She realized Brenna would persist questioning and tried to stem her tears. It had been a long time since she had cried like that. Her voice broke as she tried to explain. "I'm sorry, I just don't feel well. I think . . . I'll go to bed and rest. Maybe I'll be better in the morning."

Blowing her nose on her handkerchief, she turned her red-rimmed eyes to Brenna. "Please. I'll be fine. Sleven's got enough worries . . . tell him I'm tired." She rose and fetched her nightgown.

Brenna was totally bewildered. Dinner had not yet arrived and Jobyna's appetite had not faltered for months. She decided to leave her charge but was concerned because the girl had never been like this before, moody and unable to explain herself. Neither had she been depressed without a reason.

Jobyna pulled the covers up over her head, trying to think, trying to work out what she could do, if anything. Helpless! Hopeless! Impossible! Then she remembered. She could pray. Yes, she must pray!

Brenna carried the dinner tray into Jobyna's room, but the girl seemed to have fallen asleep so she took it back to the table. Sleven arrived, and when Brenna told him about Jobyna's strange behavior, he too was concerned. Taking a lamp into the room, he pulled the covers carefully off her head and saw she was sound asleep. He conversed in undertones with Bren-

na until they decided to retire. They would
question Jobyna in the morning.

19

A nightmare crept, unchallenged at first, into Jobyna's subconscious. She witnessed Cynara and Kenrik being brutally murdered by Elliad. Berg stood in the way, trying to stop Julian and Brian, but strong soldiers wrapped him in chains and dragged him away. Elliad held Jobyna tightly, pinning her arms behind her back. Julian pushed Cynara up on the wide stone window ledge in the northern wall of Elliad's Castle. Digging his sword into her back, she then fell down, down, down to the jagged rocks below.

Jobyna screamed out as she heard Cynara's cries in her dream. Kenrik, his hands bound with rope, was forced out of the window by

Brian. She could hear the Czarevitch yelling as he fell. She screamed at Elliad and he put his hand over her mouth. Struggling, she sank her teeth into his hand. Elliad slapped her face and her head hit against the stone wall. He pushed her nearer to the window, forcing her to stand dangerously close to the opening. His sword pressed into her back as her eyes viewed the rocks below and the two distorted, broken bodies . . .

"No, no, it's a dream!" she cried out, "I must wake up." Elliad pushed her and she felt herself fall into black nothingness. Down . . . down . . . down . . .

"Lord, help me, I'm dreaming." But she was falling, falling, falling.

"Jobyna! Jobyna! Wake up!" Sleven shook her.

The girl was screaming out. The feeling of falling engulfed her completely and she was unable to rally her senses from the horror of the nightmare.

Unable to rouse her to stop her hysteria, Sleven fetched cold water and splashed it on her flushed face.

Opening her eyes to behold Sleven's anxiety, she tried to push him away. "No. Go away. You're all traitors!"

"Jobyna, wake up! It's just a dream." Sleven shook her.

Brenna spoke to her, "Jobyna, it's Brenna! Wake up. You're just having a bad dream.

Here, have a drink of milk. You didn't eat dinner. I don't wonder you're dreaming!"

Trembling uncontrollably, Jobyna realized she had almost forgotten the tricks an upset mind could play, especially an imaginative one like hers. She sat on the edge of the bed and drank the milk, her shaking hands spilling the liquid down her chin. Sleven moved into the sitting room, poking the fire and putting logs on it. Brenna squeezed a cloth in the bowl of icy water and sponged the girl's face, mopping the milk from her neck. Rising from the bed, Jobyna pulled the cloak over her nightgown. Memories of her discussion with Lora were foremost in her mind. Stepping into the sitting room she saw that Sleven had lit the lamps.

"Brenna, go to the kitchen and get some bread or cheese, anything. Jobyna should eat. And some milk, get some more milk." The doctor sounded flustered. He had never witnessed Jobyna suffering such a violent nightmare. Brenna collected an enveloping shawl from her room and went to carry out her husband's orders.

Pacing back and forth, Jobyna still shook uncontrollably. She wanted to know Sleven's position but was sure she was not clever enough to get him to tell her. The doctor would be too sharp for her questions.

"Who did you go walking with today, Princess?" Sleven asked, reverting to her royal title.

Words in answer did not come, but Jobyna

realized he would find out sooner or later. Other servants were in the kitchen when Lora had left with her. Also, Sleven would know Frewin had come with his company from Jydanski. It would just be a matter of minutes in the morning for him to find out it was Lora she had been with in the afternoon.

"Just let me think, please." She was stalling for time. Brenna came in with a tray. Jobyna did not feel hungry at all. Her stomach churned around and around.

Sleven sat waiting. His serious gray eyes followed the captive as she paced. Brenna, eyes half closed, rocked in her chair.

Jobyna ate a little of the bread and washed it down with some milk. Taking time to clear her mouth, she then said, "Sleven, I . . . don't . . . really know you, do I?" The doctor regarded her with a blank expression. His kindly face was grave. Taking her time to think, Jobyna then continued, "When I was back in Frencolia, I had two things in mind, to be true to God and to my country." She thought hard again. How could she ask him "are you loyal to the czar?" The girl hung her head. Sleven frowned at her.

"Sleven, I heard some things today that disturb me." She paused. "My mind would be greatly troubled if I heard that people in Frencolia may revolt against Luke, their king, and seek to take over the country for their own selfish reasons."

Narrowing his eyes at her words, Sleven

waited. She was quiet for some time before he spoke, "Are you speaking about Frencolia, Jobyna?" She did not answer. Trying to journey down the same road she seemed to be leading, he said, "And I would be greatly troubled if people in my country of Chezkovia were conspiring against my czar and the freedom we have in our country."

She returned with passion, "I would give my life to save Frencolia."

Sleven said with equal fervor, "Brenna and I would do the same for our czar and our country."

Jobyna felt trapped. *Always give people the benefit of the doubt*, her father's words came to her mind. She prayed for wisdom, wishing she had done so before this conversation began.

"Today," she said, looking squarely into his eyes, "I went walking with Lora, Frewin's wife. She divulged dark secrets about your country, Sleven. She upset me greatly, although I did not let her see how disturbed I was. Lora was treating me like a . . . a woman to exchange gossip. Did you know Frewin is, well, a spy for Elliad?"

Brenna stopped rocking. Sleven leaned forward. With her father's words at the front of her mind, she told Sleven the things she had heard. When she had told him all, she said to him ardently, "If you truly love your czar and your country, you will do something before it is too late."

Sleven's eyes were misty and he took Jobyna's hands in his. "Dear Jobyna. You have no idea what this information means to me, to my country, Chezkovia. I am not just a doctor. A secret council assigned me to come here so that I may observe, for them, this . . . this El- liad, impostor. What you have told me tonight is exactly as some of us have suspected, yet the facts have not shown up clearly anywhere before. We know there have been negotiations by Elliad's spies, yet always he has the right answer, the nice, flattering things to say to Czar Kievik. The czar has been besotted by him and is blind to his treachery; he counts him as a to- tally loyal friend. The Czar's Council has been divided. We have feared Elliad would learn I was planted here at his castle. I dread to think what would happen. . . . It would surely mean my life for Chezkovia."

Dropping her hands he broke into German, speaking to Brenna. She replied softly, nodding her head. He turned to Jobyna. "Two of the ser- vants who came with me from Jydanski are in truth men of the Chezkovian Cavalry. They have a small room of their own here. There are none of Elliad's soldiers on guard in the castle. As you know, there is no need. I am going to fetch Gregory and Fritz. They must hear what you have told me, from your lips, Jobyna."

He strode to his room, coming back minutes later, fully dressed. "You must dress," he or- dered. "And thank you, Princess Jobyna. You

186

have done Chezkovia a great service." Sleven bowed and left the room.

Brenna stood and held her arms out to Jobyna. Jobyna entered them and they hugged and cried. Realizing the men would return swiftly, they hurried to dress.

"Gregory, Fritz, this is Princess Jobyna." Sleven introduced her, pulling chairs to the couch so they could sit close together. "Tell my friends all you heard today, Jobyna," Sleven urged.

After Jobyna had quoted Lora's words, explaining her own questions to the woman and describing Lora's attitude of surety about Elliad not being "king" but "czar," there was silence, each man involved in similar thoughts.

Jobyna spoke again. "Sleven, did you ever hear how King Leopold died in Frencolia?"

"He died of the plague," the doctor replied.

"No. He was poisoned, murdered by Elliad."

The two younger Chezkovians exclaimed together, realizing the significance of her words. Sleven held up his hands, shaking his head. "Let Princess Jobyna tell us what she knows about it."

Jobyna began her story from the time she found the testament in the cave, written in

King Leopold's own handwriting, his accusation of having been poisoned. She told them of King Leopold's body being there and the events that took place after this. She told them of the carnage between Frencolia and Chezkovia.

"He is so very evil. It is well within the scope of his depraved mind to murder your czar for the gaining of further position and power."

The men conversed long and intensely through the night. Jobyna fell asleep, her head slumped back on cushions on the couch. Still in a semi-upright position when she woke before dawn, a sense of dread flooded her mind. She felt sure that something bad was going to happen. Brenna slept in the rocking chair. The men sat around the map-clad table. Lingering smoke from the smoldering fire hung in the room and Jobyna rose to open the shutters, allowing the unwelcome fumes to escape and greeting the cool fresh air as it invaded the apartment. Sleven folded the maps and each man gave the other the Chezkovian salute and hug. Kissing her on the back of her hand, Gregory thanked her, and Fritz told her Sleven would share some of their plans. They must return to their room before the servants woke and suspicions were aroused.

Sleven and Jobyna sat at the table. The girl chewed on a bread roll left from the night before. Sleven spoke. "Fritz and Gregory are returning at first light to Jydanski. They will have to be so very careful. It will be like walking on thin ice. Elliad has already suggested to the czar that some of the key people in the czardom are traitors. His words caused the Chief Emir, Valerian, to be thrown in the dungeons last week. This has puzzled us greatly. We had thought Valerian to be working against the czar, that if anyone had been in league with Elliad, it would be he. Valerian had, however, been very close to Czarina Terese, the czar's wife. It seems Elliad has wound his way into the heart of the czarina and we believe he feels she is the key to his success. But it is all very confusing."

The doctor continued explaining matters at the palace in Jydanski. Jobyna knew he was taking her completely into his confidence. "Terese is the czar's second wife, a lot younger than he. She is about as scatty as a woman could possibly be! He certainly did not marry her for her logic or wisdom, for she does not have a scrap!"

He drew a deep breath. "Our country has never been in such a divided state! It's a mess! We believe the situation is deteriorating every hour. Peace and unity are being undermined and people are taking sides; yet both sides display that they are loyal to the czar! It is a very strange dilemma! Elliad is not just working for himself. We believe he has other leaders supporting him." Sleven paused for a moment, then, "Fritz, Gregory and I have decided you must escape. We want to see you safely on your way back to Frencolia."

Jobyna drew a breath of wonder, thinking, *yes, but how?*

Sleven continued. "Also, my dear wife." He looked at Brenna who was still sleeping soundly, snoring softly. "Brenna has a sister in Proburg. I am going to take her there today for her safety. At any moment, someone could inform Elliad of my dual role here and Brenna's life would be at risk as well as mine. We discussed the situation over and over. I would like to take you with me today, but Hagen would not allow it. Even with a sizable bribe, we believe he would detain us. Hagen would connect you with my treachery to Elliad for sure, and I am not prepared to place you under such a risk."

He paused for breath, frowning at the precarious position. "I will leave immediately after breakfast. The soldiers are used to my coming and going. They should not stop me if I tell them I am taking my wife to visit relatives; at least I hope they won't! This castle is less than two miles from the Proburg border. Brenna's sister lives about eight or ten miles further, in the town of Walden. It will take me the best of the daylight hours to ride there with Brenna's carriage, then back, as I must discuss the situation with my brother-in-law. Tomorrow, I will suggest you go for a ride on your horse and we will try to escape, first to

Proburg. Then we will form our next plans once safely there. Brownlea is young and swift and the horse I brought back from Jydanski would be equal. Prince Gustovas will be willing to help when he knows what Elliad is planning. The most difficult task will be to convince him of the treachery. The Prince is very close to the czar as are our two countries. Many Chezkovians have married people from Proburg." He moved to a trunk lying by the door. "I brought you some new riding boots, Jobyna."

Brenna stirred, and Sleven spoke to her, explaining the plans. Brenna was doubtful and said, "Sleven, take Jobyna. Do not worry about me! Surely this Elliad would not harm an old woman!"

Jobyna exclaimed, "No! Sleven is right! Elliad would not hesitate to kill you or have you tortured. He murdered women and small children all the way from Frencolia to Chezkovia! No one was spared! Even if you are not able to come back for me, Sleven, there is no reason why Elliad should suspect I know anything about what you are doing or where you are. Show me the maps, Sleven, and I will see for myself the way to go. If our plans change, I need to know which roads to take."

Jobyna spent the next half-hour studying the maps of Proburg and Chezkovia. Jydanski, like Frencberg in Frencolia, was near the center of the country, the most guarded place. Sleven said the roads were wide and straight. Even at night, it was not a difficult journey from Chez-kovia to Proburg. Brenna gathered up some of their belongings and Sleven packed a trunk. Brenna moved off to fetch their breakfast.

Boey addressed her at the door. "You was late, madam. I brought the tray meself." Boey looked past Brenna at Jobyna who had turned her back and was hastily folding the maps, removing them from the table to a cupboard. "Good morning, Princess Jobyna." She handed the tray to Brenna and stepped in the room to curtsy to Jobyna. "Morning, Doctor." They murmured a return greeting to Boey and Brenna closed the door.

"Jobyna, we do not know if we will sit together and share a meal again. When you thank your God for the food this morning, please pray aloud and ask Him to be with us today." Sleven spoke seriously.

"When I was at home with my family, we held hands around the table when we prayed." Jobyna smiled, extending a hand to each of them. Her hands were happily taken on either side with warm firm grips.

"Dear Father in heaven," she prayed, "thank you for this day. Thank you for our breakfast. We give this day to you and ask you to be with us. Please keep Sleven and Brenna safe on their journey. Help us to cope with all you bring and believe you are in control, not Elliad. May the good and the bad all work out your wise plans. Thank you for using my knee injury so that I may meet such friends as Sleven and Brenna. Help us to trust you completely, and your Son, Jesus Christ, Amen."

After the meal, Brenna kissed Jobyna and held her close. "You are precious, like a daughter."

Jobyna's eyes grew wide to hear these words. She knew this to be a very great acceptance and privilege.

Brenna continued, "No matter what happens, Sleven will see you are rescued."

Sleven kissed her on each cheek, reiterating Brenna's comments. They departed for their journey. Jobyna was alone—a strange feeling. She had not been alone in this castle since arriving and being locked in the room near the front entrance.

It had been decided Jobyna should not walk with them to the stables. It must not appear to be a special farewell or bring extra attention to Brenna's leaving. Jobyna sat by the window and read from the Gospel Book.

After 15 minutes, she took the breakfast tray to the kitchen and told Lora and Esme she wished to do some baking. She would make over 100 gingerbread bears for the children. Ellice worked with her and Jobyna hummed as she rolled out the dough. She put extra currant-buttons close together on their tummies. This might be the last time she could bake like this for the children. The last tray slid into the oven as Julian strode arrogantly through the kitchen doors. He bowed and as he rose, his beady frog-like eyes ogled the princess up and down.

"The Princess Jobyna? In the kitchen? Come with me, now!" he beckoned to Jobyna. Without taking his eyes off the captive, he spoke again. "You too, slave! King Elliad commands you come to the capital today. Borena is packing your things. There is a carriage waiting for the three of you."

Jobyna took the apron off and followed Julian. "May I ride my horse, please?"

Julian turned slightly, his lip curling scornfully. "Ladies of the czardom do not ride horses, Princess!" Jobyna followed him to the castle entrance. She noticed he had gained all the weight he had lost, and more. His Frencolian uniform was too tight, gaping where the buttons threatened to burst.

Jobyna thought of Sleven and Brenna and secretly prayed that they had crossed the border safely.

Hagen strode in the entrance as they arrived in the castle foyer. "The doctor has left with his wife! He told the soldiers at the gate office he was going to relatives. He left almost two hours ago."

Julian was silent. Jobyna was ushered into the reception room where she was again confined as at her arrival. She hoped Ellice and Boey would bring her new riding boots. She must remember to ask before she left if they had packed them. The girl's mind was accelerating

194

with perplexity. Elliad wanted her at the capital! Her heart felt like lead! Confusion was reigning, or was it? *Can God get confused?* The prisoner asked herself. She knew the answer. *There are no mistakes with God, only His appointments.*

20

Jobyna, Boey and Ellice sat on the one wide seat of the carriage in complete silence for the first few miles. Julian had closed the shuttered windows of the plain black carriage and none of them dared to open one lest he see them. It was dim but comfortable and Jobyna marveled at the speed and smoothness of the ride.

Boey had brought the girl's crimson cloak and riding boots and Jobyna exchanged her soft slippers for the boots. The cloak was now far too small and short. She hoped no one would see her in it as the garment appeared to belong to a younger sister and made her look awkward. Jobyna was disappointed that she would not be at the Baltic Castle to be rescued by Sleven but was consoled to think that he and Brenna were safe. She wondered why Julian wanted to find Sleven and hoped her doctor friend would not walk into a trap when he arrived back at Elliad's Castle. When Julian and Jobyna had walked to the stables she had seen many Chezkovian soldiers with Elliad's knights. That was proof enough; Elliad's power and control had expanded. It was plain for anyone to see, Jobyna thought.

Julian rode Speed and she saw a Chezkovian in his red and white uniform sitting smugly on Brownlea. The shadows of his eyes held recognition toward the princess. Jobyna wondered if she had seen him somewhere before. While composing an appropriate verbal protest for the rider of her horse, Julian silenced any exclamation as he grabbed her arm and pushed her into the carriage. The fat man locked the door from the outside and she knew she was traveling not as a princess but a prisoner!

Dull miles passed by quickly. Boey began to chatter about the weather and how much she looked forward to the warmer season. The morning was almost past when the carriage drew suddenly to a halt.

"Make way for the Princess Jobyna!" Julian called, his high raspy voice speaking in broken German.

The reply came short and sharp, "Make way for the Czarevna Cynara!"

Jobyna was able to understand their words, and she held her breath as the voices conferred. The sound of horses moving came to her ears and after a time, Julian opened the carriage door. Unfolding the steps, he announced, "The Czarevna wishes to speak with Princess Jobyna." Ellice stepped down and Jobyna could see a beautiful red carriage, ornamented with gold engravings from which two ladies-in-waiting were alighting. As Julian took Jobyna's arm, he hissed in her ear, "You must be brief!" Jobyna, wonderment on her face, climbed into Cynara's spacious carriage.

"Jobyna!" Cynara hugged her affectionately. "Is it really you? You look simply wonderful. I can scarcely believe it is the same person! Look at you! Your cloak is too small! Are they taking you to the capital? Yes. I suppose so." Jobyna did not have a chance to get a word in. "We're going to Proburg. Things are so boring at the palace. Politics. That's all I ever hear! But you look so good!" Cynara inspected Jobyna's smiling face. Once more she was overwhelmed by her natural, unadorned beauty.

Jobyna found her voice. "How did you get Julian to let me talk with you?"

"Haven't you heard of a little bribery, darling? That grubby little fat man, is that Julian? Just as well. I guessed he was greedy! His nasty little eyes lit up like diamonds when I offered him a few gold pieces. I'm so glad I saw you before we left! Do have fun in the capital."

Jobyna worried suddenly this was all Cynara had to say. "You said 'we,' Cynara. Who else goes with you?"

"My younger brother, Kedar. He was nine last week and he is beginning his training in Prince Gustovas' court." She waved her gloved hand toward the door. "He's out there on his horse somewhere. Kedar is the main reason I'm going to Proburg. Father wants me to see him settled, but if I feel like it, I may stay there for a while myself, especially if Konrad is not at Landmari. If I do see that crazy prince, I shall return immediately!" She was quiet for a moment.

Jobyna asked, "How are things in Jydanski?"

"I simply don't want to think about the place! That's another reason I'm glad to be getting away."

"How is your father?" Jobyna persisted.

"He's crabby as ever—at least with me. Has been ever since that Elliad of yours came. Mind you, he's not 'your' Elliad any more." Her voice softened to a whisper. "My step mother! She's another reason I want to get out of that place! So indiscreet! Father doesn't see past his nose! He thinks Elliad is marvelous, but . . . " Cynara broke into a long discourse in German.

Jobyna's eyes widened to think of Elliad and Terese having an affair, but most of Cynara's chatter was lost. "I have to go; we must make Landmari Castle before sunset." She did not wait for Jobyna to say more but kissed her cheeks in dismissal, speaking encouragingly, "Just keep your chin up and I'll look forward to seeing you when I return, Princess Jobyna." She knocked on the carriage door. A Chezkovian soldier opened it.

"Thank you for stopping to talk, Czarevna Cynara. I cherish your friendship," Jobyna said.

As the soldier took her arm, she glanced quickly around. They were at crossroads. Dozens of mounted soldiers waited in formation in front of and behind the carriage. Jobyna wondered where the boy, the Grand Duke Kedar, was.

The ladies-in-waiting stepped back into the carriage and Julian took Jobyna's elbow, propelling her toward the vehicle that would take her to Elliad. With a sinking heart she wished she could have gone with Cynara, but she knew it would take more than a bribe for Julian to allow that to happen. Julian folded the steps back to the inside, checked the shutters and locked the door.

The rest of the journey was uneventful. The three women fell asleep before the destination was reached. A double jolt woke Jobyna and she opened her eyes to find her head on Ellice's shoulder, but her thoughts were back at Elliad's Castle. "The Gospel Book! What happened to the Gospel Book?"

Boey sat upright, yawning. "I put it in the cupboard in the doctor's living room. Wasn't no point bringing it here. Causes too much trouble, them books."

Jobyna's thoughts were interrupted by the sound of voices outside the carriage. The door was unlocked and opened. A uniformed man with a book and quill stood at the opening. Julian watched him write. Jobyna guessed they had arrived at some gate and their entry was being recorded. The door was soon closed and the journey into the capital city resumed.

21

Late afternoon sunshine greeted Jobyna as she stepped out of the carriage. She remembered her arrival at the King's Castle in Frencberg, the first castle she had ever seen. It was difficult to believe only a year had passed since then. Jobyna imagined herself to be years older.

Holding the side of her skirt with one hand, taking Julian's hand with the other, Jobyna's vision was suddenly filled with the most amazing building. In all her wildest imagination she would never have dreamed up such a palace. The stationary carriage stood in a tremendous courtyard enclosed by a pillared clerestory which stretched as far as the eye could see.

Along the clerestory, soldiers with spears extended stood vigilantly on guard.

Julian directed her movement by gripping her arm above her elbow. His fat fingers pressed firmly into her flesh. Jobyna turned as he drew her towards a massive marble terrace which extended the width of the courtyard. Jobyna counted 10 wide white marble levels as she ascended. Pillars towered above, blocking out a complete view of the magnificent palace frontage. High arched carved doors graced the entrance.

Jobyna pulled her cloak off, pushing it into Ellice's waiting hands. Julian drew his charge along to the end door which was opened by two stately palace guards. Inside, a marble stairway greeted them. Counting the steps to 17, Jobyna walked in step with Julian. She ignored the loathsome, creepy feeling his being vibrated and concentrated on counting. Ten paces along a landing then another 17 steps, twice. She realized they were three floors up. Her riding boots resounded loudly on the pale blue marble landing.

Two guards opened a door on the fourth landing, barring Julian's way. They allowed Boey and Ellice to follow Jobyna. The guards spoke to someone on the other side of the door who in turn spoke to the three women, "Come." A wide balcony stretched out before them. The attendant knocked at a door half way along the balcony. Jobyna felt as much a prisoner as she ever had. Elliad's Castle or the Czar's Palace, it was the same. Grandeur and beauty around her were lost in the realization that she was not free. Such splendor made the stone walls of the King's Castle in Frencolia seem shabby in comparison. The captive remembered the walls and floor of the Frencolian throne room were intricately patterned with etched grey marble, but the rest of the castle was constructed of gray stone.

Opening the door, a woman nodded to the attendant. No announcement was made. The woman spoke quickly to the man who replied equally as fast. Jobyna recognized her own name, wishing she could understand their conversation.

Sensing herself under inspection, Jobyna looked at the new face. The woman's piercing black eyes seemed to remove the very skin from Jobyna's face and neck and she was relieved to see the masked doll open her mouth to speak. "Princess Jobyna. Come in."

The three woman entered the room, a small foyer decked out with vases of fresh flowers, hung about with potted ferns. "My name is Sofia. I have been assigned to be responsible for you. I belong to the palace and do only what I am told. It would be to your benefit, Princess, to do the same." The brightly painted lips spoke perfect Frenc in soft, deep tones. Long, red-tipped fingers stretched to open a door, gesturing them to go ahead of her.

Jobyna felt sickened and overpowered by the strange sweet perfume the woman emitted.

The captive stepped into the massive room. Carpeted steps led down to a huge cushioned sitting area where built-in couches encircled low tables. The other end of this sunken circle was a long dining table, polished to a glass-like shine. An elaborate, golden candle chandelier hung glittering above it. Pillars stood behind the table and archways with open doors led out onto another balcony. In other circumstances, Jobyna would have been fascinated by the dazzling wonder of her surroundings. Sofia spoke again, drawing her charge to one of the many doors stretching along one side of the huge room. Again Jobyna felt the woman's searching eyes on her face, probing every tiny detail.

"This will be your apartment, Princess Jobyna. Just go in and make yourself comfortable. I will return later." The statue-like Sofia turned to Ellice and Boey. "I will show the rest of you to your quarters."

Sofia opened the door and Jobyna entered, turning as the woman closed it soundly. She was alone. Jobyna's heart raced. The door had no handle on the inside! The girl turned back again to behold a miniature sitting room with a tiny, ornately carved table, two matching chairs and a couch. Fresh fruit and a jug sat on the table and a silver chalice stood upside-down beside the jug. Three doors were built into the far wall of the room. Jobyna pushed on the half-open door. An enormous bedroom containing one large bed met her eyes. The room seemed cold and sterile in spite of luxurious cream rugs on the pink marble floor.

Moving through another door she saw that an elaborate bathroom occupied this space. It had a door which opened into the bedroom. Frothy, perfumed water and rising vapor from the bath beckoned Jobyna enticingly. A dress lay over the back of an elaborately wrought chair. Brass fixtures held towels, hair brushes and combs, oils, perfumes and soaps. Jobyna decided to investigate the other room, discovering a dressing room displaying a completely mirrored wall. Clothes, coats, wraps and gowns of every color and style imaginable hung along one wall. The third wall was filled with shelves containing night wear, lacy petticoats, underwear, scarves, kerchiefs, shawls, hats, shoes and accessories, all meticulously placed. She wondered who the clothes belonged to? Fingering the delicate seed pearls on one of the brocade dresses, she saw it was brand new.

Returning to the sitting room, Jobyna realized how thirsty and hungry she was. Drinking the juice, she ate dates and dried apricots, sampling some of the strange shelled nuts from the sparkling silver bowl. Drawn by the fantastic fragrance of the bath, she moved back to the bathroom. Holding the dress up against her,

Jobyna thought it would be too small and short, so she went to the dressing room and chose a larger one which looked loose and comfortable. She chose undergarments. It would be refreshing to wear a clean, new set of beautiful clothes.

Jobyna had bathed, dressed, towel-dried and plaited her hair before Sofia came into the room carrying a tray bearing a covered meal.

Scrutinizing Jobyna thoroughly, Sofia spoke, "I'm pleased you've made yourself at home. I'll come back when you've eaten." Jobyna opened her mouth to speak, but Sofia had already turned away.

The prisoner lifted the silver lid to reveal roast pork and a variety of vegetables, steaming hot. Thankful for the succulent meal, Jobyna decided it was no use being afraid and hungry at the same time. A strange-looking dessert sat on a small silver platter with a miniature spoon beside it, some type of fruit cake soaked in strong wine with cream on it. Jobyna sampled a spoonful, spitting it immediately back onto the plate. Rinsing her mouth with orange juice, she tried to rid her mouth of the undesirable taste.

Cupboards were built into the sitting room wall. Jobyna opened one, cautiously. Inside were bookshelves containing books neatly stacked. Inquisitively, she explored the others. One contained a recessed oak writing desk with a fold-out table top. Parchment, ink, quills, jars of water paints and brushes sat along the shelves.

Clicking softly, the door opened wide. Sofia followed Ellice into the room. The slave wore a peach-colored brocade dress, loose, with wide flowing sleeves. Jobyna had never seen Ellice looking so lovely. Her black curly hair was damp and hung in moist tendrils around her heart-shaped face. Jobyna guessed she had been treated to a bath as well.

Sofia spoke. "Your slave will sleep in here with you." Pointing the long nail of her forefinger towards the door, she indicated a thick hanging cord, dark pink in color. Speaking directly to Ellice, Sofia said, "If you need me, just give the cord a tug and I will come as soon as I can." Sofia turned to Jobyna. "Do you have any questions, Princess?" Hundreds of thoughts flooded Jobyna's inquisitive mind. She was not sure which question to ask first or how much this woman would tell her? The hesitation was taken to be a negative response. Sofia, taking the tray with her, hastily left the room, pushing the door firmly closed behind her. There were no windows in this apartment, but the many lit candles gave a bright, warm glow.

"Did they treat you well?" Jobyna asked Ellice who nodded enthusiastically. "Did you see anyone we know?" Again a nod. Eager to know more, Jobyna gathered parchment and ink, saying, "We will use initials alone and I'll try to guess who it is you mean or they may find out what we've been talking about." There was no fireplace in the room, but it was comfortable, neither too warm nor too cold. Jobyna noticed, up high near the plastered ceiling, grated vents which she imagined kept the air circulating. In the King's Castle, along the corridors, she had noticed vents like these down close to the floor.

Pulling her mind back to her questions, she asked, "Did you see Elliad?" Ellice shook her head. "The czar?" Again, a negative. "Did you see where Boey went?" Another head shake. "Who did you see that we know?"

Ellice wrote "A" and "R," in her crude handwriting.

Jobyna guessed, "Ada and Ranee?" The slave girl nodded, placing her hand on Jobyna's arm. She opened her mouth pointing inside. "They spoke to you?" Ellice shook her head. "What then?" Trying again, Ellice made the action of pulling an imaginary tongue from her mouth and with the other palm held vertical she made the action of a blade falling in front of her face. Jobyna gasped, not wanting to express her thoughts, but desperate to know the truth, "You don't mean . . . ?" She could not voice such atrocity, and shook her head seriously at Ellice, "like Elliad did to you, Ellice?" The slave nodded. Jobyna verbalized the dread, just to be sure. "He cut . . . their tongues? Both . . . of them?" Ellice hung her head. She nodded slowly and sadly, unable to meet Jobyna's horror-stricken gaze.

The captive princess did not feel like asking any more questions and Ellice did not offer any more information. Scrawling over the "A" and "R," the letters became eyes. Jobyna drew a picture of an evil-looking bearded man. Slowly tearing her artwork to shreds, she pushed the pieces down into the toe of one of her riding boots. Frightening curiosity made her want to ask Ellice what it was like to lose one's tongue, but the thought made her stomach turn and her heart beat fast. Ellice could not explain, and there was no need to mull it over.

Jobyna paced back and forth, back and forth, and her unrest concerned Ellice. Finally, the slave took her mistress' arm and pointed to the bedroom. The last thing Jobyna wanted to do right now was sleep! Fear of having a terrible nightmare featuring Ada and Ranee and the evil Elliad made her shrug Ellice from her arm. The books in the cupboard came to her mind, and it was a pleasant surprise to discover some were written in Frenc and Latin. Reading would take her mind off Ada, Ranee and Elliad's horrible brutality. It was late when she finally decided to leave the history books and retire. If only one of them had been a Gospel Book, but she knew she was expecting too much.

Words she had learned in childhood flew to her mind. *When I am afraid, I will trust in Thee.*

After preparing for bed, she knelt down, "Lord, please keep my mind tonight. I am afraid. Do not let me have a nightmare tonight. Fill my mind with your words that I may sleep in peace. Bless Luke and bless Frencolia. If it is possible, help me to escape from this prison," she whispered. Almost choking, she continued, "Lord, please don't let them cut out my tongue." Helplessness overwhelmed her as she climbed on to the thick feather mattress. She gestured for Ellice to climb in beside her, but the girl shook her head decidedly, curling up on the lambskin rug on the floor by the bed. There was no protest, however, when Jobyna pulled a blanket from the bed and laid it over her friend, the mute slave girl.

Drifting into sleep, Jobyna's last thoughts were, *This is the Czar's Palace I am in, at Jydanski, the capital city of Chezkovia. Lord, help me, please.* She slept peacefully until dawn. Awakening refreshed, she told herself she must pray last night's prayer every night and fill her mind with the Gospel Book's words. It would prevent the terrible nightmares.

22

Twelve . . . 13 . . . 14 . . . 15! Jobyna counted the paces from one end of the sitting room to the other. Touching the door, she calculated 50 times of walking back and forth, then she began quoting Scripture aloud.

For the past two weeks each day had been the same as the day previous. Breakfast was brought. Ellice waited until her mistress had eaten, then ate from what was left. There was always plenty to spare. Each morning was spent walking back and forth in the confined space, alternated with reading, drawing and painting. Sofia brought juice about midday. Every afternoon, the bath became a frothy mist of perfume and bubbles. Ellice pulled the cord and Sofia allowed the slave to leave with the clothes, bringing back fresh towels and linen. Jobyna learned from Ellice that the slave girl was to go through the wardrobe and remove the clothes that did not fit her mistress, replacing them with garments that did. Ellice, pulling on the cord, went freely in and out, making Jobyna envious of this small freedom.

Sofia was not one to converse with her charge, and when Jobyna said brightly, "Good morning, Sofia, how are you today?" There was never any reply.

Walking, quoting the 23rd Psalm, her mind raced back to the time she had recited it to Berg and he was comforted. God knew if Berg was in heaven. If so, this captivity would be worth something! She smiled as she reached the words, "Thy rod and Thy staff, they comfort me. Thou preparest a table for me, in the presence of mine enemies . . . " She touched the wall, turning. Sofia entered the apartment, staring at the girl strangely. Smiling, Jobyna said to her, "I walk back and forth, thinking of green pastures and still waters . . . " Her voice trailed off at Sofia's stony stare of scorn.

The chamber lady opened her perfect ruby-red lips to speak to Jobyna, handing Ellice a parcel. "You will be dining tonight with the Czar's wife, Her Imperial Highness, Czarina Terese. You must properly prepare yourself to match the occasion." Sofia swept out of the room.

Ellice opened the cloth parcel, revealing a sparkling diamond tiara and ruby necklace. A tight feeling constricted Jobyna's throat. She was trapped and had to do as she was commanded! The girl determined she would control her tongue and speak only when spoken to.

It was late when Sofia entered the room. Passing a dinner tray to Ellice, her eyes scrutinized Jobyna as she spoke. "The Czarina Terese awaits you, Princess Jobyna."

Jobyna followed Sofia's lead. After two weeks' confinement, the massive dining chamber dazzled the captive princess. She focused her eyes on a woman standing beside the long dining table. Czarina Terese wore an elaborate jeweled crown on her swept-up, dark brown hair. Jobyna thought she looked very young to be the Czar's wife, and she could not forget Sleven's description or Cynara's words. Jobyna walked toward the Czarina, a few cautious steps, then curtsied low.

"Come." The czarina sat, beckoning. "Sit." She motioned to a chair that Sofia pulled back from the table. Jobyna was reminded of Elliad and his incessant commands. The table was set for two and they were waited upon by women wearing the same uniform dress as Ellice. Terese gestured once more. "Eat." Knowing she was under observation, Jobyna helped herself from the many bowls. A steaming amber fluid was poured by Sofia from a tall silver jug with a long spout into two small porcelain bowls, each with a handle. Copying the Czarina, Jobyna sipped the hot liquid.

"Tea. Have you had it before?"

"No, Your Imperial Highness," Jobyna answered. The mixture tasted like perfume. She sipped again, but as she swallowed, her face mirrored her feelings. At the click of Terese's slender fingers, Sofia brought some juice, pouring it into a silver chalice for the girl. Terese ate in silence, watching Jobyna as a cat would a mouse. An amused smirk lingered on the cosmetics of her finely featured face. Jobyna could not begin to guess what she was thinking. The meal over, Jobyna was thankful her trembling hands had obeyed the careful directions of her mind, and she had not disgraced herself by spilling anything.

Sofia poured wine at a low table in the sitting area and Terese rose, speaking as though to an inferior being. "We will recline, and I will tell you some things you need to know."

Reading the obvious warning in Terese's tone, Jobyna reminded herself to be quiet unless asked to speak. Terese reclined on a long low couch, beckoning the captive to sit beside her on a floral footstool.

215

After a short silence, the czar's wife took a deep breath and verbalized most astounding news. "Elliad John Pruwitt is dead, Jobyna. He was executed for treason against the czardom of Chezkovia." She paused, a triumphant sneer on her face, obviously awaiting the girl's reaction. There was no retaliation or joy, for Jobyna was too shocked to react. She knew it true; Elliad had committed treason! But to think he had finally been found out . . . and was dead! She had expected many things, but not this! Maybe her nightmares were over.

"You belong to Czar Kievik, now. In a few days, you will be presented to my husband in the oval crown room of Chezkovia." Terese continued to study Jobyna's face. The czarina colored to see the girl's complete composure and her flawless natural beauty. Tiring of the silence, she asked, "What do you say, Jobyna, now of Jydanski?"

"I have nothing to say, Czarina Terese." Jobyna hung her head in submission. She was going to add "maybe His Highness will send me home," but thought better of such a statement. She remembered Ada and Ranee, wondering if it was the czar who had dealt with them the way Ellice had graphically described.

Passing the girl a silver chalice of wine, Terese spoke in her commanding tone. "Then we will drink to your life in Chezkovia. May you please the czar as much as you please me."

Jobyna did not like these words. She had no desire to have a life in Chezkovia!

Terese lifted the chalice, drinking deeply. Jobyna's hand was frozen. Czarina Terese lowered her silver receptacle. "You do not drink with me?" The amused, contemptuous look swiftly turned to disdain and her haughtiness clouded with anger.

"Pardon me, please, Czarina Terese," Jobyna said, hoping she could successfully calm her superior. "I do not tolerate wine, but would be glad to drink with you if I could have some juice, please." Terese clicked her fingers and Sofia brought the juice from the table. Pouring it into a clean chalice, she handed it to Jobyna who raised the chalice and said cheerfully, "To Chezkovia. I pray for peace and prosperity for the czarina and her husband."

Terese relaxed. She was impressed and liked Jobyna. The girl was congenial and very submissive. How she could be so incredibly beautiful as well as have a peaceful personality was quite sickening! *Mind you*, the czarina thought, *without that mass of reddish hair* . . . She rose abruptly.

"Sofia will tell you when the czar expects you. It will be later in the week. My husband and I are making tours of goodwill." Terese extended her hand to Jobyna. "Just remember, you are here to please the czar."

Chilled by Terese's parting words, Jobyna rose. Taking the czarina's slender hand, she curtsied, surprised when the czarina planted a light, feather kiss on one cheek. She watched speechlessly as Terese moved to double doors with golden crowns etched into them beyond the dining table. Jobyna's hand was grasped firmly in Sofia's and she was hastily led back to her "prison."

Later, Jobyna told Ellice what the czarina had revealed about Elliad's execution. Scarcely blinking, teardrops like diamond bulbs rolled down Ellice's cheeks. Jobyna knew these tears were not out of pity or commiseration for Elliad, but due to the fact that she was finally free from his terrible tyranny.

"Maybe it was the czar who did that to Ada and Ranee." Jobyna proffered an explanation. Ellice shook her head. "Elliad?" Jobyna asked, "Did you hear someone say this?" Ellice nodded. Jobyna wondered if she had a nightmare whether it would be about the czar. *What did he look like?* She thought of Kenrik and Cynara, and decided their father would have black eyes and raven hair like his children. Maybe he was going gray. She could wait. *The longer the better*, she thought.

23

Finally, the summons came. Jobyna counted eight monotonous days since she had dinner with Czarina Terese. Fast losing her sense of time, Jobyna tried to draw up a simple calendar on parchment. Ellice helped her, gleaning information from the servant's quarters, and the captive saw it would soon be April, spring time in Frencolia.

Ellice helped Jobyna dress. The slave combed the girl's hair dry, making it jump with coppery life at each stroke of the comb. Jobyna had an icy feeling of dread and fear frozen deep in her heart. Chastising herself for being childish, she prayed for the emotional strength she needed to face her new possessor. By the time she was ready Jobyna felt calmer. Maybe Czar Kievik would allow her to go home. Surely Cynara's friendship would mean something to the father?

Jobyna was directed into the czarina's chamber for the second time. Czarina Terese waited at the door and Jobyna felt surprised to be greeted by the royal person. She had expected a servant or a knave, not the czar's wife, to accompany her. It was comforting to know that the dreaded escorts on Elliad's arm were finally over! Jobyna could not get used to the cool, contemptuous set of Terese's heavily made-up face. In comparison, Sofia's "mask" was friendly!

The captive curtsied to the czarina who commanded, "Follow me." Led into the foyer, out into the corridor, through the doors by which she had originally entered, Jobyna relaxed and mentally prepared herself to enjoy this occasion and store such an event in her memory. She was on her way to meet the Imperial Kievik, the famed Czar of Chezkovia!

Palace guards fell in step behind the two as they moved past the stairwell, along another corridor. Descending a central, open, curved staircase, Jobyna realized they were in the heart of the huge palace. The wide stairs were covered with plush, velvet-like red carpet. These were the steps the czar and czarina walked on each day. She wished Cynara were here and wondered if she would see Kenrik.

Reaching the bottom of the stairs, Jobyna's eyes beheld a circular reception room. She had to turn her head to view the whole grandeur of the auditorium. Soldiers were on guard at the entrance doors and for a brief moment Jobyna thought one of them looked like Julian dressed in a red and white uniform. Dismissing the thought as fantasy, the reaction returned spontaneously, making her heart race violently, as she found herself face to face with Brian dressed in the Chezkovian red and white. She heard his deep voice announce, "Her Imperial Highness, Czarina Terese of Chezkovia," as the doors to the Chezkovian crown room were swung to by palace guards.

Terese moved to a wide red carpet runner and began walking to the dais. Her tall graceful figure obscured the czar from Jobyna's apprehensive view. The girl glanced around. She was surprised to notice there was no reception line. Apart from Brian and four guards, the massive oval room was empty. Terese curtsied low, ascended the dais and sat on the smaller throne to the left of the czar.

Brian, his throaty voice reverberating in the empty auditorium, announced, "The Princess Jobyna." He did not say, "of Frencolia," or "of Jydanski," as Jobyna had expected. Stepping out automatically, Jobyna moved toward the middle of the oval room. Gold, red and white ornamentations glittered before her eyes, and she was aware of the brilliant crystal chandeliers blazing like diamonds around the chamber. Daring not to turn her head, she kept her eyes fixed on the dais. The czar seemed a long way away.

As she moved closer, her heart seemed to beat like a pulsating drum in her throat. The enthroned Imperial Czar wore an elaborate head piece, the Crown of Chezkovia, an incredible jeweled dome, glittering its matchless value into Jobyna's apprehensive eyes. A jeweled pattern on the top was set above a ball of solid gold. The czar's costume had a high collar and glittered gold with thousands of red, green and blue jewels set in dazzling intricate embroidery all over the royal chest.

She could see his thick black beard, streaked with silver, his face, his eyes. He smiled at her. Jobyna took another hesitant step. The dais became a blur and the ruby red carpet rose rapidly beneath her. Jobyna's knees turned to water. Her mind fogged and completely blanked. She pushed her hands forward as the floor became a crushing crimson wall. The girl's head dropped with a jerk and she closed her eyes as an engulfing wave of anguish flooded through her frame. If only she could feel the relief fainting would bring. How could she endure this? Frozen stiff, she could not move to rise. Time and space were utterly lost in her deep despair.

The czar strode from the throne. He stood in front of the prostrate figure. Jobyna opened her emerald eyes to behold the jeweled hem of his robe gracing the red carpet. Her head would not turn to look up at him. The czar dragged her to stand on her trembling feet, holding her close to him as she swayed unsteadily. With his free hand under her chin, he forced her to look at his face.

"Would you swoon in front of the Czar of Chezkovia, Sparrow?" he murmured. A sneer distorted his features.

As Jobyna looked up into the icy blue eyes of Elliad, her lips trembled to find appropriate words, but there were none. His charade complete for her sake, he chuckled cynically as he characteristically tucked her arm under his, holding his other hand to the czarina. With one woman on each arm, he walked out through the reception room, ascending the stairs. Every step Jobyna took was a mechanical, instinctive reaction. She felt completely lifeless, void of all emotion and energy.

The main table in the banquet room was set for three. Elliad sat in the middle, Jobyna on his left, Terese on his right. Jobyna did not recognize any of the servants who served the delectable, elaborate meal. Elliad spoke to them in German, speaking to Terese also in her native tongue.

They were discussing Jobyna, and Terese sneered as she told Elliad, "The maid should be taught common etiquette. She doesn't even know how to have a social drink!" Terese snickered, her ensuing words were lost as

Jobyna tried to piece together all that had happened in the last month. The awesome fact that Elliad wore the czar's crown and sat on the throne of Chezkovia was trouble enough to deal with. She must try to block this terror from her thinking and pretend it was all an optical illusion, the result of her overactive imagination. Maybe she was dreaming? One feeling she knew was real came from the aroma of the food. Hunger! Jobyna nodded to everything the waiters brought and ate it all.

"The sparrow has turned into a vulture!" Elliad commented. The triumphant look in his mesmeric cobalt eyes made her squirm uncomfortably. Unable to wait any longer, he queried, "What thinks the daughter of Chanec of the czar of Chezkovia?"

Jobyna was tempted to spit out all kinds of derogatory comments, but she bit her tongue, swallowing the words. "The grandeur of it all overwhelms me." She answered truthfully, her eyes looking around the oval banquet hall. Elliad ignored Jobyna after this and continued conversing with Terese. The royals drank copious amounts of wine and Terese leaned heavily on Elliad's shoulder. Jobyna was thankful when Elliad clapped his hands twice, bringing Brian swiftly through the doors.

"Have the guards escort the princess back to her room!" he commanded. Jobyna obediently stood and curtsied low to the two, departing to the accompaniment of Terese's shrill laughter.

Jobyna threw her tiara to the floor and tried to pull the ruby necklace off so that it could join the hated headpiece, but the tricky catch prevented such a tantrum. She paced up and down, back and forth, her agitation making her totally unable to rest. Ellice followed her mistress, turning when she turned, constantly crossing the girl's path.

"Please, Ellice! Please leave me!" Jobyna folded her arms. "I don't know if this is what anger feels like, Ellice, but I'm sure I feel angry! So you had better stay out of my way!" Ellice mimed herself as begging Jobyna to talk to her. Slamming the door soundly between them, Jobyna ordered, "Stay out of my room!"

Jobyna hated Elliad! She loathed everything about his entire being! Especially all he had done, she finally conceded. She completely despised the Czarina Terese! The captive would not let her active mind imagine what they had done to the czar, or the czarevitch, Kenrik. She wondered why there weren't people protesting and doing something about this facade? Calming herself, she thought, *Maybe it isn't as I think. After all, maybe Elliad was just pretending. Perhaps the czar is away some-where. Terese had said they were "touring." He may even have left the palace in Elliad's hands while he was absent.* Entering the sitting room once more, she spoke to Ellice.

"Did any of the servants speak about Elliad's execution?" Ellice nodded. "Have you ever seen the czar?" Ellice shook her head. Jobyna dared not tell her what she had experienced in the oval crown room, or at dinner.

A few hours later the beginnings of a horrible nightmare made her sit up suddenly. Jobyna lay fully clothed on the bed. Kneeling down, she prayed for freedom from bad dreams and climbed under the bed covers.

Jobyna had no idea of the time when she was awakened, but on later reflections, she calculated it to be the early hours of the morning. She was soundly shaken from her slumber.

"Come with me." Sofia pulled back the bedclothes as Jobyna tried to turn over. Swinging her legs over the side of the bed, Sofia pushed the girl's slippers on.

"But you are dressed!" Sofia exclaimed in surprise, holding out a satin robe. "This is one time, Princess, we do as we are told!"

Jobyna did not reply, partly because she had no idea why Sofia made such a statement, but principally because she was still half asleep.

Pulling the robe on over her brocade dress, Jobyna followed Sofia like one sleep-walking, numbly moving with the woman's footsteps. Like one comatose, she did not notice Ellice lying on the couch in the sitting room, or the long walk along the corridor and their ascent of numerous stairs. Huge doors with golden crowns engraved on them were held open. Jobyna's eyes met Brian's. She did not feel afraid. She was sure this was part of one of her many dreams. The doors swung closed and she was alone in the room, or was she alone?

Jobyna jumped when someone grasped her hand. Her eyes quickly adjusted to the dimness. She inquired, "Ranee?"

Jobyna was drawn along, through another set of doors, to a room with brighter lighting.

Elliad rose from a huge, cushion-clad luxurious velvet couch. He dismissed Ranee with a nod and took Jobyna's hand, pulling her to sit with him on the couch. He pulled her sleeve up and touched the scar of her brand. Running his fingers through her hair, he buried his face in the copper strands. Her captor's breath was thick and stale with wine. His blue eyes were glassy and his words slurred as he whispered, "You are mine, Sparrow. You will always be mine." She struggled to pull away, but he held her, his fingers entwined in her long locks. His body suddenly stiffened as the sound of heavy footsteps resounded from the corridor. The doors were flung open.

Brian ran towards them, shouting, "Your Highness, Czar Kievik, there is trouble in the dungeons! Large numbers of soldiers are trying to free some of the prisoners! We cannot hold them! Our prize prisoner is escaping!"

Elliad almost pulled Jobyna from the couch in his haste to untangle his fingers from her hair and depart with Brian.

Jobyna found herself alone on the cushion-covered couch. She was shaking uncontrollably and crying great soul-shaking sobs. This was a living nightmare. She was sure she was awake, but the terror continued!

Ranee stood beside the girl, pulling her roughly to her feet, both hands grasping the maiden's. She held a crumpled note that read, "An escape is planned. Follow me." Jobyna shook her head in disbelief, struggling to pull away. She did not want to give this woman the benefit of the doubt ever again. Ranee turned the paper over and Jobyna read, "How are my children?" This question loosened Jobyna's tongue, and she told Ranee that she had not been allowed to get close to the children but had seen them in the garden some days. Ranee's two girls looked to be full of energy and good health. She remembered the baking, but Ranee was leading her through the rooms of the royal suite to a door at the far end of the apartment. Ranee removed a bunch of keys from her belt, selected one and unlocked the door, locking it again behind them. Jobyna's feet flew down the stairs after Ranee's fleeing figure. Dream or not, this was one part she could deal with. Every step she trod, she prayed would take her further away from that madman, arrogantly pretending he was the czar of Chezkovia.

24

Ranee, I did baking every day in the kitchen at Elliad's Castle . . . the Baltic Castle." she corrected herself. "I sent gingerbread bears and cookies to the children." Ranee paused briefly to listen to this information. "I wanted to read to them, but Hagen refused it." Continuing down the stone stairwell, they were breathless when at last they arrived on the ground floor.

"Princess Jobyna." The light was dim, but Jobyna could make out a group of soldiers. One of the men took her hand. Intertwining his long lean fingers in hers, he held her tightly, his sword at the ready in the other hand. "We have no time for protocol. I am Sleven's son, Michael, and this is my brother, Adolf. Our father told us you are a sister because you have helped Chezkovia. We are going to help you escape." A soldier held the door slightly ajar, peering cautiously out into the courtyard.

The watching man called, "The signal!"

Jobyna was dragged at neck-breaking speed across the marble courtyard, her feet scarcely making impact on the slabs. She was swung up onto a horse's back. Grasping the animal with all her might, she felt the accelerating hooves break into a gallop. As they clattered past a blur of torches and soldiers, loud voices called out for the escapees to halt! Jobyna thought of Ranee who had given up all to save her this night, and she prayed they would make a safe escape, not daring to imagine the consequences if they were apprehended.

Chilled night air stung her face. The sheer robe and thin dress were no match for the cold breeze. Goosebumps rose on Jobyna's arms and legs causing the girl's teeth to chatter uncontrollably. She leaned close to Michael, absorbing some warmth from his body. Brenna had spoken of Michael and Adolf, her two sons. They were both married with young families. What a risk they were taking! Some of the horses veered off in another direction. Before long, the posse was at the city wall. Soldiers with flares waited by a small gate. Michael swung the girl from the horse's back.

"You ride, don't you!" Michael's words were not questioning, but stating a known fact. He removed his red and white jacket and Jobyna turned as he held it open for her to enter its warm recesses. She rolled the long sleeves back from covering her hands, and Michael helped her do up the tricky toggles. "Do you know which is your horse?" He asked. There were many horses in the company. She whistled softly, a special low whistle, and heard a familiar whinny in reply. The animal found his mistress before she located him, and Jobyna jumped with fright as Brownlea nuzzled affectionately into her tangled hair.

Michael guided her to Brownlea's side. "Wait a minute," Jobyna said. She reached down and gathered the cumbersome brocade dress and robe, pulling it up between her legs as she had done when a child, tucking the hem into the wide belt of the jacket. Sleven's son lifted her onto the horse, and she sat astride, ready to depart with the men. Other horses arrived and Jobyna looked to see if she recognized any of the riders. Meeting Kenrik's eyes, her eyes beheld his severely bruised and battered face.

Holding Brownlea's reigns with one hand, she reached across, placing her small hand on his. "I'm sorry, so sorry," she murmured.

Kenrik did not speak. His immense suffering and pain was obvious. Jobyna recognized a defeated but defiant gleam in his black eyes. His arms had numerous lash cuts on them. On his neck, thick streaks of clotted blood had congealed in angry raised and reddened welts.

Kenrik wore a simple, oversized, sleeveless brown tunic, and Adolf helped him put on his red and white jacket. The girl remembered Brian's words about the "prize prisoner."

The horse under Kenrik quivered, turning its head towards Jobyna who recognized the animal. "Speed!" she cried reaching to pat him.

Michael, now mounted, spoke quickly to her. "Our father waits for you at Walden, Princess. We wish you good speed to make it there before dawn. Tell him we battle for Chezkovia, but are not winning yet." He turned to Kenrik, "Czarevitch Kenrik, you must listen to us and stay in Proburg, for the sake of your life and for Chezkovia. We will gain a hearing from your father, be sure of that, but for now your safety in Proburg will be our first victory."

The thunderous sound of horses' hooves broke the stillness of the night. Mounted soldiers galloped toward the company. One of the riders yelled, "The czar's cavalry! Quick, through the gate and bolt it."

Jobyna spurred Brownlea on and on. The soldiers in the front were leading and she held the horse back as he galloped. Kenrik rode alongside her and she was reminded of the times she rode with her brother Luke. Speed could outrun Brownlea. He was older and there would come a time when Brownlea would outstrip him. After the initial burst, they eased back to a pace more tolerable for the distance they would travel.

Ruby-tinged dawn streaked the cloudy sky as they cantered to a border tower in Proburg. Challenged at the first gate, the soldiers conferred in German. Distant horses' hooves could be heard in the cool morning breeze and the company was monitored quickly through the gates. The Proburg soldiers in their brown uniforms saluted Kenrik, gazing at Jobyna in open amazement. Her long wind-whipped and knotted hair lay loose across the shoulders of the oversized red and white jacket. The robe-covered dress formed two gathered pockets on each side of the horse, her bedroom slippers poking out beneath the dusty hem. They trotted the weary horses through a narrow pass between high cliffs where the road had been painstakingly cut from the rock to make this difficult border entrance easier to traverse.

While a group of soldiers conferred with Kenrik, one of the soldiers spoke to Jobyna in Frenc. "Just eight of us will accompany you now; the rest are going to warn other border guards of the danger to the czarevitch's life. We will be able to ease back a little, Princess. There are other ways into Proburg, though not as direct as this one, and they will very likely be unguarded. It will set our pursuers back

234

several hours, and we are hoping they will turn back."

Now that it was daylight, Jobyna gave Brownlea complete freedom to set his own pace. The horse drew ahead of the soldiers, but she did not care what they thought. She let the gelding have it all, leaning into his neck.

"We're on our way, Brownlea," she whispered, "Go for it, boy. Every step is one step closer to Luke and freedom!" Then she remembered. "Thank you, God." She turned her head to the sky, now with soft blue patches here and there. "Thank you, God!" She realized, for the first time since leaving Chezkovia that like Daniel, she had been rescued, unharmed, from the lion's den. She prayed that nothing would happen to take her back there!

Upon reaching crossroads they took the narrower road. The eight miles to Walden took less than an hour, as the hard clay road was good to ride on.

People had begun their day, moving toward the market. Four soldiers moved to the front of the small company and four stayed behind Jobyna and Kenrik. Officials at the gate motioned them to stop, but with some quick, quiet deliberations, they were allowed to enter. Soldiers quickly closed the gates behind them. Walden was a sprawling town built inside a towering wall. Jobyna could see a moated castle looming ahead. Dread swamped her at the thought of another castle, but she knew she must go where she was led. She had not imagined Brenna's sister to be living in a castle, in fact she had not given much thought as to where she would live at all. Every castle was so different, but all had gates, walls, entrances, courtyards, stables and guards! *Dungeons as well*, she thought with a tremor. The portcullis lowered with a ground-shaking thud behind them, and Jobyna shivered involuntarily.

I will never live in a castle when I get to Frencolia, she promised herself.

Stable hands took Brownlea with eagerness and Jobyna cautioned, "He mustn't drink yet. He needs a rub down. . . . " A groom interrupted her, in German, looking at the soldiers, shrugging his thin shoulders.

One of the soldiers set her mind at ease. "He does not know Frenc. Don't worry, they know their job well."

Kenrik swung himself limply off Speed and two soldiers helped him to the castle entrance. Brenna hurried down the central stairs and Jobyna found herself enveloped in her fervent embrace. They cried together as Brenna drew her inside the castle.

Kenrik murmured something to the soldiers and one of them came to Jobyna. "His Highness wishes to speak to you right away, Princess, if you would follow us . . . "

Jobyna was introduced to Brenna's brother-in-law, Count Segar and sister, Countess Cadence. They spoke to the girl through Brenna as interpreter, making her feel at home. Servants brought food and drink. Kenrik ate hungrily and Jobyna realized how tired she was. Brenna brought her a large tumbler of warm milk which made her more sleepy.

Once Kenrik's hunger was appeased, he began to question her. Had she seen his father? Where did she last see Elliad? She relayed to Kenrik what Terese told her about Elliad's execution, how she was presented in the crown room before the thrones where Elliad and Terese were seated. Jobyna described the crown Elliad wore.

Kenrik was furious. Clenching his fists, he shouted in German. Storming around the room, he threw a plate at the wall, smashing it into small pieces. A tumbler flung into the fireplace sent hot embers flying out on the hearth rug. The soldiers, agreeing with his statements, tried to calm him as he banged his fists against the wall.

Jobyna, wide awake, answered all of the questions they asked of her, but because of her constant confinement in the small apartment, she knew very little.

Once the czarevitch was composed enough to sit down again, Jobyna described the czarina's large sitting room to Kenrik. He told her it was Terese's own rooms that she had been kept in, part of the czar's harem. Kenrik became overwhelmed with fury once more when he realized Elliad was now occupying the czar's royal

suite! Having exhausted her knowledge of Elliad at the palace, the men ignored the girl and
conferred among themselves.

Brenna drew her to the side of the castle
dining hall. "Sleven was not able to come here.
He is with Prince Gustovas at Landmari Castle,
speaking to the prince about joining with Chezkovia to stop Elliad from gaining the throne.
Prince Gustovas is most reluctant to listen to
statements of treachery. He says he must have
proof before he will take any action. We are
hoping that the czarevitch will persuade him to
help. Sleven will be sad to think it is already
too late to prevent Elliad from taking the
throne. I cannot comprehend it myself. What
has happened to our czar?" She wrung her
hands, trying not to cry.

The soldiers moved toward the door, and
Kenrik came toward Jobyna. "We are riding to
Landmari. Prince Gustovas must help us. We
are grateful, Princess Jobyna, for your information." He indicated the count and countess.
"You will be well cared for here and we will
help you return to your country as soon as possible." He took her hand and kissed it as she
stood to curtsy.

Jobyna spoke earnestly. "I pray that God will
return to you what is rightfully yours and deal
with our enemies."

He bowed and left the room. They were
taking fresh horses and would be at Landmari
Castle in little over an hour.

Brenna told Jobyna that Czarevitch Kenrik had said he had been Elliad's prisoner in the palace dungeons for over two weeks. Elliad had personally visited him in the dungeon and when Kenrik had requested to see his father, Elliad told the czarevitch that his father did not wish to speak to him again. He was leaving his son's fate to his friend and counselor, Elliad himself. Kenrik now believed that Elliad, posing as his father, was planning to have him killed. He had been beaten and whipped because of the anger he displayed. Kenrik's anger was stronger than ever now.

Restlessly, Jobyna told Brenna she would like to go out to the stables and check Brownlea. Brenna wanted her to rest, but like Kenrik, rest was far from Jobyna's mind. She felt a new burst of energy and hoped to ride as far as she could from Chezkovia and Proburg, especially as far as possible from her treacherous enemy, Elliad. To see her brother was foremost in her mind. To reach Frencolia's safety was her overwhelming desire.

She requested Brenna to speak with the stable hands to find out when Brownlea would be ready to ride again. The answer was, "Anytime, if he is not pushed too hard, and not too great a distance." Brenna wrung her hands once more, realizing Jobyna's mindset. She spoke to her brother-in-law and he ushered them to his office, bringing a map to his desk. He explained to Brenna and she told Jobyna,

"Segar says you could reach Audric Castle by nightfall. My daughter, Belle, and her husband, Dael, live there. The castle belongs to Prince Gustovas and Dael is the overseer. You would call him a knight, I suppose. Dael is part of Proburg's 'National Guard.' It will be as well for you to tell Dael what is happening. Proburg is very much involved with Chezkovia and our battles are their battles."

Segar pointed out places Jobyna could stop along the way between Proburg and Frencolia. The southern border of Proburg was the northern border of Reideaux, the country north of Frencolia. The tracks were narrow with two difficult mountain passes to traverse, but at this time of year, there should be no real difficulties.

Noting her soiled dress and robe, Jobyna asked Brenna if there was something she could wear that would be less conspicuous than the red and white jacket over her evening dress and filmy robe. She giggled and added, "Especially in a country where women do not ride horseback!" Brenna conferred with Cadence, but it was Segar who left the room, returning with a Proburg soldier's uniform. Shaking her head, Brenna held her hands up in horror. Jobyna was delighted. Segar said he would send two of his trusted castle guards with her. She would be quite safe. He hushed Brenna's protests with a final command, "Stop making unnecessary fuss when there is nothing to fear!

Has not the Princess Jobyna ridden all the way from Jydanski? What is there to be afraid of?" Brenna would not answer.

The uniform was on the large side, and the padded shoulders of the jacket gave Jobyna a masculine appearance. Emblems on the front and right sleeve were inscribed with Segar's only son, Moritz's special insignia: an embroidered castle and the letters "M.W." Moritz was Prince Konrad's bodyguard and had outgrown the jacket several years previous. Brenna told Jobyna that Moritz was her favorite nephew. Cadence gave Jobyna two woolen vests to wear under a thick tunic, thus filling out some of the extra space in the uniform. Tucking the ruby necklace securely under the vest, Jobyna felt sure it would be worth keeping, even to trade on her way home if necessary. The woolen trousers felt prickly and Cadence found two pairs of long thick socks to help fill the boots which were several sizes too big.

"You'll need the extra warmth on those mountains," Brenna advised.

Jobyna plaited her hair in two long braids, winding them around the top of her head. The bearskin hat fit right over her head, covering her ears. She carefully folded the brocade dress and the robe, thinking it would be good to have something feminine to wear when she met Luke. She owned not another stitch of clothing. Brenna and Cadence stared silently as

Jobyna looked in the mirror. Her face betrayed her. It was most unlike a man's, but from a distance who could tell, she asked them? Cadence packed some of her own clothes, together with Jobyna's dress and robe, into a leather pack to strap on Brownlea. Segar introduced Jobyna to Delmer and Gyles, telling her he had briefed them. They were willing to escort her to Audric Castle where Dael would take over. He gave Delmer a pouch containing a brief note for Dael, telling Delmer to have Jobyna explain to Dael about Elliad being in control of the palace in Jydanski.

A castle guard came hurrying from the main gate, speaking to Segar in German. Count Segar ran toward the tower with Delmer and Gyles following. Jobyna drew Brownlea out into the courtyard. Gyles would ride Speed. Jobyna hoped she could take Luke's horse all the way to Frencolia as she knew her brother would appreciate this. She turned as the clatter of horses' hooves sounded on the cobblestones. Two men, wearing Chezkovian soldiers' uniforms, dismounted, speaking in urgent tones to Segar. The count informed them of Elliad posing as the czar. They moved to Brenna who indicated Jobyna. They hurried over to the figure in brown, looking at her with wonder in their eyes. Jobyna recognized their faces as the "servants" who had been with Sleven at the Baltic Castle. She racked her brain for their names.

"Fritz and Gregory!" She gave them her hand and they bowed to her.

Gregory turned to Fritz who spoke. "Princess, we have come from Jydanski to warn you. The czar, if not Kievik, then Elliad, is furious about your escape, more so than the czarevitch's escape from the dungeons. He knows already that you are in Proburg. It is said he is riding here himself with countless numbers of the cavalry, demanding your return. It is just as well you are ready to leave, for he will be here in Walden within an hour."

Jobyna turned to Segar, "It will be well if you can secure the castle and the town. I have seen Elliad wipe out a whole community, men, women and children. Do not listen to his soft talk. He lies." She paused, looking at the ground, biting her lip while Brenna translated. Time stood still for a minute as the men absorbed these words.

Brenna saw Jobyna's concern. "What is it, Jobyna?"

Jobyna looked at Segar. Her next statement cost so much, she could scarcely believe it was her own voice. "Count Segar, if you would rather give me into his hands to save bloodshed, then you must do so." She did not say she was willing, for she would have lied!

Brenna translated to Segar but he cut across his sister-in-law's words. Brenna translated back, "My brother-in-law says, 'Get on your horse and good speed to you Princess Jobyna. We are not cowards here! That lunatic will get what's coming to him!' "

Brenna kissed Jobyna, crying uncontrollably. Jobyna's emerald eyes were bright and tearless, but she hugged Brenna fervently. Segar moved to help Jobyna on to Brownlea's back, but with a grasp of Brownlea's mane and the reigns, and a light spring of her feet, she swung herself unaided to sit on the horse's back. Delmer and Gyles led the way around the stables to the less obscure back exit over the moat, through the gates in the thick walls, out into the farmland, Fritz and Gregory following.

Jobyna could feel Brownlea's tiredness. She leaned forward, patting his sleek neck as he cantered. She was tired, too. The few hours of sleep the night before had not given her rest. She felt the incline of the land and saw the looming mountains in the distance. Just beyond the visible mountains was another mountain ridge where Audric Castle was built on the border. She urged Brownlea into a gallop.

Fritz and Gregory had taken fresh horses and when Jobyna, Delmer and Gyles joined them on a crest, they were pointing back, looking the way they had come. The distant horizon was dotted with red and white uniforms, hundreds of Chezkovian soldiers on horseback!

25

"They have seen us, but may not know how many we are," Gyles said. "We must work an alternative plan."

They drew the horses out of sight, Fritz on watch. The men spoke quickly. Delmer gave Jobyna the small pouch and she pushed it inside her jacket. Gyles said to her, "The left road at the fork leads to Audric Castle, Princess. We will wait until you are safely out of sight, then we will make sure they see us ride toward Maynard Castle, to the right. Hopefully, they will follow us, especially if you are out of sight, but we will need the four of us or they will see we have divided. Tell Count Dael what is happening and he will secure the castle. Audric is impenetrable and you will be safe. We will join you as soon as we can."

Jobyna did not need extra bidding. Digging her boots into Brownlea's sides, she was gone, down the other side of the ridge and off between the rocky outcrops. After the "Y" fork, there was only one road to follow and she urged Brownlea on as fast as she dared. To be captured now! She could not imagine how Elliad would treat her. She wondered why he bothered; why did he not let her go?

The path grew narrow as she approached the high, rocky cliffs. Pulling Brownlea around sharply, she dared to look back. She could see the four men had almost reached the "Y" turn-off, but there was no sign of red and white uniforms. Turning Brownlea once more, she disappeared into the gap between the cliffs. It was dark, dismal and dangerous, and Jobyna was glad to come out into the sunshine on the other side. Another three miles and she would be at the castle in the mountains and safety.

The road grew wide again. Brownlea was climbing beside descending rapids. At one place the horse had to ford the river. Thankfully the water was shallow at this spot and he experienced no difficulties. Moving more slowly, Jobyna did not drive Brownlea as before. She looked anxiously at the mountain peaks ahead. Rugged crags were enveloped with ominous black clouds which swirled down into the valley she was in. The road pulled her up into the narrow stony pass Count Segar had spoken about. Brownlea's feet trembled as they climbed, and he picked his way cautiously over the shifting schist. Soon they were descending the other side of the pass. Ahead, built into the side of the mountainous cliffs, Jobyna caught her first view of Audric Castle.

Colored naturally, the same as the rock it was built into, the mountain castle displayed tall round towers on either side of the front gate with a high wall topped with battlements leading to two more towers. Behind this was a tall, round stone building, crowned once more with battlements. Higher on the mountainside were two more towers. Jobyna realized that guards in the battlements and on the towers would be monitoring her approach. However, she did not hesitate at this thought but urged Brownlea down the path, wishing him an extra lease of strength. If only she could keep going, through the castle gates, toward home. She hated the thought of yet another stone monstrosity.

Startled by a sudden movement in the corner of her right eye, she turned to see two mounted men in the Proburg soldier's brown uniform galloping toward her from a side path. They had seen her, but she did not wait for them. Flicking the reigns she urged Brownlea, "Go, boy, go!" He was aware of the horses behind and increased his speed as much as he could, but the others gained swiftly, one on either side of her. Knowing herself to be cornered, with the huge closed portcullis looming up ahead, she slowed Brownlea down, patting his neck to reassure him. However, they beckoned her on, and she entered the barbican feeling once more like a prisoner.

A guard shouted from the tower house and the two men called back. They spoke to her, and she said, "I do not speak German. I speak Frenc. I come from Frencolia." The men looked at each other. The larger, whose build reminded her of Berg, shouted angrily at her in German, pointing to her uniform. His words were too fast, but she caught his question as to why she was wearing the uniform. She shook her head, as he spoke quickly again. Reaching in the jacket, she pulled out the pouch. Instantly he drew his sword, holding it with the point at her throat. Jobyna dropped the reigns and put both hands in the air, holding the pouch up. The other man swiftly grabbed the pouch and reigns. Grinding and whining, the portcullis began to move. Brownlea was led through the barbican, under the gate house and through another set of gates swung open by watching soldiers. The courtyard was full of soldiers in brown uniforms, and Jobyna prayed someone there would speak Frenc.

The big man, whose name she later learned was Moritz, Count Segar's son, waved his sword at her, issuing orders to the soldiers who moved toward her. Guessing he wanted her to dismount, she swung herself down and found herself held firmly by a soldier on either side. Moritz dismounted, growling at her once more, pointing his sword at the emblems on the jacket she was wearing. Again she told him she did not understand, he was talking too fast. She did not know it was his jacket she wore. He grew impatient and barked out orders. Hearing his anger, Jobyna was sure he hated her and she felt he was the ugliest brute she had ever laid eyes on, Berg included! To her utter dismay, she was taken to a stairway under the tower, down, down, down and locked in a dark, damp dungeon utterly void of light or air vents. Feeling her way down the six steps, she found the room to be small, the only furniture a stone bench. Her one consolation was that they were in possession of the pouch and would take it to Brenna's son-in-law, Count Dael, the overseer of the castle. If this were the case, Count Dael would come and set her free.

Exhausted, she lay on the stone bench. If tired enough, Jobyna could fall asleep anywhere. Her father had scolded her nearly every night at family prayers, for she inevitably fell asleep.

When Moritz descended with Count Dael, Jobyna was sound asleep and had to be shaken to rouse. Moritz carried a torch which lit up the small cell. The girl sat up, disoriented for a moment. Dael spoke to her, questioning her in German.

"I speak Frenc." She stared at Brenna's young son-in-law, chastising herself for her negative thoughts. In the light of the flare, his face seemed a subtle mixture of cunning and greed. His small eyes narrowed as he looked at her, puzzled, she was too young to be in uniform, her voice too soft.

"You are not Delmer!" Dael exclaimed in Frenc. "My Uncle, Segar, wrote that Delmer would deliver the message. Where are the other men and the princess?"

"Are you Count Dael?" She asked.

"Yes, I am Count Dael."

Jobyna's face broke into a smile and she took his hand, shaking it. She pulled off her hat, tossing her two long braids free. The men's eyes widened in complete amazement. "I am Jobyna Chanec of Frencolia and I am pleased to meet Sleven and Brenna's son-in-law." Dael's reaction was not as she had expected. He wheeled around, uttering an exclamation, looking up the narrow steps. He gabbled something to Moritz, saying her name, and the big soldier raced out, bolting the door behind him.

"Put the cap back on!" His shaky voice ordered. She gathered her braids, winding them around her head once more, leaning forward and pulling the hat over the top, securing the band under her chin. "We have Chezkovian

soldiers all over our courtyard. They are looking for you. It is known that we have a man
who rode with the princess." He paused, trying
to sum up the situation. Moritz returned, and
Count Dael joined him at the top of the steps.
They conversed urgently.

"We must get you across the courtyard to the
safety of the castle keep where we can talk.
Moritz will bring Proburg soldiers and we will
say we are taking you for questioning.
Cooperate with us, Princess, and keep your
head turned down to the ground." He motioned for her to ascend the steps first, and
there was no alternative but to do as he asked.
Moritz took one arm, another soldier grasped
the other firmly, and she found herself dragged
out into the darkening courtyard. A voice
Jobyna instantly recognized, came to her ears,
speaking in German. It was Brian!

Thinking of Elliad being here, her heart
began to race. Keeping her head down while
Count Dael spoke to Brian, Jobyna then found
herself jerked off across the courtyard, half carried into Audric Castle itself, up steps, along a
corridor and into a room. Dael, coming in behind them, pointed her to a chair. Moritz locked the door. Dael sat at the desk, conferring
with Moritz for some time. With the intensity
of their conversation, the meaning was lost to
the prisoner. Moritz left the room, and the
other soldier—she heard them call him Vincenz—once more locked the door. There was

silence as Dael gazed at her, his face a mixture of carefully concealed agitation.

She dared to speak. "I recognized the voice of the man you spoke to in the courtyard. He is Elliad's right-hand man." Her voice quivered, "Is Elliad here?"

"What do you mean? King Elliad was executed!" Dael looked at her, surprised. "That emir out there serves Czar Kievik."

Jobyna remembered Delmer asking her to explain what had happened. She realized Segar must not have said very much in the note, except maybe to explain who they were. Jobyna told him where Delmer, Gyles, Fritz and Gregory had gone, trying to lead the soldiers away from her. They would verify her story when they arrived. Explaining the events at the palace in Jydanski, she told Dael that Kenrik believed Elliad had either killed his father or imprisoned him. Jobyna added that she believed many of the soldiers wearing Chezkovian uniforms were, in fact, soldiers Elliad brought with him from Frencolia. Brian most certainly was! Dael's countenance grew white and drawn. He stood to pace the room, banging his fist several times on the walls.

Wheeling around, trying to compose himself, he stammered, "I will quote to you what this 'Emir Brian' told me, Princess! He said the czar is anxious for the return of Princess Jobyna and will give 1,000 gold pieces to the company that brings her back safely to him." This time,

Jobyna's face grew deathly pale as the significance of these words sunk in. "You must be very valuable to this Elliad, Princess."

"Does he want me dead or alive?" She ventured the question.

"Oh, very much alive! Brian said that for every bruise you had, Czar Kievik would deduct a hundred gold pieces!"

"Then I should like to find the highest mountain and throw myself from it!" she declared, standing to her feet. "I suppose you have told them I am here?"

"Actually, not yet, Princess. We told Brian that we have one of the men who rode with the Princess, and that we would question him first. We told him you are our prisoner. He is waiting to question you next." Dael rubbed the point of his black beard. "But we do support our friend, Czar Kievik, and I am interested in the one thousand gold pieces for myself! I do not know if I believe what you say or not. I will have your story checked out before I decide what I will do with you." Jobyna's eyes showed she was deeply hurt. Ignoring her green pools, he continued, "However, if what you say is true about this Elliad posing as the czar, that throws a whole new light upon the matter!"

A soft knock at the door was followed by a voice from the corridor, announcing himself, "Moritz!"

Vincenz opened the door. Two men entered,

the other also dressed in the Proburg brown, but he was not wearing the jacket or hat, and his appearance was that he was a soldier, off duty. Count Dael bowed to him, gesturing with his hand, palm up, to Jobyna. The young man walked right around the girl, amusement on his face as he looked the soldier's uniform up and down.

"Princess Jobyna?" His voice held disbelief. "In your uniform, Moritz?" He stood in front of her, his blue eyes searching deep into the green depths. The blueness instantly reminded Jobyna of Elliad and she made up her mind she did not like this fair, curly-haired man who showed utter arrogance toward her. He rubbed his clean-shaven chin and stroked his forefinger and thumb on his moustache as though trying to read her thoughts. She wondered who he was. This query was answered as though he did, indeed, read her thoughts.

His deep voice resounded, in Frenc, "It pleases me to meet you, Princess Jobyna. I am Konrad of Proburg. Some call me 'The Crazy Prince.' My value is not as great as yours, Princess. One thousand gold pieces! My father cannot give me away let alone pay someone to take me!" He laughed loudly, holding his hand out to her. She ignored his hand, upset by his humor. His suntanned face was pleasant when he laughed and his eyes glittered beseechingly with mirth, but she chose to dislike him still.

The captive felt he laughed at her, making fun of her predicament.

He shook his hand as though it stung and turned to Dael, speaking in German. They were soon involved in deep conversation, excluding Jobyna once more. Jobyna turned, spying a bench in the corner of the room. Feeling a victim condemned in a man's world, knowing she could do nothing herself about her situation, she sat on the bench. Pulling her hat off, she unbraided her hair, combing it with her fingers. The soldier, Vincenz, standing on guard at the door, watched her in silent surprise. Turning to the wall, she lay down and fell asleep.

The men debated hotly for over an hour. Dael explained Jobyna's claims about Elliad posing as Czar Kievik. When they had exhausted their conversation, getting nowhere and unable to agree, Prince Konrad turned to look at their "prisoner." He crossed to the bench where her long hair fell to the floor. Bright copper hues glowed in the light of the lamps. Seeing she was sound asleep, Konrad felt sorry she had not been given anything to eat or drink. He turned to the men in the room, speaking in German. "No one in this room is to go after those gold pieces, do you all hear?" His eyes stared into Dael's. "My Father must be contacted before any decisions are made! Is this clear? We will stall this Brian man and tell him our prisoner is unconscious. Tell him we had to beat him and still he would not give us the answers we wanted." He turned to Moritz. "Tell him we think they must have taken the princess to Maynard Castle or somewhere else." He looked at the soldier guarding the door. "Don't get ideas, any of you! There will be no treason coming from this room!"

26

Having sunk to the uttermost depths of sound sleep, Jobyna's rest was peaceful and dreamless. Konrad shook her gently, speaking her name, but she would not rouse. It was after two in the morning and Konrad had crept back to the room. Exhaustion and tension combined to render the girl almost unconscious. The Proburg Prince ordered Moritz to carry her.

Moritz conveyed her down into the heart of the dungeons, through many doors. Konrad locked them carefully again, checking that each was secure. Still she did not wake. The prince opened a "bookshelf door," moving into a dimly lit room, locking the wall behind them.

The chamber had another door in it and they entered a large, well-furnished room. Konrad fetched a sleepy eunuch from a nearby chamber. Informing this "caretaker" that they would be back in the morning, they left Jobyna lying on a couch, securely locking the doors once more as they exited.

Jolted into reality because she had no idea where she was, Jobyna woke with a start, her eyes exploring the room. The servant scuttled over to her as she sat up. She drew herself back from his strange, inquisitive stare. He came close to her, too close, she thought. Pointing at her hair and her clothes, he spoke, but she could not understand his words. Telling him she did not speak German, she said she was from Frencolia.

"Frencolia?" his voice was soft. A strangely sorrowful shadow crossed his recessed, hazel eyes. She nodded wonderingly at him. He was an old man with a smooth, unlined, young face. He scampered back across the room. She noticed the bookcases which lined the walls where he foraged, bringing a map, pointing to Frencolia. Jobyna nodded again and placed her forefinger on Chanoine.

He left the map with her and again scurried across to a bookshelf. This time he brought a heavy book, causing her eyes to light up with pleasure as he put it on her lap, drawing the pages open. It was a Gospel Book, written in Frenc. His solemn hazel eyes burning with sensitivity, he watched as she turned the pages gently.

His hands took hers and he pointed first to the middle of one palm, then to the other. With his first finger pointing up, he placed the other hand on his heart. Repeating his childlike actions, Jobyna pointed to her heart. He smiled and shook her hand. Embarrassed that he stood so long gazing at her, she rose from the couch. There was a whole shelf of Gospel Books written in Frenc! Jobyna caught her breath, wondering if someone, maybe Konrad, was collecting them up like Elliad had. The servant here may be a prisoner! Turning to see where he was now, she saw he had taken one of the Gospel Books off the shelf and was polishing the engraved leather cover which looked brand new. No, she thought, he did not look or act like a prisoner. Testing the door handle, she found it to be locked. So they were prisoners! Returning to the couch, she studied the map once more. Turning it to allow maximum light on it, she traced the road she would take through Reideaux to Frencolia. Home seemed a million miles away.

Metal clicking against metal sounded in the lock and the door creaked open. Konrad entered with Moritz who brought a tray which he set on the small table. The prince spoke to the servant who scampered quickly to fetch goblets, then a large, full pitcher. Jobyna realized how hungry and thirsty she was.

"Go ahead, we've eaten," Konrad said, holding the goblets as the servant filled them. "Wine?" he asked her.

"No thank you. I don't drink wine," She said, feeling uncomfortable as his glistening blue eyes once more met her resolved green gaze.

"This is new wine," he said, holding the goblet out to her. She looked puzzled so he continued, "You know, fresh grape juice, not fermented." She took it, sipping a little. Her face broke into a smile.

"Thank you." She looked across at the Gospel Books. "Why are there so many Gospel Books in here?"

Perturbed, the prince did not answer but rose, talking to Moritz and the servant. They were discussing her, and she knew enough to understand they were somewhat upset by her presence in these chambers.

Scrambled eggs, large chunks of cheese and bread took her attention, but she could not help thinking how good it would be to be in Frencolia where everyone understood exactly what was being said. The servant came and helped himself heartily from the tray.

Konrad pulled a chair to the table and sat down. "My friend, Count Dael, does not know you are down here. There is quite a to-do going on upstairs because you are missing. I told them I was sure some of my men helped you escape last night. Moritz, Vincenz and I have been helping Dael organize a search to find you. Later, we plan to ride out with some of the men to search for you. Dael does not know this room exists. The dungeons down here belong to me and are off-limits to everyone else. I allowed Dael and his men to search as far as they could which was to a bookshelf concealing a door in the wall. The cells under the towers, such as the one you were put in last night, are used for prisoners." He paused now and then, watching her eat. She wondered if he thought her to be rude, but she was too hungry to worry. "For the meantime, you are safe here, Princess."

Swallowing a mouthful of the deliciously sweet grape juice, Jobyna asked, "Why are you protecting me?" She was wondering if he wanted the gold pieces for himself. Again he did not answer. He stood and spoke with Moritz. They moved away, across the room, and she heard the sound of a key in a lock. The servant went with them, and the door was again secured. She was alone.

Exploring the room, she found it led through an archway into a larger chamber. Writing desks were fixed around the walls. She could see them in the bright light from the room where she had slept. Fetching a lamp, she investigated the new room. Wonder filled her as she realized it was a place where Gospel Books were being copied, three in Frenc, two in Latin, the rest in German. She counted 12 tables and realized 12 people could work at once. The thought of it took her breath away. Thoughtfully returning to the couch, she took the Frenc book to the table where she placed the lamp. It was a large volume and she was interested to find it contained new writings. She had never known of "The Acts of the Apostles" or "Letters to the Romans" and was fascinated to read letters written by Paul the Apostle. The story and message in the book of the Acts absorbed her whole thinking. Jobyna became so engrossed she forgot the place, the time and the soldier's uniform she was wearing.

This was the account of a man who openly killed Christians yet became a believer and protector of the faith. Some hours later when Prince Konrad quietly emerged with Moritz and the servant, she did not notice, so involved was she with Paul's writings, sitting at the table with her back to the door. Konrad had spoken to her twice, but she had not heard him.

"Does your horse have a white triangle on his forehead, Princess?" he asked, louder, coming over to see what it was that possessed her total attention. Touching her shoulder, he added, "And an 'E' brand on the shoulder?"

She spun around, catching only the last few words, brushing his hand away fiercely. "How do you know about that?" She felt guilty for having been so wrapped up in reading.

"About what?" he asked, folding his arms, amusement returning to his boyish face.

"The brand," she said, not thinking.

"Where?" he asked.

"On my shoulder." She shook her head at his blank blue gaze. "But you don't know about that! What are you talking about?"

"What are you reading, Princess?" He asked.

"The writings of Paul, the Apostle. The Letter to the Romans." Her face lit up.

"And what do you think about such writings?" he asked, his attitude skeptical.

"Such wonderful words! I wish I had known about justification before. The footnote, 'Just as if I'd died.' What an awesome thought! I would like my brother to read these writings." Great happiness glowed from her green eyes and excitement flooded her face as she thought of Luke's reaction to the words she had read.

"You don't believe the Gospel Book?" Konrad's question was sarcastic and full of disbelief. He wondered if she were trying to trap him.

She nodded at him saying, "I surely do, Prince Konrad. Without the comfort of this book, I would not have survived to this day!"

Shaking his head at her unexpected answer, Konrad claimed, "But we have heard from good sources that Frencolia bitterly opposes the book! The people are against its writings; every copy was burned, people killed . . . " Konrad narrowed his eyes. He thought she was a very clever actress.

"That is Elliad you heard of. For the two years of his reign of terror, that is what he did!"

She began to tell him about the self-pronounced king and his proclamations against the Gospel Book. Konrad questioned her more and she found herself telling him about her parents' murders and how Elliad had sought to capture Luke and her as well.

"But that is over. Have you not heard the good news? My brother, King Luke Chanec, is a believer!" Realizing she was baring her heart to this stranger prince, she asked him, "Do you believe the Gospel Book, Prince Konrad?"

His blue eyes looked seriously into hers. "With all my heart, Princess. That is why I am called the 'crazy prince!' " Konrad realized she was not lying. It was hard to believe, but she told the truth. The innocence on her face and in her wide green eyes was for real! He sat beside her. "My father, I think you have met him, you made quite an impression on him." (Konrad did not tell her what his father had said, or how his father's over-zealous descriptions of Jobyna had completely turned Konrad against such a match. He tried to keep his thoughts on the incredible revelation that this beautiful Princess believed the Gospel Book!) "Father has banned me from reading the Gospel Book or speaking of it! He once ordered that I be decorated with nine lashes for 'preaching' to him. He is almost as fervent against the book as your Elliad."

She retorted strongly, "Elliad is not 'my Elliad!' How I wish people would not call him that! He has never been 'mine,' and I pray I am never 'his.' I would have jumped off the mountain yesterday rather than be captured by him!" She turned her mind back to the Gospel Book and Konrad's words. "You disobey your father. Aren't you afraid he will find out?"

"He is too busy to bother about me and my crazy pastimes, too occupied with his court and his women." Konrad's tone was bitter. "It is my eldest brother, Gustav, I worry about. When he comes to the throne in Proburg, as Gustovas the Second, he is likely to be the one to sniff out our operation here at Audric Castle, not Father. I feel quite safe while Father is on the throne. He thinks I would not dare disobey his command. He treats me as his failure son, the recipe that flopped." Without realizing it, Konrad was baring his heart. "Father hates blue eyes!" He looked into her emerald eyes. "He was most taken with your eyes." He laughed and she thought of the previous night when he had laughed. It had not been at her, but at himself. He asked her, "So how did this Elliad, who is not yours, come to capture you, Princess?"

Jobyna told him all that had happened: the treasure cave, the capture of Luke, King Leopold's body, her capture and her sickness at the King's Castle in Frencburg. She did not tell him about the Seal to the Kingdom. That was Frencolia's secret. Jobyna told him how she had prayed and God had given her spiritual

265

strength through her illness. She told him of the great pile of Gospel Books, how she tried to hide them in the secret tunnel from Elliad but his cunning and greed were greater than her strength. Prince Konrad listened. He was consumed with her story.

When Moritz interrupted, apologetically, Konrad handed over the keys and told him to take care of the matter. The servant poured more grape juice and they talked the day away. Jobyna told him about Berg and the verses she quoted him. Her voice grew soft when she spoke of Berg's apology. Konrad looked at the deformity of her hand, the scar. She drew back as he sympathetically reached for it. She childishly put her hand behind her back. Making light of the brand, she said emphatically she would never want to become part of Elliad's harem, she would rather die.

"The thought of dying and being with Father and Mother has been a comfort that has helped keep me secure this past year," she said, forgetting she was speaking to a prince of the kingdom of Proburg, considered to be an 'enemy' country by Frencolia. "Now, the thought that keeps me going is that of being back in my country with my brother." Jobyna explained Luke's letter to her, that Scriptures were being read daily in the village squares and children taught to read. Konrad's attitude and expression had totally changed by now, and his sapphire eyes glowed warmly as he listened. He asked questions about her parents, her upbringing in Chanoine and Luke.

In a brief silence, Jobyna queried, "How then, did you become a believer, Prince Konrad?"

"Just call me Konrad, Princess. I do not like the title of prince."

She returned, just as fervently, "Then please do not call me princess. No one is less a princess than I. You were born to your title, Konrad, but I have no such royal image!"

He would have disagreed, but instead answered her question. "The evangelist went to Reideaux after Frencolia, then he came to Proburg. I was 12 years old and drank in every word he said, believing in Jesus Christ as the only way to heaven. It was then I began to read the Gospel Book. There are less than 100 believers in Proburg and it is difficult to become a believer here. Father does not send soldiers out to hunt for the book. He pays people to inform him, then the book is confiscated and destroyed. All adults from the home where the book is discovered are put in stocks and whipped, but no one has been deliberately executed so far. We are producing books as fast as we can, but the demand is greater than the supply. We send a few to Muldaver and Strasland. Our greatest hope is to do what your brother is doing, to teach the children so when they have children, they in turn, will teach them."

Moritz returned with a tray, setting it on the

table. He drew Konrad aside for a few minutes, speaking in undertones. Hot stew and warm bread rolls emitted an enticing aroma. As Konrad ate with her, he told Moritz some of the things Jobyna had said. Moritz beamed at her and the smile softened his harsh features, transforming him. Jobyna decided he was not quite as ugly as she had thought. The day was over, but they talked on into the night.

Konrad, his voice reluctant, finally announced, "We must go." He brightened and added, "I will pray before we part." To Jobyna's dismay, he prayed in German, but she joined with Moritz and the servant in the "Amen."

"Now you know why people call me 'crazy!' But I'd rather be a fool for God than one whom God deems a fool. I'll see you in the morning, Princess Jobyna." Konrad emphasized the "Princess."

"Good night, Prince Konrad." Jobyna smiled at him and he laughed. Kindness crinkled the corners of his cobalt eyes. He left with Moritz, locking the door.

Concerned at being left alone with the servant, whose name she did not know, she pointed to herself, "Jobyna," she said, "Jobyna."

The flat of his palm against his chest, he said, "Franz, Franz." Turning on his heel he walked through the archway, out of sight. Jobyna pulled the boots off, and the two pairs of socks, also the jacket. She lay the jacket around her shoulders, over the tunic. Wondering how long she would be kept here, she thought, *I really don't mind. I have a Gospel Book, and Prince Konrad is a believer. This is the first place I have been in since leaving Frencolia that I feel really safe.*

Falling asleep quickly, she woke hours later, screaming in terror from a nightmare. Riding the tiring Brownlea, hundreds of soldiers chased her endlessly. Every corner she turned, thousands of soldiers were waiting with swords drawn. Brownlea was exhausted but she would not let him slow down because they were gaining on her. She jumped with fright to see Franz bending over her. Shaking and crying, she knelt down in front of Franz and prayed for sound sleep. Climbing back on the couch, she pulled the jacket over herself again, hoping the servant would go back to wherever he slept. He did.

27

Before Jobyna awoke, Konrad arrived with the breakfast tray. Franz told him about the nightmare and when she awoke, he questioned her. "You weren't afraid of Franz, were you?" he queried, not waiting for an answer. "You mustn't be afraid, for he is harmless."

Jobyna said to him, "I suffer nightmares due to my terrible imagination. My mind plays dreadful tricks on me. It helps when I pray, and sometimes in my dream, I realize God is with me. He reminds me it is just a dream and I sleep properly. Most of my nightmares are about Elliad and torture. I am sure they will cease when I get home."

"Doctor Sleven is coming today. It will be difficult to bring him down here, but we are going to try tonight when everyone is sleeping. You must see if you can catch some extra sleep today. You look tired." Konrad noticed dark rings under her eyes. "Brian is using Audric Castle as headquarters for the search for you, and it is too dangerous for you to be moved at this stage."

Jobyna asked, "Brian knows Sleven; won't he be suspicious?"

"Sleven is pretending to help with the search for you. He will work with Brian to gain the reward so he can receive a portion. Just think, Jobyna, you are worth five hundred horses!" He laughed, then asked, "Thinking of horses, Jobyna, what does your horse look like?"

She remembered now. It was Brownlea he had been asking about when she told him about the brand. "He has a white triangle on his brown forehead and two 'E' brands. One brand is placed over the Chanec 'C,' and the other is burned into his foreflank."

"I thought so. I have had him transferred to my stables. Dael has over a hundred horses, and yours will not have been noticed or missed. No one is allowed in my stables but my men," Konrad assured her.

"I had a small pack with clothes in it," she remembered, "I wonder where it is?"

Konrad told her that the pack was in Dael's possession. One of the stable hands had given it to him. To ask about her clothes would immediately arouse suspicions. He told Franz to bring his cloth, bowl and pitcher of water so she could wash, telling her it was the best he was able to do for now. The kitchen staff had always accepted the fact that food was brought below, but suspicions would be aroused if a collection of other items was transported to the dungeons. Dealing with Dael's present mistrust was difficult enough! Telling her he would be back with Sleven later in the evening, Konrad departed to help Dael and Brian in the search.

Jobyna washed in the icy cold water. She was thankful to feel refreshed, but wished she had a comb. Wetting her hands, she raked them through her hair, braiding it carefully. She wanted to be ready to put her hat on and leave when the moment came.

The day passed quickly. Jobyna read more of the writings of Paul, the Letters to the Corinthians, Galatians, Ephesians, Philippians, Colossians and Thessalonians. She turned back to Romans and worked on placing some favorite verses into her absorbent memory.

After midnight they woke her and she was overjoyed to see Sleven, who hugged her close. "You are looking well, my daughter. How do you feel?"

"Actually, I feel good. I've not been getting any exercise, though. I've been reading," she told him.

"The rest will be good for you. You have a long journey ahead."

Sleven told her that most Chezkovians believed Elliad was Czar Kievik and that the usurper, Elliad, had been executed. "Czar Kievik" had ridden to the Proburg border, in pursuit of his son and his captive, before returning to the Baltic Castle. The Chezkovian Cavalry accepted this man as their czar as there was no obvious change in the czar's appearance. The "fact" was being reported that Kenrik had gone insane and was acting in treason against his father. Prince Gustovas was not willing to listen to Kenrik's accusations against the czar. He said all rumors must cease. Elliad was dead. Before Jobyna and Kenrik had escaped, Elliad sent to Proburg for Cynara and Kedar to return to Chezkovia, writing that he, their father, was not well and needed them in Jydanski. The letter was in the czar's handwriting and Sleven said he suspected it was forged by Terese. Additional communications to Prince Gustovas were further evidence to the Proburg monarch that his friend, Czar Kievik, was alive and in control. Kievik's "attack of ill-health," the czar wrote, was due to his son's treachery. Cynara and Kedar had been sent back to their "father" the day before Jobyna's escape.

Sleven said it was reported, unofficially of course, that they were prisoners at the Baltic Castle, but verified information was very sketchy. Jobyna was sad to hear about Cynara and Kedar, but she could well imagine that Elliad would want them kept out of his way! Breaking into her thoughts, Konrad told Jobyna that Brian had received word today from the "czar" that the reward for her capture was now increased to 2,000 gold pieces!

"So, I'm worth 1,000 horses now," she said, laughing at the thought. She was feeling so much safer now that Sleven was here, for she knew she could trust him completely. The men did not share in her laughter.

Konrad spoke seriously. "It is impossible to escape from Proburg. Brian has set up road blocks into Reideaux. He has even sent a company to King Kelsey." He paced across the floor, stroking his chin. "We need a diversion to hasten your escape! But even when you get back to Frencolia, Jobyna, there may be people there who would be very interested in Elliad's 2,000 gold pieces. That is a lot of gold!"

She laughed. "If someone other than his own men captured me and claimed the gold, Elliad will likely kill them and keep the gold. I wish people knew what he is really like! I cannot make out why he wants me. He has achieved all his sick goals by sitting on the throne in Jydanski!" She looked at Konrad and Sleven, both staring seriously at her innocent face.

Thinking of Cynara and Kedar, she added, "It must be that he wants to get rid of anyone who can identify him." She thought of Kenrik. "The czarevitch is not safe. I wonder how much Elliad has offered his men for Kenrik's capture?"

Konrad changed the subject, "I have sent six men to Landmari Castle. They are going to start rumors among the right people that my father or one of my brothers is keeping you there, waiting for the czar to raise his price. Hopefully in a few days, all the soldiers will head that way. Landmari has many hiding places and they will be kept busy searching for you. The men are going to have sightings lined up that will keep them busy all over the north of the country. My father will be out of his mind sorting out where you are, who is loyal to Proburg, who is loyal to Chezkovia and who is working for the so-called czar!" He chuckled loudly at the thought of such pandemonium.

Jobyna asked Sleven about Fritz and Gregory and he said they would join them at Audric as soon as possible, as would Delmer and Gyles who were lying low at Maynard. The evening passed quickly and Jobyna was greatly comforted to be with Sleven, who claimed she was family. The conversation exhausted, Sleven's attention went to the bookshelves in the room. Konrad and he talked about the Gospel Books. The prince took one from the shelf and Jobyna fell asleep in the early hours of the morning to the sound of their quiet, friendly discourse.

Franz's gentle shaking woke her; the men were gone. She ate bread, cheese and fruit. Jobyna spent the day reading the rest of the New Testament. She wrapped Moritz's jacket around her feet for warmth. She wanted to save the socks until she needed them in the boots. It would be wonderful if Konrad's plan worked and Brian left Audric Castle with his troops. The prince or Sleven did not come that day, nor the next. Moritz brought the food and Jobyna was frustrated not to be able to communicate enough with him to hear any news. *Patience,* she thought, *and prayer!*

As she lay down that night, she tried to calculate how many nights she had slept on that couch, in the same clothes. She counted five!

Breakfast eaten, Jobyna began reading from the Psalms of David. Suddenly, the door opened. Konrad led the way into the room with Sleven, Fritz and Gregory following. She started when she saw the red and white uniforms enter, bowing to her.

Pulling her to her feet, holding both hands, Sleven's eyes danced into hers. "It worked! All the soldiers have raced off to the capital! Do you remember Julian?" (He need not have asked.) "Well, he sent word from Landmari that he believes you are being held prisoner somewhere there, that there has been a definite sighting. The soldiers almost trampled each other to leave Audric. Brian led them out over an hour ago. The road blocks have all been abandoned and we hope to see the way clear to leave very soon."

Konrad spoke to her. "I am coming with you, Princess. I am interested in visiting Frencolia and meeting your brother, King Luke Chanec. I will send word to my father, telling him I am going into the mountains with my soldiers for a few days, which is true. Only I will not tell him it is to be the Frencolian Mountains!" He smiled his stunning smile, then continued seriously, "I have sent four soldiers on ahead to speak with King Kelsey of Reideaux, to make sure we will not meet any Chezkovian troops. If we leave within the hour, it will keep our men one hour ahead of us."

Sleven took over the conversation. "I am coming too, Princess, as well as Fritz and Gregory. We will talk with King Kelsey while in Reideaux, and to your brother in Frencolia, about sending troops to help Chezkovia get rid of the impostor."

They departed from the Audric Castle dungeons by a rarely used exit which led to

Konrad's stables. Jobyna traveled the Proburg/Reideaux border pass on Brownlea, disguised in Moritz's soldier's uniform. Two soldiers in red and white and six in brown accompanied her. To anyone watching, it was just a group of soldiers going on a mission with a landowner, Sleven, who appeared to be a baron or a duke.

The Castle of Kelsey stood out against the distant horizon like a child's stone model play toy. Jobyna knew it would grow to gigantic proportions before they entered the walls. The journey had been hard and drizzle began to fall. She was weary and the day reminded her of the time Julian escorted her to the King's Castle in Frencolia. The thought made her shudder. How could she ever eliminate such memories from her mind? Glad of the warm Proburg jacket that repelled the rain and the bearskin hat keeping her hair dry, she leaned into Brownlea's mane, snatching a little comfort from the familiar animal.

Minutes before sunset, the company was welcomed through the castle gates. There had been no signs of pursuit. Dael had not seen the small cavalcade leave Audric Castle and Jobyna was thankful to feel freedom once more.

King Kelsey himself greeted them, waiting at the stables with Konrad's soldiers, welcoming each one, listening to their names and asking questions about the journey. He hugged Konrad affectionately, calling him "My son." Konrad had told Jobyna he visited Kelsey Castle often. When Jobyna was introduced to King Kelsey, she was not sure whether to bow or to curtsy. In keeping with her disguise, she bowed.

King Kelsey moved closer to Jobyna, whispering in her ear, "It's all right, my child, no one here knows who you are. We are keeping it a secret so the word will not get back to Proburg." His kind chestnut eyes spoke a thousand words of welcome and comfort. His voice became apologetic when he told her he was alone in his greetings to her. His wife had died of the plague, and they had been childless.

The kind king spoke again. "Now, this part is a little difficult, Princess. We have chosen two trusted women servants to care for you, but they do not know who you are. It is better that you do not speak to them. It would please us to have you dine with us this evening. Also, we have arranged for your room to be guarded and we hope you will feel secure here." Konrad interrupted, saying he would have his men share some of the guard. King Kelsey turned his warm brown eyes to stare at him. He looked back at Jobyna, then he was silent, but his eyes twinkled brightly.

Many times in Jobyna's life, a hot bath had felt like a life-saving luxury and this was one of them. The women servants did not speak but stared in awe as she removed the soldier's uniform, the woolen singlets and the ruby necklace. She soaked her tired, saddle-weary limbs with pleasure, enjoying the steamy perfumed waters. A dress of adequate fit was found and she was transformed from a soldier back into a princess!

The rooms in King Kelsey's castle were small and plain, more so than those of the King's Castle in Frencberg. Ancient muted tapestries adorned the walls, and the furniture was well worn. Jobyna felt it was homey, rather like a large manor house. The main dining room was small and cozy.

King Kelsey introduced Jobyna to his court as "A friend of Prince Konrad." She noticed she was the only female in the room. The king made her feel relaxed and escorted her to a chair beside his. Konrad, not waiting to be directed, sat on the other side of her. The meal was served and eaten in complete silence. Servants brought finger bowls of warm, scented water, and towels, between the courses. When the wine was served, fruit juice was also brought, and the men began to talk quietly to those alongside.

King Kelsey asked her questions about her country, but it was surface conversation, and Jobyna guessed this was for the sake of those present who did not know who she was. The king turned to the man beside him, making conversation with him.

Konrad took up conversation with Jobyna, telling her once more that he came to Reideaux often. King Kelsey was more like a father to him than Prince Gustovas. It was an extreme privilege for her to be seated next to the king, Konrad informed her, with sparkles in his sky-blue eyes. Usually, in Reideaux, the women did not eat at the same table or in the same room as the men. There was a separate kitchen and dining room for the womenfolk.

"Right after dinner, King Kelsey and the Reideaux Council will be meeting with us to discuss the Chezkovian problem," Konrad told her in undertones. Jobyna was aware of the way Konrad was looking at her, as though his eyes saw her for the first time. She knew the difference the dress made. The brown uniform had lied about her figure.

King Kelsey stood, taking Jobyna's hand and kissing it. As though switched on by multiple mechanisms, all the men stood and bowed. Jobyna stood and curtsied to the king who turned and led the way from the room. Bowing to her, Konrad offered his arm and she walked happily with him as he escorted her to her room.

She slept well that night, feeling safe in this castle belonging to kindly King Kelsey.

28

King Kelsey bade a warm farewell, sending six of his knights with them for added protection and to join in the discussions in Frencolia to bring reports back to him. His men wore dusky blue uniforms, making the entourage more colorful than ever.

The king's eyes laughed as he took Jobyna's slender hand. "The Soldier Princess. We shall never forget you, Jobyna of Frencolia. Bring your brother to visit us sometime, won't you?"

Jobyna thanked the king for his hospitality and said if it was possible, they would accept his invitation. New-born, golden sunrays radiated from the distant hills as they rode out of Kelsey. Jobyna was more excited than ever at the prospect of reaching the last stop before Frencolia! The day grew gray, misty and cool. Brownlea lacked his usual zest and it was with relief they arrived at Ira Castle near the Frencolian border in mid afternoon. Konrad's soldiers had preceded them by an hour, and when the company arrived, preparations had been made for them. Count Ira and his wife welcomed them and Jobyna was taken into the considerate care of Countess Celia. The constant traveling was beginning to tell, and Jobyna was thankful when the Countess had servants serve dinner at a table in her sitting room. Jobyna was pleased to retire early, and after her fervent prayers, she slept peacefully until the morning.

A servant woke her before dawn and Jobyna dressed once again in the soldier's uniform, the thrill of anticipation sweeping over her. Ira Castle was four miles from one of Frencolia's northern border castles. They planned to traverse the mountain pass early, report in at the Border Castle, ride through Valdemar, then Samdene and to Frencburg that day. She would see her brother, Luke, at last!

Sir Felix, the knight in charge of Valdemar's Border Castle, was called suddenly to the Northern Tower about an hour after dawn. He saw the colorful cavalry picking its way up the rocky path towards the Frencolian Border Castle. The foreigners were carefully counted and the different uniforms noted. A soldier quickly helped Felix don his armor and he prepared to meet the visitors.

It had been decided for Konrad to make the first approach and Jobyna would follow to give proof of her identity. Konrad handed his sword to Moritz and drew his horse towards Felix who was also mounted. Twenty soldiers lined up on either side of Felix, their swords drawn. Konrad dismounted slowly and approached Felix.

"I am Konrad, son of Prince Gustovas, from Proburg," he said.

Felix dismounted and bowed, not taking his eyes off Konrad. "I am Sir Felix, a knight of the kingdom of Frencolia. What is your business?"

"I have come to escort the Princess Jobyna from her captivity back to the safety of Frencolia." Felix side-stepped to view the mounted soldiers some distance behind Konrad. "The princess is disguised as a soldier. She rides the nearest horse behind me." Felix looked again, disbelief clouding his countenance. Konrad turned, beckoning Jobyna. She dismounted quickly. Leading Brownlea, she walked to them, pulling off the hat and shaking her braids free.

Felix bowed, his face breaking into a huge, relieved smile. He took her hand. "This is a great day for Frencolia!" He stared into Jobyna's face and his mind was flooded with memories from an unforgettable past.

Jobyna, sensing his recognition, held his hand

in both of hers, "This is a great day for me! This is the day that the Lord has made!" she exclaimed, smiling back at Felix. The absolute happiness she experienced made her tremble. She was overcome by the magnitude of her emotion.

Felix led the colorful cavalry through the border gates and they entered the castle courtyard. Konrad, Jobyna and Sleven went with Felix to the office. The knight would have liked to question them but knew he must leave that to others. Instead, he issued orders to his soldiers. Konrad told Felix there was the possibility of Chezkovian troops in pursuit and all Frencolian borders should be secured. Felix left them in the office and when he returned, he was accompanied by another knight.

Leaving the castle in his care, Felix rode out with 10 Frencolian soldiers, escorting Konrad, Jobyna, Sleven and the foreign soldiers. There was no way Felix was going to miss out on being present at this reunion! The conglomeration of uniforms was now green and gold, brown, red and white and blue. Jobyna had replaced the cap on her head, realizing there would be many stares cast her way if she left her braids hanging down and the hat gave her extra warmth on this gray day.

Brownlea sensed her happiness, and in spite of his limited fodder over the past week he responded with a burst of extra energy. They rode through Valdemar later in the morning.

When they reached Samdene just after noon, the sun suddenly broke through the clouds as though to wish them a special salutation. People stared and pointed and Jobyna knew the party made quite a spectacle. Secretly glad that Felix had not sent word ahead, she looked forward to surprising Luke. On later reflections, she realized it would have been more comfortable for her brother, the king, to have been forewarned!

By late afternoon Jobyna could see the rear of the King's Castle ahead, and fearful fascination filled her flushed face.

Sleven asked her how she felt and she answered, "Words cannot explain, Sleven. It's hard to believe I am really here!"

The moat bridge was down and the Frencolian soldiers led the way with Felix stopping to check in with the guards. They crossed under the northern gate house and were soon in the castle courtyard. Felix drew them around the right of the castle towards the stables. Jobyna noticed Frencolian knights and soldiers watching the procession with interest. When they had all dismounted, the prince spoke with Sleven and Moritz and they organized the men into two lines. Konrad took Jobyna's arm and they went to the front of the group with Sleven and Moritz behind. Felix motioned for his men to form an escort, and they all moved off toward the castle entrance. Jobyna shrugged off the familiar feeling of being a guarded prisoner and tingled with the truth of the contrast now.

King Luke Chanec had been in the Frencolian throne room all day with the senior knights and court counselors. In the morning they had discussed news that had arrived from Chezkovia declaring Elliad's execution. Word about his sister was that she was being kept at the Jydanski Palace by Czar Kievik. Luke felt relieved to know she was still alive. A letter was written to the czar requesting her release. This communique had been dispatched at noon.

King Luke had especially requested that they have an afternoon session this particular day, the 22nd day of April. He wanted to keep his mind totally occupied. To think of his sister in captivity on this day was too painful. The afternoon was spent writing new laws regarding punishment for crimes. Luke wanted to abolish the cutting off of limbs and tongues, changing these punishments for minor offenses to lesser disciplinary measures. The discussion was long and involved. Some of the counselors quoted the Gospel Book in defence of the old laws.

Prince Dorai looked up from his desk beside the dais in the throne room. A messenger, unbidden, was walking toward him. It must be of extreme importance, dismissing protocol in such a casual manner! To disturb this council was unheard of except in matters of unprecedented urgency. The court messenger bowed low to Luke, who ignored him, continuing his discussion with Lord Farey.

Bowing to Prince Dorai, the man bent to whisper, "Prince Dorai, there are soldiers in the reception room to see the king. Soldiers from Chezkovia, Proburg and Reideaux. They willingly surrendered their weapons at the gate. Sir Felix is with them and he requests an audience immediately." Prince Dorai rose, bowing to Luke, who paused momentarily, then continued.

Prince Dorai's surprise was followed with disconcert to see the group standing before him in the reception room. He drew Felix aside, reprimanding him, "Why did you bring them in here?" His eyes fell upon one young Proburg soldier and the face disturbed him. He had seen such a face somewhere before . . .

Jobyna had never met her uncle, Prince Dorai. She had no idea of the events of the past year, the revelation to Luke of their dead mother's brother. Her many pleasant surprises were just beginning.

Felix nodded to Konrad. "Prince Dorai, let me present to you, Prince Konrad from Proburg." The Frencolian knight turned to Konrad, "Prince Dorai, Crown Prince of Frencolia." The two men bowed to one another.

Konrad turned, beckoning to Jobyna, who came shyly forward. "Prince Dorai, I am pleased to return to the care of Frencolia, King Luke Chanec's sister, Jobyna."

Almost losing his composure, Prince Dorai gulped as she pulled off her hat, letting her long braids fall down her back. She did not know what to say, and he was speechless for a few moments.

"Jobyna?" He finally found his voice. She reminded him totally of his sister. She nodded and held out her hand. Trembling, he kissed it affectionately.

"I am pleased to meet you, Prince Dorai, and I am glad to be here. May I see my brother?" Her face was eager and he knew he could not make her wait.

"He is with the counselors of the land, . . . if I could have a word with him first, . . . and you shall see him in a moment." The prince turned, motioned the guards to open the doors and moved back into the throne room.

Luke saw Prince Dorai return, but continued listening to the men debate. He leaned his elbow on the arm of the great throne, totally absorbed in the subject being discussed.

Prince Dorai interrupted, bowing. "Your Majesty, excuse me, but we have a matter that cannot wait." The silence was instant. "A . . . your . . . my . . . an important person . . . has arrived from Chezkovia with Prince Konrad of Proburg. I request your permission to present them in the throne room now." He did not wait for Luke's answer but returned to the doors, commanding the guards to open them.

Luke stared, frowning, as his uncle walked

toward the doors. It was unacceptable to interrupt a session of the council. He had no idea what was going on. No preparations in his mind had occurred to make ready for this occasion.

Prince Dorai himself made the announcement, "Prince Konrad of Proburg . . . and . . . Jobyna Chanec, Sister of King Luke Chanec." The council turned to the door. Luke stood involuntarily as he heard the sounding out of his sister's name. He saw his uncle enter with two men dressed in brown uniforms, or were they two men?

Jobyna began walking toward the Frencolian throne. This was a moment she had never dared to dream about. She remembered the last time she had been in this room with Elliad and his soldiers. She saw her brother rising to his feet, staring at her, incredulity all over his face. Suddenly all protocol disappeared. They were a brother and sister who had been grievously separated for a year.

"Luke!" Jobyna cried, forgetting where she was and who was with her.

"Jobyna?" His feet practically flew down the steps. They had both changed, she more than he, but recognition flooded their faces as they moved towards each other.

She was hugging him and crying. He kissed her cheeks and held her close. His eyes met Konrad's, and Luke murmured, his voice husky, "God be praised. Thank you."

It took some time for Jobyna to stop crying. She was so happy, yet she was weeping, clinging to her brother, sobbing into his broad shoulder. Luke nodded approval to his uncle who was dismissing the overawed council.

In defence of Jobyna's tears, Konrad said, "We have traveled for many days and today has been the longest. Your sister is tired and will need food and rest." Luke, with his arm around Jobyna, moved nearer to Konrad who bowed and continued, "My men need to eat and we must talk with you, King Luke Chanec. There are urgent matters to discuss."

Prince Dorai sent a messenger to fetch his wife and he suggested Luke go into the reception room to greet the other men. Luke was introduced to Sleven and Moritz and the other soldiers one by one. Jobyna sat down on one of the padded chairs, watching him. Her sibling conducted himself in a way that was entirely new to Jobyna. He had grown taller and was more manly. There was little of the reckless Luke of the past. The crown on his head made Jobyna realize the power he held. His kingly authority was obvious. Jobyna turned her eyes to Prince Dorai whose attentive gaze was upon her.

Luke walked to the older man's side. "Jobyna, this is Prince Dorai, your uncle, our mother's brother."

Jobyna looked in amazement at Luke, then at Prince Dorai who nodded.

"That is all the more reason to be glad for this reunion!" she exclaimed, tears still glistening on her rosy cheeks.

Minette arrived and was introduced to Jobyna who embraced her aunt joyfully. Sir Dorai suggested Minette take Jobyna to her quarters and take care of her there.

Luke, beaming broadly, announced, "We will have a celebration dinner tonight!"

29

King Luke Chanec himself escorted Prince Konrad, Moritz and Sleven to the guest rooms of his royal suite, encouraging them to bathe and change. He left Prince Dorai to take care of the other men and commanded they meet in the main castle conference room in an hour.

Luke was anxious to know the details of the escape and journey to Frencolia, but his mind was focused mainly on his sister's timely presence. Calling his chief servant, Sabin, he issued orders for the preparation of the castle dining room and the decoration of the throne room.

Jobyna waited with her aunt in her sitting

room while the servants poured hot water into the bath in Minette's suite.

"Mommy, who's that lady wearing those men's clothes?" A soft voice came to their ears and Jobyna's eyes turned to see a little girl skipping into the room, followed by three other children.

Minette pulled the girl toward her, putting her arm around the small frame. "This is your cousin, Jobyna." Minette turned to Jobyna, "This is Elissa, named after your mother." The little girl hung back from her, shy and scared. Minette stood to her feet, directing the children to her niece. "This is Doralin who is seven years old, and our son, Charles, is nine. Maia, our oldest, is 11. Children, this is King Luke's sister, Jobyna."

The children scrutinized her with wide, serious eyes. They had heard much about Jobyna and had prayed with their mother for their cousin's safe return.

Doralin spoke up. "God does answer prayer, doesn't He?"

Jobyna smiled at them in happiness, "Cousins! You all are my cousins!"

She looked at Maia who was quite grown up for an 11-year-old. Maia stared back at Jobyna, both thinking how alike they were, almost the same shaped face and long brown hair highlighted with gleaming copper hues. Jobyna hugged her look-alike, saying, "We are like sisters, Maia."

Minette sorted through her gowns while Jobyna bathed. She chose the new one her seamstress had recently completed for her. Jobyna had told her aunt that she had only what she arrived in and would obviously need something more appropriate to wear to dinner. The gown Minette brought into the suite had been specially designed but she had no feelings of regret in giving it to her niece. It was woven of fine pale green wool, the bodice and sleeves were decorated with tiny seed pearls sewn in an intricate pattern, embroidered here and there with threads of fine silver. Jobyna showed Minette the ruby necklace, declaring she would not wear it, because by rights, it belonged to Frencolia. Memories of the ruby necklace were painful, and she would be glad to be rid of it.

When Jobyna had dressed, Minette brought her a simple pearl choker and a cream rose for her hair. Jobyna was a grown-up version of Maia. Minette fussed over her as she would a daughter, brushing her damp hair, plaiting the side pieces. The young mother wove some of Jobyna's hair into a fancy knot at the back, tucking the rose into the top, leaving the rest flowing loose and long. The effect was breathtaking. Minette drew a breath at her niece's stunning beauty.

Jobyna chatted with the children while Minette dressed, interested to hear what they thought about life at the King's Castle.

"Charles is better at sword fighting than Luke." Elissa said with triumph in her voice.

"Luke doesn't sword fight, does he, Elissa?" Jobyna asked, concerned.

Charles answered the question. "Father is teaching him, and he says Luke has too soft a hand. Luke and I fight for fun."

Minette entered with two nursery maids who bustled the children off after waiting for them to kiss their mother good night. Maia hung back. She curtsied to Jobyna, stating very seriously, "I am so pleased you are here, Cousin Jobyna. I hope I am as beautiful as you when I grow up."

Luke stood at the door to Minette's apartment, a large bouquet of roses in his hand. Konrad waited self-consciously behind him, wishing he was the one who carried the flowers. Luke bowed and held the flowers out to his sister who took them and curtsied, thanking him, smiling to see him again so soon.

"I am sorry we are late, little sister. The discussion took longer than we expected, and we have scarcely begun." He extended his arm, finding it difficult to believe how wonderful she looked after all she had been through during the past year. Sleven had told him some of it, and Luke had become so angry he could scarcely control himself and sit still. Konrad was present and was mortified to hear the doctor's account of Elliad's ill treatment.

Minette took Konrad's arm and they began

the walk to the dining room. Konrad's eyes followed Jobyna's every move. She was so beautiful and looked very much like a princess.

"King Luke Chanec and his sister, Jobyna Chanec."

Jobyna was faced with a reception line. The first person to greet her was Sabin, and she could not help but embrace him, much to his ecstatic embarrassment. He beamed at her, tears rolling down his suntanned cheeks. Jobyna was introduced to the court officials and their wives. Seven senior knights were present, and three lords who were able to come at short notice. Luke indicated for her to stand with him while Prince Dorai and Princess Minette were announced, then Prince Konrad, Doctor Sleven, all the foreign soldiers, one by one, each announced by name and country.

With introductions completed, Luke took Jobyna's hand and said, "Tonight, we are celebrating the greatest occasion for me since I was crowned King of Frencolia: the return to this country of my dear sister." He paused while everyone applauded, then continued, "When we were together in our home at Chanoine, we always held hands around our dining room with family, as well as visitors, and gave thanks to God. That is what we shall do tonight."

There was a shuffle in the great hall as the people formed a large circle, joining hands. Konrad could not believe such a thing was really happening! Prayer of thanksgiving was unheard of among royalty in Proburg or Chezkovia. He found himself with Minette on one side and Sleven on the other. Luke began to pray. He thanked God for the safe return of his sister and for blessings on those who had helped her return. He gave praise to God that He, the Lord God, was King over all kings and Lord of lords. Konrad's heart raced and great joy welled up inside his being. Luke gave thanks for the food and the Frencolians reiterated a hearty "Amen."

After the meal, through which everyone was encouraged to converse, Luke stood to his feet and the room grew quiet. He requested they all move to the throne room. Taking his sister's hand, he led the way.

Decorated with pillars holding up huge receptacles of spring flowers, the throne room was a mass of brilliant colors and flickering lights. There were 15 floral arrangements on one side and on the other were 15 great candelabras, each containing 15 rose-scented, glowing candles. Jobyna gazed at the decorations in wonder as Luke led her into the fragrance-filled chamber. He drew his sister up to the dais and stood with her on the steps. The people silently congregated in the great room.

Luke smiled and turned to his sister. "Jobyna, I have a surprise for you tonight. I will tell you some things you did not know before." He turned to include everyone. "Fifteen years ago, this very morning, my mother gave birth to a baby girl. This tiny baby was six weeks premature and the doctor said she would die. Mother wrapped the babe in lambswool and carried her inside her bodice close to her breast. This baby survived, but mother did not name her or register the birth until six weeks after she was born. 'Jobyna' means 'afflicted, persecuted, as the gem cannot be polished without friction, so a man—or woman—cannot be perfected without trials.' My sister has had more than her share of trials and we see the gem in its brilliance here tonight." Luke turned back to Jobyna. "You shall be known from this night on as 'The First Princess of Frencolia, Princess Jobyna Chanec.' " Jobyna drew a deep breath. Luke, sensing her disapproval, spoke decisively and sternly, "The king has spoken!"

He turned to a knave bearing a simple gold coronet on a plush, black velvet cushion. Luke took the head-piece and placed it on Jobyna's head, solemnly kissing each cheek. Taking the princess' hand, he turned her to face those watching. "It is your birthday, today, Princess Jobyna, and we welcome you home. What would you like to say?"

Jobyna felt stranded. She did not want to be a princess, but Luke had pronounced her such before she could speak to him. Her secret hopes were to live in a manor house, to be a farmer's wife. She looked at Konrad whose blue eyes sparkled into hers. He was smiling at her, and she felt indignant. Maybe he had told Luke what she had said about not being a real princess. She looked around at the people who were waiting to hear her voice.

Her thoughts said to her, *This is not your doing; it is out of your hands. Will you fight what God is working out for you?* She voiced, "I am happy to be here tonight, and I need to remind myself that God works His good will in spite of what man may seek to do. His thoughts and ways are not our thoughts and ways. I do thank God for the trials that are now past, and I thank God for my brother, my king." She turned and curtsied to Luke. "I look forward to serving my country in whatever way I can. This day is made by the Lord. Let us rejoice and be glad in Him."

Luke extended his arm to her and they walked to the doors, standing to speak with people as they passed by. Konrad waited until last. "I was hoping I may escort Princess Jobyna Chanec to her quarters, with your permission, King Luke Chanec." He held his arm to Jobyna and Luke indicated for them to walk by. However, he followed behind, walking with Moritz all the way. Luke kissed his sister's hand and cheeks affectionately before she entered the room.

"I will look forward to your company at breakfast, Sister. I pray you sleep well." Luke turned to Konrad. "We have called the council to meet immediately after breakfast, Konrad.

You must get all the rest you can." However, the two talked all the way back to the royal suite where they continued their conversation late into the night.

Jobyna settled down in the bedroom beside Minette's, completely happy and content. She was home! This was the first night of the rest of her life in Frencolia. Her trials were finally over! She was safe. As she closed her eyes, she could see the 15 candelabras glowing in the throne room. Fifteen years! Such a long time. God had been gracious to extend her life for so long. She fell asleep with praise in her heart and peace permeating her contented mind.

30

Taking fruit and bread for Brownlea and Speed, Jobyna sought out her two faithful friends in the stables. She was pleased to find them rested and content. Luke, Prince Dorai, Prince Konrad, Doctor Sleven, the other visitors and the Frencolian Council had been in conference for two days and she wondered what the outcome would be.

Disturbing memories descended depressingly on the princess as she walked the corridors of the King's Castle. Deciding she needed to conquer her fears once and for all, she ascended the stairs to the great battlements. Jobyna strolled to the places where she had walked as a prisoner of Elliad, a year ago. Across the moat, she saw the city of Frencberg and the high cliffs encasing the valley where Luke and she had discovered the treasure cave. Jobyna's hatred of castles was still strong, but with Luke, her uncle and aunt and cousins around her, maybe she could tolerate this fortress.

Luke said he had commissioned the manor house at Chanoine to be rebuilt and he would take her out there to view the progress as soon as possible. She could help choose furnishings. A monument had been erected over their parents' graves and he wanted to have a memorial service there.

The outcome of the conference was that a contract was being drawn up and would be taken to the various kingdoms who had been negatively affected by Elliad's pillaging. If all nations would join together against Elliad as a murderous lunatic—not against Chezkovia or Czar Kievik—then an end could be brought to the matter. Whether Czar Kievik was still alive or not remained to be discovered.

Sir Dorai verbalized the situation aptly, "Once the kingdoms sign the contract, Elliad is as good as dead!"

The thought of men preparing for battle made Jobyna shudder and she hoped no one would get hurt in the carrying out of the contract. Her concern did not extend to Elliad and his men—she hoped they would receive all they deserved.

Jobyna was delighted to be home, and when

Luke told her they would ride to Chanoine the next day, she could scarcely sleep for excitement. Sleven, Fritz and Gregory would return to Proburg, taking the contract to Prince Gustovas. They would meet with Czarevitch Kenrik and his men from Chezkovia. The delegation from Reideaux would take a copy of the contract to King Kelsey. Other Frencolian knights would take copies of the contract to the kingdoms of Strasland, Zealavia, Bavarest, Danzerg and Muldaver. As for Konrad, he and his men would stay in Frencolia. The Prince wanted to discover more about Luke's kingdom, to climb some of its mountains and to see for himself how Luke was using the Gospel Book to guide the way he reigned. Konrad wrote a message to his father, confessing he was in Frencolia and requesting his father's approval to stay for a while.

Residents of Chanoine were out in full representation to greet the royal party. The road to the manor house was blocked with crowds. Soldiers had to clear well wishers out of the way to allow the celebrities to enter. News that Princess Jobyna Chanec was visiting brought inquisitive Frencolians from neighboring villages. They cheered and shouted, throwing flowers in her path. Many tried to pass bouquets and gifts to the beautiful princess.

Jobyna, full of joy, held her breath as Brownlea carried her across the flower-decorated moat to the home she loved. Luke had ordered the builders to make the house as near the original as possible. The only difference was the extra security. The young king planned to stay there himself when he was able. Pleased to have Speed back, Luke drew the horse alongside his sister, nodding toward the front garden. Konrad was instantly at her side to help her alight.

The memorial service was brief. Luke read from the Gospel Book and his clear voice resounded across the moat.

"Jesus said, 'Let not your heart be troubled, believe in God, believe also in me. In my Father's house are many mansions. . . . I am the Way, the Truth, the Life.' Jesus said, 'I am the Resurrection and the Life, he who believes on Me, though he were dead, yet shall he live.' "

Surprised that she did not feel any bitterness at all, Jobyna was able to wholeheartedly join Luke's prayer of thanksgiving that God was in control. The road had ended for her dear father and mother, as one day it would end for them. To die was not something to fear; it had been living that had been hard.

Jobyna viewed the glass case containing the Gospel Book beside the two crosses. A handsome reflection joined hers and she stared into the raised glass lid. Konrad stooped to whisper in her ear, "You are the most beautiful princess on earth, and surely the most courageous and wise." Luke's reflection appeared on her other side, and Jobyna turned to face him.

"It is so good to be home!"

With a king on one arm and a prince on the other, Jobyna turned towards the manor house where they would share the first meal to be had within these new, yet memory-filled, walls. In spite of its unfinished state, the manor house already felt like home.

Together in Frencolia, Jobyna and Luke looked forward to the freedom and felicity of the faultless future.

NOTE—BEWARE: Elliad is still scheming! Read what happens to Luke, Jobyna, Maia, Konrad and Kenrik—and Elliad—in *Kingdoms*! In *Treasures* Elliad sought, as king, the famed treasures of Frencolia. In *Castles* Elliad conquers castles and becomes the czar of Chezkovia! In *Kingdoms*, Elliad has a new occupation—he wants to gain power over the surrounding kingdoms!